CO

DOCTOR WHO – THE NEW ADVENTURES

Also available:

THE NEW

DOCTOR WHO

ADVENTURES

CONUNDRUM

Steve Lyons

First published in Great Britain in 1994 by
Doctor Who Books
an imprint of Virgin Publishing Ltd
332 Ladbroke Grove
London W10 5AH

Reprinted 1994

ISBN 0 426 20408 5

Cover illustration by Jeff Cummins
Typeset by Intype, London
Printed and bound in Great Britain by
Cox & Wyman Ltd, Reading, Berkshire

With thanks to Paul Cornell, for showing it could be done; to the Manchester and Liverpool Societies of Cult Television, for friendship; to John and Claire, although John won't appreciate finding his name in a *Doctor Who* book; to mum and dad, for everything else; and to Steven Moffat, for writing *Press Gang*.

conundrum: *n.* riddle esp. with punning answer; hard question. [16th c.; orig. unkn.]

The Concise Oxford Dictionary of Current English

Hello? Are you there? Are you reading this?

I hope so. I'm afraid I can't tell, from where I am. But I know you have a printer set up there, in that weird freezing room of yours, with the glass sphere and the rods and the pentagrams. I know it tells you everything that happens here, relates to you the stories that I write. I hope that sometimes, now and then, you find the time to read just one or two; perhaps gain a little amusement from my characters and their tales.

Well, maybe you do. Maybe you've been keeping tabs on me all this time. Maybe that's why *he's* here now. Because you finally think I'm ready for him.

I can see him already, that blue box of his caught helplessly in our grip. Do I detect your hand in this fortuitous arrival? I know that bird-woman-thing you keep has all sorts of powers. I mean, it brought me here from Earth, didn't it? I even watched as it reconstructed this place from ashes.

And finally he's here, like you always said he would be. So this is what it's all been for, right? I'll tell my final story, write him into my trap, and close the book on him forever. No epilogue, no sequel, no next volume in the series. And I hope that doesn't spoil your enjoyment, but I thought you'd want to know.

Besides, I hope you'll find this entertaining anyway. I've brought back all my best characters from the past, especially for my swan song. And who knows? You might still find a few surprises if you care to read onwards.

Remember, only the ending is certain. The Doctor is finished. Like you wanted. Beyond that . . .

Well, you'll have to wait and see.

Chapter 1

Stories So Far

I'm going to start my tale in a small town called Arandale.
I expect you remember that? Only this time, things are
going to be a little different. A little colder, a little
darker . . . a little more deadly. You see, the happy, sunny,
friendly little town that we've journeyed to so many times
before no longer exists. Not for the moment. It's winter
now – and winter in Arandale means a change for the
worse.

By the time October and November have rolled around,
the tourists have stopped visiting. The flowers no longer
bloom and the leaves have dropped from the trees, free
to drift into the grey hills which enclose this bleak little
settlement. The once picturesque buildings now seem
frightened and alone, huddling close against the onset of
the dark as the long nights press inexorably inwards and
the first flakes of snow cling tenaciously to the rain-soaked
ground.

In a candlelit room at the rear of Rosemary's shop, a man
who called himself Shade was experiencing a range of
emotions, none of them his own.

Confusion. Fear. Anger. Resentment. Finally, a dull and
miserable acceptance. It was happening again.

He blinked, and suddenly the Death card was staring
up at him, hollow black sockets glaring out from its white
skull face. Rosemary stifled a gasp and her eyes flicked
up to meet his, finding no comfort in their black depths.

The card was a grand one; part of a unique set, hand-

3

painted by a distant ancestor over three hundred years before. The skull-faced figure was holding a brightly lit globe, its gnarled hand reaching out of the picture as if to offer its prize to the onlooker. Rosemary forced herself to concentrate on that, seeing nothing besides the exquisite artwork – trying desperately not to make eye contact again.

'The card doesn't necessarily signify an actual death,' she explained, stammering slightly as she began her familiar chat.

'I know,' he said quietly.

'Like many of the cards in the tarot,' Rosemary pressed on (remember the drill, keep those eyes down), 'it signifies a change. The proffered orb represents the chance of a new beginning, a fresh start – but it is necessary to embrace Death, in some form or other, before that fresh start can be achieved. The card is saying that it is time for something to end – a belief, or a career perhaps. Although that may cause grief, something new and worthwhile will come from the sacrifice.'

Her spiel completed, she trusted herself to look up again. She cursed her own feelings as she did. Something about this man unnerved her, in a way she had never been unnerved before. Something about that face, almost devoid of emotion, or those ebony eyes, their secrets shrouded in glistening darkness. She suppressed a chill of fear and reached hurriedly for the final card. The Knight of Pentacles. Better, much better.

'The paramount quality of this card is perseverance. The Knight of Pentacles is an achiever, he sets himself realistic goals and works diligently towards reaching them. What it could mean to you, erm . . .'

'Matthew.'

'Of course. In your case Matthew, it could stand for an event – something which has dragged on for a long, long time, and is about to reach a satisfactory conclusion.' Rosemary paused again, floundering now. She needed his feedback to interpret the card, but none was forthcoming.

4

'Or it could represent a person. Someone who is about to come into your life.' She was fishing desperately for information, and she had the uncomfortable feeling that he knew it too. 'So – well, that's something to think about,' she finished lamely, gathering the displayed cards hurriedly and shuffling them back into the deck.

'Yes. Thank you.' Still no hint of emotion.

'Just one more layout, then. This will tell us . . .'

'No. I must go.'

The interruption was abrupt, and Rosemary jumped involuntarily as Shade pushed back his chair and rose. His actions were accompanied rather ominously by a sudden loud and inexplicable bang from somewhere without. The candle flickered and died and she could see only his pale white face hovering eerily in a mist of rolling grey smoke. He left silently, and for a long moment she dared not even move. Then the nervousness she was feeling grew into a full-blown fear, its icy fingers working their way up her spine. She leapt to her feet, propelling herself swiftly across the darkened room. Her fingers fumbled for the wall switch and the overhead light snapped on, its electric glow dispelling the nightmare shadows in an instant.

Rosemary fell against the wall then, her heart beating loudly in her ears as her brain tried to rationalize her feelings. Yes, Matthew Shade had frightened her – only it wasn't just him, was it? It was the Death card, too. Over the last three weeks it had made its unwelcome presence felt in every reading she had done. Over and over she had found herself comforting disquieted customers, calming the understandable fears that the card inevitably caused. She was beginning to feel those fears herself now, more so with each new reading and each new appearance of the Grim Reaper. The card didn't have to mean death, she kept telling herself. Not an *actual* death. But she knew that some time soon, things were going to change. For all of them. And she doubted it would be for the better.

From somewhere outside, another small explosion shattered the evening calm, followed this time by a series of sharp cracks. Calmed by the comfort of the light, Rosemary now recognized the sounds of fireworks, and this at least was some small relief.

The dark evening sky was bathed momentarily in fiery red. From somewhere on the far side of Arandale a streak of yellow blazed into the sky, scattering burning trails far and wide. Guy Fawkes' Night was still three days away, but impatience had spurred some of the townspeople into beginning the celebrations early.

Shade barely noticed the pyrotechnics as he left Rosemary's shop, his feet crunching on drifts of compacted ice and his breath freezing into tiny droplets before him. He drew his thick black trenchcoat protectively around him and plunged his pale, cold hands deep into his pockets. Coming here had cost him valuable time, but the information he had gained might soon prove useful. He had wanted to ascertain whether Rosemary Chambers really possessed the mystical powers she laid claim to, and he now had his answer. But other things were more urgent.

The psychic cry had left him with only a vague impression of its position of origin. It took him forty-seven minutes of walking to pin-point it exactly, in one corner of a dark passage beside the Indian take-away. He had been right, of course. Valerie Jones was dead. Just like the others. Sprawled unceremoniously in a sea of litter and blood.

He looked at the body for a moment, feeling something only slightly akin to pity. Then he headed back to the bright lights of the street, and to the telephone box on the far corner. He knew the number of the police station by heart.

'Victim number three,' he said softly into the receiver. 'In an alley-way off Piccadilly Road.'

He paused for a moment, just to be sure his message had been heard. 'Who is this?' came the voice of a startled operator on the other end of the line. 'Where are you calling from?' Loud and clear.

He put down the telephone and waited.

That's enough of the prologues. Right now, I've more important things to attend to. You see, on a frosty slope just a short way outside the small town, a phone box of a different kind has arrived, appearing literally out of thin air.

And you know what that means.

'We're on Earth,' announced the Doctor curtly.

Ace sighed and checked the instruments for herself. 'The English Midlands, November the second, 1993. A Tuesday.' (And how your pet thingumajig tricked them into believing that, I'll never know – but nice one anyway!) 'So we're through the time-storm okay.'

'Seems like it.' The Doctor flipped on his fedora hat, operated the door control and strode out of the TARDIS without another word. Ace watched him go, her face without emotion. He had been like this since they had returned from the *Titanic* – all moods and sulks, with hardly a civil word for anyone. Okay, so he'd spent a week in the sick bay, he was entitled to be a bit off-colour, but this was ridiculous. It was like he'd just given up on everything. On her, especially.

Well, sod him, thought Ace, there were more important things to worry about in this life than the Doctor. Strange dreams, for one thing: a woman in red. And a door she couldn't open, for another. She ran her fingers across the TARDIS console, and a large keyboard catapulted obligingly out before her. The recently repaired chameleon circuit.

She had work to do.

I must say, the Doctor looks nothing like any of the versions I've seen. Still, you said he'd be different, I suppose. It seems he's in his seventh body at the moment – quite short, dark-haired, bright-eyed... What else? He comes from Gallifrey: a Time Lord. Not that that'll help him. Hence the blue box, his TARDIS. An acronym for Time And Relative Dimensions In Space. I suppose you'd know more about that than me. It looks like he's had a hard time of it recently. Someone playing with his past, meddling in the timestream, causing discrepancies . . .

That's you, isn't it?

The others? Ace, for one – or Dorothy, as she doesn't prefer to be known. You've just met her. A bit of a cold bitch, I think. She's seen a lot of things, fought a lot of fights, killed a lot of people too. She doesn't talk much nowadays, not about herself, and she keeps her feelings well hidden behind mirrored glasses. It's tempting to peel back that mind of hers layer by layer, and see what really makes her tick. Still, I don't suppose you want sixteen pages of my psychoanalysing her to death.

So finally then, our resident Professor – though she'd die if anyone found out that the qualification isn't a real one. Bernice Summerfield is her name – Benny, they call her. Compassionate, intelligent, intuitive, quick-witted . . . no threat to us whatsoever. She's in the bath at the moment, but I'm sure she won't mind if we drop in.

'I take it we've landed,' Bernice surmised.

'That's right,' came Ace's voice through the intercom. 'Earth, 1993.' No further information was forthcoming, nor indeed had Benny expected any. Nowadays, it seemed that the TARDIS crew communicated mostly on a purely functional level.

The bath was a majestic one, all gilt trim and perfect contours, sunk deep into the velvet-carpeted floor of a room the size of Westminster Cathedral. Benny had spent a great deal of time here since discovering it a few days before. She considered its existence to be the single advantage to the Doctor's sudden change of TARDIS, a change which had left her otherwise quite disoriented and strangely homesick. (Just trust me on that one, will you? It's far too long a story to go into at this juncture.) When the pressures of life began to get to her, she would come here and allow the swirling hot waters to ease away her tensions, to give her time to think and plan.

What she was planning now was her future, and specifically where she would spend it. She had, after all, made herself a firm promise that the next time the Doctor took her to any place remotely suitable, she would pack her bags and go. Now she was suddenly back on Earth, in what just happened to be her favourite period of history, and it felt awfully like her bluff had been called.

Somewhere along the line, she had to make a decision – and she knew it wouldn't be an easy one.

The wheel spun out of control, slipped out of his grasp, and Corrigan screamed as the car flew sideways. He found the brakes by instinct alone; worked them once, twice, three times. Stop. Handbrake on, yanked upwards with more force than necessary. Then finally he allowed himself to be frightened, slumping breathlessly against the steering wheel and sweating hard despite the bitter cold of the evening air. Over the next few minutes, he indulged his anger by cursing everything; curse the dumb Brits and their right-hand drive cars, and the midwinter weather which froze a guy to the bone and left treacherous black ice on highways which were too blasted narrow in the first place. And curse his rat of a partner, crying off this job at the last minute with flu and sending muggins here, Jack Corrigan, across the ocean in his stead. But most of all, curse the blasted town of Arandale, to which his search had brought him, almost too quickly for comfort.

He could see it down there now, all laid out like some sort of picture postcard. It probably snowed all year round in Arandale, he thought – snow that stuck, covering the ground with a white fluffy coat that wasn't at all wet and uncomfortable like the brand that landed everywhere else. The townsfolk probably danced around their snowmen on May the first, whilst the elders roasted chestnuts on warm open fires and the kids went skating on the frozen lake, but never fell through the ice. He hated the place already

9

– and his black thoughts eventually proved to be quite cathartic. In a slightly better mood, he finally gathered his resolve and gunned the engine of the old Morris Minor. The car spluttered into life for but a moment, before the battery light flickered and lit and the engine died whining. A second try brought only the hoarse choke of an ineffectual starter motor. Dead.

For a moment Corrigan just stared disbelievingly at the dashboard, cursing his luck, cursing the car rental company and cursing the weather, his partner and Arandale once more for good measure. Then he punched the steering wheel hard enough to make his knuckles bleed.

Five minutes later, he began to think about finding a telephone.

The Doctor stormed back into the TARDIS, barely controlling his anger. 'Well, thanks for giving me a door to use at last!' he snapped.

Ace feigned innocence. 'Sorry, did you want to come back in? I was just trying out a few defensive formations. It worked then?'

'That's why we have a lock on the door!' answered the Doctor sourly. 'We don't need belt and braces. And we certainly don't need to look like any of those ridiculous weapons of yours!' He pushed her to one side, swiftly punching in a series of instructions which first erased Ace's lovingly plotted graphic of a twenty-fifth century Axmeister tank, and then returned the chameleon circuit keyboard to its housing. 'I'm switching back to the default setting. The TARDIS can pick a form for itself, one that blends in with its surroundings. That will be perfectly adequate! Where's Bernice?'

Ace shrugged. 'Breezed in, checked the external temperature, breezed out again . . .' She turned away from him, with a scowl. Not that she was really that angry, despite his wanton destruction of a good few days' work. Ace had used her memory and the telepathic systems to reconstruct parts of the new TARDIS, and her motive in practising with the chameleon circuit had not been to change the ship's outer shell at all. Rather, she hoped that, given familiarity with the device, she could maybe turn it in on itself, alter the TARDIS's internal configuration and finally find and get through the frustrating locked door that was a product apparently of her own subconscious mind (another long story, I'm afraid).

'I'm here,' Benny announced, appearing at the interior doorway immaculate in a red and black trouser suit and a long, clean overcoat. No high heels, no flapping lengths of fabric; stylish but practical, as always. 'All ready?' The Doctor and Ace glared at each other silently. 'Good,' said Benny. 'Then let's get out there, shall we?' Without waiting for a reply, she walked quickly past her companions and through the exterior doors.

By the time the Doctor and Ace joined her on the grass outside she was standing, arms folded, and looking back towards them with a hint of amusement. 'Okay,' she said, nodding towards the TARDIS. 'Which one of you wants to explain this?'

Ace grinned. ' "Blends in", eh?' she taunted the Doctor.

' "Blends in"?' echoed Benny. 'Doctor, that thing "blends in" like a rhinoceros at a goldfish-only drinks party. I mean . . .' She looked up at it again, as if checking that her eyes hadn't deceived her. 'Of all things . . . *the gingerbread cottage!*'

'Can you eat it, too?' Ace wondered, experimentally breaking a piece of candy from the side of the construct. The Doctor whisked it from her hand, jammed it forcibly back into place and stomped moodily back inside the ship. Moments later the unlikely-looking fairy-tale house gave the briefest of shimmers before transforming into the more familiar sight of the battered blue police box. Ace and Benny exchanged a look, and Benny couldn't help thinking that the two seemed closer in that shared instant than they had been for days. The moment was lost as the

11

Doctor returned, jamming his hat firmly into position as he pushed briskly between them.

'Perhaps now,' he muttered darkly, 'we can all just learn to leave things the way they should be!' And he set off towards the small town without a backward glance, leaving Ace and Benny to follow him in silence.

'Same as the other one,' the police surgeon confirmed. 'Knife wound in the chest, body drained of blood. Looks like she died about an hour ago.'

Blyth nodded, the freezing wind numbing his face into a permanent scowl and giving no comfort to the hard, cold knot which had formed in the pit of his stomach. One death could be put down to a lunatic; two was the work of a serial killer. And two on consecutive nights meant there were more to come. Soon.

'That's very interesting,' mused the Doctor, insinuating himself upon the scene as if he had been there all along. 'And this is the second victim, you say?'

'That's right,' confirmed Blyth, a short, stout man with thinning hair and a thick moustache, clothed in the uniform and insignia of a police sergeant. He regarded the new arrival uncertainly. 'The first was found last night, over by the pizza parlour.'

'Pizza parlour?'

'On the corner of Mitre Street and St George's Crescent.'

'Ah, yes. And that was a knife attack as well?'

'Yes.'

'And no blood left in the corpse?'

'None.'

'Anything off the autopsy report yet?'

'No. Do you mind if I ask you something?'

'Go ahead.'

'Who are you?'

The Doctor grinned and doffed his hat politely. 'I'm the Doctor. These are my friends, Ace and Bernice. I'm here to help.'

'We've had experience with vampires,' Ace put in, distracting Blyth's attention from her companion. He hadn't noticed her arrival either, though that was perhaps unsurprising in the midst of the general mêlée of police, reporters and curious onlookers. He couldn't say he particularly cared for her appearance; mirrored glasses which hid her eyes, a rucksack stuffed with devices unknown and a tight leather combat suit which gave him the immediate impression that she was looking for trouble. The man seemed far more approachable, very much the explorer in his cream linen suit and hat, a white tie slung casually around his neck – although Blyth couldn't help but wonder about the large silver spoon which protruded from the Doctor's breast pocket.

'Now, Ace,' the man was saying. 'No one said anything about vampires.'

'No blood in her, though. Mind you, no holes in the neck either.' Blyth realized with a start that the woman had been allowed to examine the body. What were his men thinking of?

'Well, there's nothing we can do here,' said the third stranger impatiently. 'For now, anyway.' Blyth liked the look of this woman a lot more, if only because of her relatively conservative choice of clothing. Perhaps also because she was the only one of the three who seemed rightly uneasy in the presence of the blood-drained corpse.

'I think perhaps my friend is right,' the Doctor agreed, much to Benny's obvious relief.

'But . . .' Blyth began. The Doctor silenced him with a wave of his umbrella.

'I'll look in at the station tomorrow and you can give me an update then. No, no, don't worry, I'll find it.'

It was a good ten seconds before Blyth found his voice again – ten seconds during which the new arrivals had weaved their way through the crowd, on to the main street and round the corner out of sight. 'Some weird people in this town,' he finally confided to one of his constables.

13

'You can say that again, sarge. You should've seen the other one that was here.'

'Other one?'

'Aye, just a couple of minutes ago. All dressed in black and white, pitch-black eyes, pale skin. Just stood over there looking at us, like one of the living dead.'

Blyth shivered and pulled his overcoat tightly around him. It did him no real good – but then, the feeling of coldness which had set his teeth to chattering had very little to do with the temperature.

News travelled fast in Arandale – certainly fast enough for it to have reached the Black Cat Tavern within minutes of Ms Jones' body being found. As the Doctor and his companions hurried into the hospitable warmth of the public house, they were acutely aware that few conversations failed to include the words 'murder', 'blood' and 'shocking'.

The landlord smiled at them as he deposited their drinks on the bar. 'Shocking business these murders, eh? No blood in either of them bodies, they say.'

'So I believe,' said the Doctor. He found a table and looked around for his companions, sighing as he realized that Ace had already abandoned him in favour of a card game on the far side of the room.

'Interesting places, pubs,' he commented, taking a seat opposite Bernice. 'If you look for the right things, that is.' Benny merely grunted in acknowledgement; she too had other things on her mind. Thoughts of leaving pricked uncomfortably at her, and she wondered if this cold, unfriendly community could ever be a better home to her than the TARDIS.

The Doctor didn't seem to mind. Idle conversation was far from his thoughts, too, and he was occupied for now with looking for those 'right things' he had mentioned. The Black Cat Tavern was of genuine Edwardian construction, and despite a series of modernizations over the years, a lot of the heart of the place had remained. Nowadays the building was more homely than it was grand, but its beautiful cut-glass panels and its genuine mahogany fireplace served as magnificent reminders of days past. On a winter mid-week night like this, the hostelry attracted little more than a dozen customers, most of them hardened regulars. The Doctor cast his eye over each of these in turn, gleaning who-knew-what information from their appearances and actions. He found his gaze lingering longest on the small group of card players with whom Ace had settled. In the company of others her old smile had returned, and the Doctor could almost see the happy and carefree young girl who had long since been lost to him. He wondered where he had gone wrong.

'I'm out,' Ace announced, flipping her cards into the centre of the table. 'I can see why everyone plays for matches now,' she added to the attractive young black girl at her side.

'No one ever plays for money when Mel's in the game,' Karen laughed, treating Ace to one of the sparkling bright grins which had won her instant friendship. 'For most of the people round here, it'd be enough of an achievement just to beat him two games out of three.'

Ace smiled back, a rare genuine smile. She had hit it off with Karen Davies immediately – somehow, that cheerful nature of hers seemed contagious. Ace had even jeopardized her poker face by removing her shades, well aware of the barriers they placed upon communication.

'So,' she said, 'what's the night-life like around here?'

Karen rolled her eyes and took on an expression of mock suffering. 'What night-life?'

'Oh. Like that, is it?'

''Fraid so.'

'Well, let me get them in again before last orders,' offered Ace, getting to her feet and reaching for her money before the other girl could object. Good job they hadn't been playing for cash, she thought. It never seemed to matter when the Doctor handed out local currency on

15

other planets and in other centuries, but in her own time and place she found it vaguely embarrassing, a bit too much like asking for pocket money. The last thing she wanted was to have to go back to him cap in hand and ask for more. She was aware of his eyes upon her now, and she shot him a look back across the room. The distraction was just enough for her to walk straight into somebody.

'Sorry,' muttered Ace, a little embarrassed. At least she hadn't spilt his drink, that was something.

'You want to be more careful, young lady!' growled the stranger. A holy man of some sort, at least at judging by the collar and by the crucifix which hung on a chain around his neck. His hair was grey, his clothes were black and something gleamed disconcertingly within his sharp green eyes.

'I said I was sorry.'

'I don't mean just your deportment, my girl. I mean your mode of dress, your whole appearance.'

'You what?' Ace's embarrassment had turned into irritation.

'This – outfit of yours,' said the priest, with obvious distaste. 'Hardly suitable attire, don't you think?'

'What I think is that it's my own bloody business!'

The man sighed and cast his eyes skywards in despair. 'Well, so long as you have been warned,' he told her. 'But you should try to remember, my girl, that murders most foul have been committed here these past days. Mark me well, there is Evil walking abroad.'

'Well,' said Ace, 'as long as it stays there.' She didn't wait for a reaction to that. Instead, she pushed past the priest and completed her journey to the bar.

'Sorry about Father Sheridan,' the landlord murmured furtively. 'He's like that with everyone.'

'A regular, is he?'

'Thankfully, no. He's just here for the week, on what he calls a Holy Mission. Some sort of sabbatical, I suppose.' Ace chanced a look over her shoulder but Sheridan

16

had returned to his table, sitting alone in the furthest corner of the room. He seemed no longer interested in her supposed misdemeanours.

By the time she returned to her own seat, the card game had broken up and the participants had split back into their own little groups. Karen was sitting with the victorious Mel Joseph, who she now introduced properly to Ace as her fiancé. There was something about Mel that Ace liked, too – something about those sparkling, sincere eyes which peered out from behind wire-rimmed spectacles, or the unruly blond hair which had avoided the touch of scissors for a year or two at least.

'Are you always this lucky?' she asked, as Mel shovelled his hard-won matches into a pile in the centre of the table.

'Just had a lot of practice,' he answered cheerfully.

'Yeah, at that and everything else!' said Karen, elbowing him affectionately in the ribs. 'From Monopoly to chess to snakes and ladders – he thinks of nothing else. I don't know why I put up with it!'

'It must be love,' opined Mel, slipping an arm around her waist.

'Well,' said Karen, huddling up against him, 'after everything we've been through, it better had be.'

'Want to tell me about it?'

No response.

'You look as fed up as I feel.'

The words came from Bernice who, waiting morosely at the bar for her third vodka and tonic, had decided that the quickest way out of her depression was by conversation.

'Don't mind me,' muttered the intended recipient. 'This is my natural state of mind. Ask anyone.'

Having already chosen her target, Benny had no intention of doing anything of the sort. 'Bernice Summerfield,' she introduced herself.

'Philip Chambers. You've probably heard of me. Or of my wife, at least. Rosemary Chambers?'

17

'Erm, no – don't think so.'

For the first time, the man lifted his head to look at her. He might almost have been handsome, thought Benny – mid-thirties, pleasant face, mousey hair – but his skin was pale and lined, and it seemed like he was weighed down with the worries of the world.

'Makes a change then,' said Philip. 'Usually that's all the tourists come here for, to get a look at the "world's wackiest witch", and the poor old bloke that married her.'

'I'm sorry.' Benny's mind threw up an unwelcome image of Phil slaving over a hot stove whilst his elusive wife hopped astride a broomstick and flew cackling over the village.

'It'll be worse tonight,' he continued morosely, 'what with these murders and everything. It'll be all occult signs and contact with the devil; probably have the whole village round till well into the morning, trying to raise the spirits of the victims with her stupid Ouija board.' And there was more – plenty more – to be said about the trials and tribulations of being married to the neighbourhood witch, with the list of complaints running on for long after Benny's brain had switched into neutral. So much for a meaningful dialogue, she thought. And if she had hoped that the Doctor might come to her rescue, she now realized that she was to be disappointed. He had already left.

Jack Corrigan arrived at Arandale Police Station at twenty minutes past ten, a tow-truck depositing his useless car ungraciously in the cold yellow pool of light which illuminated the entranceway.

'Cheers, buddy,' he grunted half-heartedly as his rescuer unhooked the vehicles and swung himself back into his cab. He paused briefly to remind Corrigan once again that a visit to the garage would be a wise course of action.

'Yeah, yeah, thanks,' he said, 'I'll bear that in mind.' He wouldn't, of course, but he would certainly be giving the hire company a piece of his mind.

The station was a small one, to say the least – in a place like Arandale, there was hardly a need for the facility at all. And with a small station came a small complement of staff; just one uniformed sergeant in charge of a few constables, which was why the officer at the desk seemed so pleased to see a genuine detective, albeit a self-employed one, and hey, perhaps while he was around, he could maybe help them with this little problem they seemed to have – two murders unsolved and the promised arrival of CID delayed by the ferocious winter weather ('roads into the village are impassable they reckon, you'd be some sort of an idiot to try it . . .')

By the time he got out of the station, Corrigan had spent almost thirty minutes trying unsuccessfully to cajole the man into giving him the address he needed and to persuade him that no, thank you very much, he'd love to help out with the murder enquiry but he really had more important things on his mind at the moment. To make matters worse, the man in charge was nowhere to be found. Sergeant Blyth had returned from the scene of the murder and hurried straight off to pick up his kids from the lake. Ice-skating, apparently. Corrigan bit his lip and fumed in silence.

There was a parking ticket on the windscreen of his car, but at least that meant it couldn't get another. He left the useless pile of scrap where it stood and headed for the lights of the Black Cat Tavern across the road. He was in urgent need of a drink and if he hurried, he might just be in time to get one.

The cold, brittle grass crunched harshly beneath Shade's feet as he tramped slowly from the outskirts of the town towards the small dark shape on the horizon. He halted only when he was near enough to identify it positively; a weather-worn blue shell, a light on its top and the words 'Police Public Call Box' picked out in white on the side. An unusual sight, one might have thought, for this time and place. But Shade had known exactly what to expect.

19

He thought of the Doctor and his two companions, and he thought of the Knight of Pentacles, and – briefly – smiled his thin-lipped smile. Finally, having seen all that he wanted to, he turned and slipped silently away into the darkening night.

Into the shadows.

And with that, as they say, the stage has been set. The players are in position, the introductions have been made and it's time for the action to begin. For what can the Doctor do? Nothing, but walk further into my trap and eventually succumb to his inevitable fate. Remember, all he sees are the things I write for him to see; the characters and the situations to which I have decreed he should be exposed. And all of it just words on the page, just a collection of related stories.

So far.

Chapter 2

Nocturnal Admissions

By now, it had become something of a ritual.

As the distant town hall clock struck ten hollow chimes, Norman Power climbed once again onto the wrong side of the old wooden bridge and forced himself to look down.

Oblivious, the river continued in its ages-old path. As it always did. For what could it know, after all, of the pain and the anguish he was feeling? Of the hollow shell that his life had become?

It wasn't very deep, he thought, as he had thought a hundred times before. Not very deep, but a long jump away. And if the fall didn't get him, the bitter cold of the water certainly would.

It would work. He could do it.

He *would* do it.

But not just yet . . .

For the longest of times then, Norman Power sat in silence – as he always did. His frail arms pulled his dufflecoat tightly around his shaking body and he wondered again why he had bothered to wear the costume beneath it. Hanging uneasily from his wiry frame, the flimsy white garment offered scant protection against the harsh air.

And eventually, as he always did, Norman found his attention wavering, shifting away from the dark waters below and turning instead to the dark sky above. It was a good night tonight – a good, clear night – and his eyes shone in wonder at the majestic splendour of the sparkling firmament. As they always did. And again, his mind turned to the meteor storm, and he imagined it once

21

more; a thousand tons of compacted rock whistling softly through the atmosphere, beautiful trails of orange blazing in the air behind them like the most magnificent of the season's fireworks.

He wanted to see it again but no matter how he willed it, there was nothing up there. No rocks, no whistling, no trails of fire – no heaven-sent salvation from his pointless existence. So eventually even the trails in his own mind's eye burnt out, and he sighed a deep and painful sigh of regret as he realized that his heart's desire was never to be.

By the time the clock struck eleven, Norman's attention was given over fully to the stars – shining so far away, yet seeming so tantalizingly close. When he closed his eyes, he fancied that he could hear their siren songs, reaching out to him like a set of homing beacons back to an old and better life.

So that was what he did. He closed his eyes and he listened to the stars, knowing that he would hear their calls until long after the dawning sun had driven them away with its cruel morning light.

And he tried, once again, to remember which of those stars he had visited.

It was well past last orders when Ace said goodbye to her two new friends on the pavement outside the Black Cat. Indeed, the Doctor had left quite some time before, heading for the local guest-house into which he had booked his party – in something of a foul mood, as she recalled.

'I think he expected us to go with him,' Bernice had commented uncertainly, but Ace had replied that that was his own problem, and that she was only just beginning to enjoy herself. Benny had followed him anyhow, and Ace had decided that she wasn't really interested in *her* problems either.

Right now, she had other things to occupy her. With Mel and Karen out of the way, she could turn her attention to someone whose appearance in the pub some fifteen minutes earlier had immediately aroused her curiosity. He was still sitting by the now-closed bar, she noticed; a broad-shouldered man with a rugged face, a sour expression, a battered brown hat and a trenchcoat that had seen better days – most of them during the nineteen seventies.

'Hi,' she said brightly, tapping him on the shoulder. 'I'm Ace, and you're a detective.' Nice timing, she congratulated herself, as her victim choked comically on the mouthful of beer he had just taken. She waited with smug patience as he recovered his composure, turning towards her with an expression that was fierce and threatening.

'Smart mouth, sister,' Corrigan hissed, waving a warning finger under her nose. 'But I suggest you keep it buttoned. You don't know zip!'

'An American one too,' said Ace, unfazed. She pushed the offending hand aside. 'Either that or you've been watching too many imported cop shows. Is that your real accent?'

The man glanced quickly around him before grabbing her arm and pushing her roughly towards a corner table. Anyone else might have lost their manhood for that, she thought. Still, she would play along for now, if only to hear what this strange-looking character had to say for himself.

'Jack Corrigan,' he muttered, flicking his identification briefly before her eyes. 'The hardest-boiled dick in the States!'

Ace smirked. 'If you say so.' So Benny didn't have the monopoly on reading non-verbal communication. Of course, she would have to be blind to have missed the signals that Corrigan was putting out. 'So what are you doing out of the States and sitting in a pub in a quiet English town? On vacation are you?'

'That's about the size of it, yes.'

'Liar!'

'Believe what you like,' Corrigan said, 'but I came in here for a brew, and that's all there is to it.'

'Fine,' said Ace, with exaggerated politeness. 'Tell you what then, you come back in here tomorrow and I'll introduce you to all my friends; Benny, the Doctor, Mel, Karen . . .'

The detective's eyes widened and his expression froze. 'Oh no you won't, missy. You're not gonna breathe a word about me to anyone. Understand?'

'Aha! So you *are* watching someone, then?'

Corrigan glared at her, venomously.

'Okay,' said Ace, 'but I could help you, you know. And either way, I'm going to find out exactly what it is you're doing here.' She got to her feet and headed back out of the pub.

Jack Corrigan watched her go and reflexively pulled at his chin, as his mind ticked its way through a number of promising scenarios.

Elsewhere, Bernice awoke shaking from a dream in which . . .

She didn't want to think about it. She rubbed her eyes and stretched her arms and yawned loudly, and remembered *lying face-up in the mud, and the hands around her throat, and* . . .

She banished the image, concentrating her eyes on the peeling yellow paper which seemed to decorate all of the rooms in Mrs Shawcross's guest-house. She forced her ears to hear nothing but the wailing wind without, and she waited for the dream to recede into the untappable depths of her mind, as such things always did.

It was no use. No matter what she did, she could remember it as plainly and as vividly as if it had been real.

Ace had tried to kill her – hurled her to the ground, choked the life out of her struggling body – and all the time, the Doctor had just stood calmly by and told her that it was all for the good of the universe and she really shouldn't be fighting it, you know.

So that was it. Well, okay, she had admitted it to herself now. She had had a bad dream and that was that. It didn't

24

mean a thing. Right? But she knew that there were no such instant solutions to the anguish she was feeling. Indeed, she had found herself increasingly of that opinion for as long as the night had progressed. She had arrived at the guest-house almost two hours before, but had so far been able to settle into little more than a light doze, her nightmares awakening her whenever restful sleep seemed on the horizon.

Her problems were twofold. Firstly, the TARDIS's internal clock had still said 'noon' when she had stepped out into the dark Arandale evening. Although the ship seemed to protect its crew from the effects of jet-lag as such, it was still a little difficult to adjust to such a change.

The second problem had been well documented in her dreams, and right now it was something she didn't want to think about too hard.

Instead, she just lay for a while longer, staring at the ceiling, listening to the wind – until finally, she came to terms with the fact that, for the next few hours at least, the possibility of sleep was non-existent. She got quietly out of bed, slipping quickly into her trouser suit and overcoat. A brisk walk around the village was what she needed; if not to actually solve her problems, then to at least enable her to view them a little more clearly.

As she passed along the landing, she wondered if she should perhaps look in on the Doctor. Bernice had learnt by now that her companion rarely spent the night hours actually sleeping, particularly not when confronted by a fresh problem into which he could intrude.

In the end, she decided against the idea. Things had not been the same between the pair recently, not since Silurian Earth and the way in which the Doctor had condemned that other-dimensional planet's billions of life-forms to certain, lingering death. Not that she was even quite convinced that that decision had been the wrong one, under the circumstances, but it was as if the incident had opened a door to her; a door through which she had suddenly, and with startling clarity, seen all the shadows and the stains which hung upon the soul of her one-time friend and mentor. She had seen only through the cracks in that door before, and she had never truly comprehended just how alien, how amoral, was the man she had chosen to travel with.

It was a disturbing thought, and one which brought thoughts of leaving inevitably back to the forefront of Benny's mind. Sometimes, she reflected, it was so hard to know what was the right thing to do. But she did know that the thing to do now was to pass the Time Lord's room by and head out of the building alone – because the last shoulder she wanted to cry on right now was that of the Doctor. Not when she felt, with all her heart, that he was no longer somebody she could trust.

Trust? Nowadays, it felt like she didn't even know him.

Bernice had been right about one thing, though. The Doctor was not asleep. Neither though was he truly awake. He was sitting now, crosslegged on the floor beside his bunk, and his eyes were wide although he was seeing nothing. His deep dark thoughts, alas, were not meant for humankind to know . . . which is to say that I can't actually read them at the moment. An unusual fellow, this Doctor.

Well, I suppose you told me he would be.

Ace's mind was on the Doctor as well. She imagined him standing at the head of the guest-house stairs, tapping his foot impatiently as he pointed to his watch and demanded to know where she had been all night. The image was a ludicrous one of course, but she nevertheless quickened her pace slightly and wished she'd paid a little more attention when he'd given her the directions to Mrs Shawcross's establishment. In any case, the picture was quickly destroyed – not by her own angry attempts at denial, but rather by the sudden screech of brakes and the realization of imminent danger. She dived by instinct to one side as a battered white Datsun car barrelled around the corner, skidding to a frantic stop with three wheels on the right-hand pavement.

'You stupid bitch!' yelled its passenger, hurling open the door and flying out into the road. 'Crossing the bloody street like that, you could have got us all killed!'

Ace instinctively checked the driver's whereabouts, but he was still in his seat, staring straight ahead with eyes glazed by shock and by alcohol. Good, she thought. Just one to deal with, then.

'Oh, excuse me,' she said, with exaggerated politeness. 'I'm obviously too drunk to walk home. Perhaps I should have brought the car with me, eh?'

'Don't get sarky with me, you stuck-up bitch!' the woman seethed, waving a painted finger under Ace's nose. Ace recognized the harridan, albeit only from having her pointed out across the Black Cat's lounge. Her name was Tina Grimshaw, her drunken husband was called Mason and neither of them, according to Karen, were very much fun to be with.

'Move that,' Ace calmly instructed, staring at Tina's finger, 'or lose it.'

'Come on, love. Leave it. Let's get off home.' The slur-red speech came from Mason Grimshaw, now partially recovered and hanging unsteadily out of the car window.

'Keep out of it, you!' Tina retorted, and her husband flopped indelicately back into the car and kept his silence. She, on the other hand, was just getting started.

'I should bloody well report you, you dozy bitch!' she raged, jutting her face so far towards Ace's own that the younger woman recoiled involuntarily from the pungent scent of over-applied perfume. 'Coming into our village dressed like some sort of whore and swanning around here like you own the place, with no mind for where you're going and what sort of accidents you're causing. You ought to be . . .!'

There was plenty more, but Ace paid little attention. Much as she enjoyed a good argument, she could well do

27

without the directionless tirade of abuse which seemed to be Mrs Grimshaw's conservational upper limit.

'Okay,' she interrupted finally, reaching beneath her jacket. 'I'm going to give you a count of five to shut up, get back in the car and leave.' And Tina's furious rejoinder was stifled as Ace produced the blaster gun which the Doctor so hated her carrying. 'Well?'

'You bitch!' hissed Tina, disbelievingly. Ace wondered if that was the only insult she knew. She was actually rather enjoying the way Tina's expression of horror spread slowly from her eyes to the rest of her face. Flicking her weapon to its lowest setting, she fired a blast of energy at a nearby litter bin, producing a pyrotechnic display as impressive as any of that night's fireworks. 'Now,' she said, tucking the blaster back into its concealed holster, 'we'll say no more, shall we? Goodnight.' And she turned to continue her journey, noting with satisfaction that Tina was still standing stock-still, her jaw agape, as she turned the far corner of the street.

As Ace finally reached the guest-house, found her room and settled into a deep and dreamless slumber, others not so very far away were just beginning their nocturnal activities.

In a deep, dark cellar, a robed figure stood triumphantly before a rough stone altar, breathing deeply of incense and candle smoke and controlling his shuddering body for as long as he could, until . . . until loud, hysterical laughter burst from his lips and he shook no longer with fear, but rather with a mirth born of delirium.

'Thy bidding has been done!' he shrieked with triumph, lifting his watery gaze towards the heavens. And the chant was taken up by the crowd behind him, their voices starting low but rising steadily, higher and higher, reaching upwards towards fever pitch.

'Thy will be done. Thy will be done. Thy will be done.'

'It is all as was decreed,' their leader whispered, but his words were lost, drowned out by the exultant cries of his legion of followers. He leaned carefully forward, his palms pressed flat against the altar before him, and he stifled a moan of almost sexual ecstasy as the Force flowed into him, rippled through him, became one with him, made him its own.

'Thy will be done . . .'

The Force reverberated through the town, and even the Doctor was stirred momentarily from his meditation. His sharp, inscrutable features took on a look of slight puzzlement, and the shadow of a doubt flickered momentarily across his eyes.

Norman was jerked suddenly out of a dream world, his body charged with ice-cold energy, feeling suddenly empty as the sensation drained out through his feet. He shuddered and fought back an inexplicable tear that welled in response to some tremendous sense of indefinable loss. He almost cried out loud when he realized that somebody was sitting on the bridge beside him.

'Hi,' said the stranger, laying a steadying hand on the startled man's shoulder. 'My name's Bernice Summerfield. Benny to my friends. Tell me, is everyone in this place a chronic depressive?'

It took a long moment for Norman to gather his wits; a long moment staring into Benny's reassuring eyes. Then he tore his gaze away, and concentrated instead on the drop before him. He shifted his weight on the handrail, uncomfortably.

'You're not going to jump,' said Benny.

'Try and stop me!'

Benny smiled. 'That wasn't a threat, it was a statement of fact. I'm sorry, I didn't catch your name.'

'Norman,' he said, almost ashamed. 'Norman Power.' His eyes were on the water below him, but he knew as well as Benny did that the rest of him wasn't about to follow.

'So what's the problem, Norman?'

'Problem?'

'Oh, well pardon me for jumping to conclusions. I just sort of assumed that you were sitting on the side of this bridge here because you were thinking about hurling yourself off it and dashing yourself into bloody little pieces on the rocks in that river down there. I do apologize, I must have been mistaken.'

'It's a long story,' insisted Norman, changing tack.

'Aren't they all?' returned Benny. 'But you're dying to tell someone – almost literally. So go ahead.' I hope this one isn't as bad as Phil Chambers, she thought, somewhat uncharitably.

Norman was still reluctant. 'You wouldn't understand,' he told her. But it seemed that Benny had an answer for everything.

'That's what my old maths teacher used to say when she was trying to explain the concept of applying differential equations to matrix calculations,' she told him.

'And?'

'And she was right. But I've always been a lot better with the more practical side of life. So try me.'

Norman looked at her, his brow furrowed. 'Is this some sort of an act, or do you always approach strangers like this?'

'I can honestly say,' said Benny, 'that whenever I've happened upon a fifty-year-old man about to fling himself off a bridge at one o'clock in the morning, I've reacted in just this fashion.'

Norman sighed, and turned his attention back to the sky above. 'Anyway,' he said softly, 'you really wouldn't understand. You couldn't know what it's like to have been out there.'

Benny followed his gaze. 'Out where?'

'Out there!' Norman's finger stabbed upwards. 'Out amongst the stars, visiting new planets, new galaxies . . .'

'Oh, out *there*!' Benny inspected her fingernails nonchalantly. 'Just came from there a few hours ago, actually.'

Norman jerked back, startled, and for a frightening

moment Benny thought he was actually going to topple off the bridge by accident. 'You're a shape-changer!' he accused her, breathlessly. 'From the planet Zog!'

'I most certainly am not.'

Norman seemed to calm down a little, but he was still on his guard. 'Then where . . ?' he asked.

'That,' said Benny, 'is a long story.'

And for the first time in a long time, Norman's wrinkled face creased into something approximating a smile. 'Aren't they all?' he said.

In one white-walled room of a hotel a little more expensive than Mrs Shawcross's converted semi, a scarlet-cloaked figure with an even longer story to tell knelt close against an untidy bed, and with hands clasped tightly together, prayed fervently to a God of whom the more legitimate members of his profession would never have approved.

He prayed long and he prayed hard, for the safety of his flock and for the delivery of the world from the forces of Evil which beset it. Most of all, he prayed that he, Father Kenneth Michael Sheridan, would be able to find within his own tainted heart the strength and determination which he would sorely need if he were to succeed in his crusade against the Dark.

Finally, by the light of a single blood-red candle, he made a solemn declaration of intent. 'That I will confront the servant of the Evil One in this cursed place, and thus rid the gentlefolk of Arandale from the scourge which walks amongst them. Amen.' The Christian word of praise never sounded more ominously out of place than when used in this room, by this man.

Father Sheridan spent the night then in silent supplication, far beyond even the eventual death of the guttering candle flame. For his heart was as steel, and his mind in preparation for the ultimate test of the unbending faith which was his. The shining golden crucifix on its chain remained in the tight grip of his good right hand, and his

31

eyes never moved from the printed image of the one he was sworn to destroy. The picture was torn from a newspaper, a few months old now. Just a filler story about an amusing curiosity, quickly and easily forgotten by most.

'Arandale's witch' read the headline. And the photograph was that of Rosemary Chambers.

Norman was still trying to take it all in.

'And you're really from the future?' he asked, for what seemed like the thousandth time. 'I mean, the real future? My future?'

'If you have one,' said Benny, looking pointedly down at the river. 'That's up to you.'

'What's it like?' asked Norman, urgently. 'I mean, how do we all end up? Do things get any better?'

'I . . . I can't tell you that. At least, I don't think I can. I'm sorry.'

Norman's enthusiasm was undiminished. 'What about the planets, then? Which ones have you been to?'

Benny laughed. 'Oh, I shouldn't think the names would mean anything to you.'

'They might,' he answered, perhaps a little too quickly, too eagerly for comfort.

Benny didn't know whether she should say what was on her mind now, but she did so nevertheless. 'You said you'd been out there. To other planets. What exactly did you mean by that?' Did she really want to be perpetuating this topic of conversation?

'Mercury,' Norman announced, after a moment's thought. 'Oh yes, I remember Mercury. I fought Volcanus and his Magma-Men there. Nearly died too, but I managed to save the whole blasted planet in the end. They even gave me the keys to Mercurion, their capital city. You'll have been there, of course?'

'Erm, no,' admitted Benny, 'I've not quite got round to that one yet. We tend to travel in, erm . . . other circles.'

Norman's eyes lit up. 'Oh, you mean Mars, Jupiter, Saturn, all round there?'

'Well . . .'

'I fought in the War of Attrition out there, you know,' he said, wistfully.

'The War of Attrition? Where was that?'

Norman looked at her strangely. 'On the planet Attrition, of course. The secret eleventh planet of the solar system. Don't tell me you've never been there either?'

'You know, oddly enough, I don't think I have.' But Benny's sarcasm was totally lost on her companion.

'It's quite funny actually,' he continued, unabashed. 'I don't know quite how I survived that one either. Things certainly looked pretty black for a while.'

'I can imagine.'

'I used to think I had a guardian angel watching over me, making sure that nothing too bad could ever happen. Does that sound stupid?'

'Not at all,' Benny assured him. Actually it seemed like the most sane thing he had said thus far.

'I sometimes wonder if she's still out there,' said Norman, 'watching down on me from the stars. But I can never see her there, no matter how hard I look. I think . . .' He paused, blinking back tears, then continued in a slightly lower voice. 'I think she must have gone. I think she went a long, long time ago.'

He lapsed into silence after that, and for perhaps as long as five minutes the pair sat side by side, unspeaking, each lost in their own miserable thoughts. By the time Norman resumed the conversation, he had made one of the most important decisions of his life.

'I'm going to tell you something,' he said, obviously still a little uncertain.

'Yes?' Benny adopted her best listening expression, her eyes encouraging him to take the plunge and open up to her.

'It's something I've never told anyone before.'

'Aha.'

'And you've got to promise, promise me faithfully, that you'll keep it a secret. Can you keep a secret?'

'You should hear some of the ones I've kept in the past,' Benny joked. 'Not that you can, of course. They're all . . .'

'Secret, yes. But this one . . .' Norman paused, for dramatic effect more than anything, Benny suspected. 'This one could be a matter of life and death.'

Benny nodded, her expression suitably serious.

'You see, it's like this,' said Norman, taking a deep breath before he continued. 'I used to be a hero.'

He let the words hang in the air for a moment, as if expecting a response of some kind. Benny, not having the faintest idea what he was talking about, was unable to give a particularly coherent one. 'What, you mean a policeman or a fireman or something?' she asked finally.

'Oh no, no. I mean a super-hero!'

'A what?'

'A super-hero. The White Knight. Perhaps you've heard of me?'

'I . . .'

'No. No, I don't suppose you have. My name won't be going down in history, then?'

'Well . . .'

'I shouldn't have expected it to, I suppose.' Norman laughed mirthlessly. 'Most people don't even remember me in this century, never mind through the next few. 1959, it was, June the fifteenth. I remember it well.'

'Remember . . .?'

'The meteor storm. Part of it hit just outside the town; almost demolished the old castle over there.' He pointed, but the buildings of Arandale lay firmly between him and the structure in question. 'That's where I got my powers from, naturally. I went up there to see what was going on – yes, I know that doesn't sound very sensible, but I can't explain it. It's like something was calling to me. And then I touched one of the fallen rocks, and I felt sort of strange, as if something had just leapt inside me and . . . and, well . . .' He tailed off sadly, as his bright memories of the past became swamped in the miserable shadows of the

34

present. 'I suppose you think I'm making a fool of myself. Just a sad old man, throwing his life away pining for the gifts he used to have.' Then he turned to Benny, and his eyes were sparkling with a fierce enthusiasm. 'Oh, but if you'd been able to *fly* . . !'

He was lost in memories again and Benny, finding herself strangely drawn to this ridiculous character, reached out a comforting arm. 'No,' she said. 'No, I don't think you're making a fool of yourself. Not at all.'

Norman smiled gratefully. 'You know what I think?' he asked.

'That isn't one of my abilities, no.'

'I think you're my guardian angel. I think you've come back to me, after all this time.'

Benny squirmed slightly under the weight of implied responsibility. 'You have to look after yourself,' she muttered, uncomfortably. 'And you can start by getting off this bridge and getting a grip on your life.'

Norman had turned away again and the eyes which looked back towards the stars were now painfully moist. It was a difficult decision, but in the end Benny felt it best to leave him be. So without another word, she climbed slowly down from the rail and began the journey back to the warm bed she had left behind and the long sleep which she now felt truly able to cope with.

As she stepped beyond the village limits, she made the final mistake of looking back over her shoulder. Norman was still there all right, his position unchanged, his gaze still skywards. He might as well have been some petrified gargoyle, maintaining a silent vigil from the side of the bridge, spending the whole of his life just waiting for a repetition of an event that could never have happened in the first place.

And in the moment she thought that, she felt her heart reach out towards him, and she knew that her good night's sleep would be a long time in coming.

By half past five, the sky was beginning to lighten in

the east, the faint prelude to dawn starting to banish the glorious firmament into invisibility, at least for the daylight hours that followed. Norman climbed slowly down from the bridge, like he always did, and sank his hands deep into his pockets. His eyes focused firmly on his feet, seeking out little in the way of landmarks as, by habit more than by guidance, they trod the familiar path back towards his home. Like they always did.

Tonight, he told himself. He would come back here then, and this time he would have the courage to do what was necessary. Tonight, he thought, he would end it all forever.

An explosive splutter drew his attention sharply upwards, to where a bright streak of orange shot high into the early morning sky. For a moment his heart soared, but it was just a firework. Nothing more.

Tonight, he thought. Definitely tonight. And he made himself a firm and binding promise to that effect before continuing on his journey with the enlightenment of a difficult decision finally made. Like it always was.

This morning, there was just one change in the familiar routine. One important change. This time, Norman had a real live guardian angel watching over him – and not from quite so far as he might once have imagined.

Chapter 3

Five Go Adventuring Again

At nine o'clock that morning, the Adventure Kids assembled for their third meeting of the holidays, gathered as always in the relative privacy of Tim's back yard.

Well, four of them did, anyway. Displaying her usual total disregard towards all matters important, Mrs Mitchell had decreed that Carson wasn't to leave the house that morning. He needed a bath, she claimed, so the rest of the team would have to conduct their business without him.

'Okay,' said Tim, admirably concealing his disappointment at this horrendous turn of events. 'So what do we do?'

The others looked at him blankly.

'I mean, we can't just sit here all through the hols, can we? I want to get back into action.'

'Well, I don't see why we have to go looking for another stupid adventure,' protested Michelle. 'I mean, we're always running off chasing robbers and looking for ghosts, and I'm sick of it! Can't we just get through the holidays without a mystery, for once?'

She certainly had a point. As you'll know from the Kids' previous appearances, danger and excitement were never far away when they were around. Formed by Tim during the summer holidays two years before, they had since gone on to prove themselves invaluable to the tiny local police force; it seemed that hardly a vacation passed when the four friends (and Carson) didn't find some sort of fascinating mystery to unravel – and indeed, they had now participated in over twenty such cases.

Ah – on second thoughts, I think they must have had *two* adventures in each holiday. Or three. Or ... well anyway, this is their last one, so it really doesn't matter.

'Don't be such a cry-baby!' Gary Chambers scolded his younger sister. 'We formed this club to have adventures, didn't we? Well, I say we should get out there and look for another one!'

'I agree,' said Tracey Daniels. 'But we'd better hurry – it's Wednesday already, and we're back at school on Monday.' She furrowed her brow in concentration and there was silence for a moment as they all thought hard. Somewhere in Arandale, they knew, there was at least one gang of crafty smugglers – probably dressed in unconvincing ghost costumes and scaring the local populace silly – just waiting to lead them into another of their hair-raising exploits. But how to find them?

'I know,' shouted Gary suddenly. 'What about Vampire Castle? You know, that great old building on the top of Blood Hill, right outside the town – the one that's supposed to be haunted!'

'Gosh yes,' cried Tim. 'You're right. I don't know why we haven't thought about investigating that before. Good idea, Gaz.'

'Then that's settled,' said Tracey, jumping eagerly to her feet. 'We'll go and have a look round there after lunch, shall we? Say about two o'clock?'

Of course, they all agreed heartily, and after another hour or so of excited chatter about old adventures, ghost stories, the probability of their ever getting membership cards drawn up and so on, the children parted and went their separate ways.

Until the afternoon.

The Doctor and Ace shared a subdued breakfast in Mrs Shawcross's small dining room. Bernice, having finally got to bed less than three hours before, was still deep within

38

an exhausted, dreamless sleep, and the Doctor had decided that it was best not to wake her.

'What are you up to today?' he asked Ace, in an attempt to break the silence between them. His companion just shrugged, her concentration reserved for tackling the mound of toast she had shovelled onto her plate. 'Seeing your two friends again?' the Doctor tried.

'Might do.'

'What about that private investigator chap, Corrigan?' How had he known about *him*?

'What do you mean?' asked Ace, guardedly.

'Well, what do you think of him?'

She thought about this for a moment. 'Pretty unconvincing,' she concluded, before turning her attention back to her meal. Obviously not in the mood for conversation, thought the Doctor – as if she ever was these days. With him, anyway. He sighed, pushed his half-empty plate to one side and, with a murmured goodbye, headed purposefully into the hallway and out through the front door. The expression on Ace's face was an inscrutable one as, peering over the top of her shades, she watched him go.

'Good morning,' said the Doctor cheerfully, doffing his hat and grinning broadly.

Hung-over and already late for work, Mason Grimshaw gave only a low grunt in response, pushing past the smaller man without sparing him a second glance. Showing no further reaction to the brief encounter, the Doctor continued his casual stroll up to the gift shop and peered attentively into its well-stocked window.

The shop, small though it was, sold quite an impressive array of goods, most of them utterly useless. Nevertheless, the Doctor strolled breezily into the establishment, looked politely around the displays of practical jokes, novelty fridge magnets and neon telephones, and finally made a purchase.

'Is that a spoon in your pocket?' the sales assistant

asked, as the Doctor managed somehow to cram the Travel Scrabble set into the inside pocket of his jacket.

'It appears to be,' he answered, and left.

One chore completed, he thought. Now what was his next move to be?

At eleven o'clock, Ace kept a previously arranged appointment at the home of Mel Joseph and Karen Davies. It was a far more impressive building than she had actually imagined; a white brick semi-detached house with red-painted window frames and a polished oak door adorned with shining brass. She vaguely wondered, as she slammed the lion's head knocker against its housing, how the young couple had been able to afford such luxury – especially when they were both to be found at home at this time on a Wednesday morning.

'Hi,' beamed Karen as she opened the door. 'Come on in.'

'Nice house,' Ace complimented her as she stepped over the threshold.

'Thanks. We only rent, but we've tried to do it up nice. Well,' Karen added after a moment's reflection, 'I have, anyway. I've had to hand the front room over to Mel for his games. They're wall to wall in there!'

Ace gave an inward whistle of astonishment as they stepped into the room in question. 'You're not kidding, are you?' she said, quite impressed.

Karen grinned. 'I warned you. A complete fanatic, he is. He had half of this lot carted straight up here as soon as we got the place. The rest he's bought since.'

Ace moved slowly around the room, picking out just some of the names on the vast array of multicoloured boxes which formed cardboard towers rising from every conceivable surface. ' "Baker Street", "Game of Life", "Champions", "Ker-Plunk" – is there any game he *doesn't* have?'

'Not many, I shouldn't think.'

'How do you put up with it all? I mean, he's got this room well filled.'

'And half the cupboards upstairs,' Karen assured her. 'Still, it's all harmless, I suppose. And it keeps us alive and in clothes.'

'Sorry?'

'Oh, didn't I mention? Mel designs games for a living – freelance work. He doesn't get very many contracts, but those he does get earn a fair amount.' That was the house explained, at least.

Karen glanced around for the nearest example of her fiancé's work, finding it teetering on the top of one of the piles of gaudily painted boxes. 'NIGHTSHADE' the box read. 'The official game of the popular TV series.'

'He did this one a few years ago,' she explained. 'You know, when there was that big "Nightshade" nostalgia thing, the videos and the books and the repeats and all that.'

Ace nodded. She had never actually seen the programme, but she'd once met its star. A very long time ago, she recalled, in a part of her life remembered chiefly for its pains and frustrations.

'And there's plenty more where that came from,' announced Mel from the doorway. 'Hi, Ace. Come for the two-cent tour? Or would you like a quick game of something first?'

Ace smiled. 'Maybe later. The two-cent tour, please.'

'Okay,' said Mel. 'We'll have a quick wander around the town, lunch at Ted's Caff, and then we'll introduce you to the star attraction.'

'Which is?'

'Our very own local witch, of course!' Karen told her. 'Rosemary Chambers.'

'I'm still not sure about this,' complained Michelle, lagging behind the others as they struggled up the steep incline of what youthful imaginations had traditionally labelled Blood Hill. All of the Adventure Kids had turned out promptly, of course – well, all except Carson, who had apparently shown signs of moulting and was being kept indoors for suitable treatment. Still, Michelle at least was none too keen on the idea of poking around in haunted castles and throughout the journey there, she had made a frequent habit of saying so.

'Look,' snapped Gary, irritably. 'I don't know why you don't just go on home and leave this mystery to the *real* investigators.'

Michelle scowled at the back of his head, holding on tightly to a thick, leather-bound book she had found in her mother's shop. She'd show them, she thought.

'Come on you two,' Tim called back, encouragingly. 'Stop arguing, can't you? We're nearly there.' And sure enough, another minute's walk brought them right up to the doorway of the ancient castle – or at least, of the castle's ancient remains.

'Not much of it left, is there?' commented Tracey, wrinkling her nose up in distaste. 'Just a few half-demolished walls and doors and stuff.'

'It'd be a bit draughty for any ghosts,' Gary pointed out, drily.

'Maybe so,' said Tim, 'but I still think it's worth checking out.'

The others nodded in agreement – all except Michelle, who brandished her book importantly. 'You want to try looking at this before you go running in there!'

'Oh get lost, cry-baby!'

'No, Gary,' Tim interjected, 'let her have her say.' At eleven years old, he was the eldest of the group and well used by now to fending off quarrels between the siblings.

'What have you got, Mish?' asked Tracey, trying to peer at the faded title of the volume.

'A book,' said Michelle proudly, 'on Vampire Castle.'

'On the castle?' echoed Tim, genuinely interested.

'Yep.' With a sidelong smirk at her brother, Michelle squatted down onto the grass, leading the others to do likewise. 'Of course, they use its real name, Arandale

42

Keep – and it says here that Blood Hill was really called *Fern* Hill . . .'

'But what does it say about the ghosts?' interrupted Gary impatiently.

'Not a lot actually,' said Michelle, flipping through to the relevant page. 'All that happened after the castle was demolished.'

'By some sort of meteor storm, wasn't it?' put in Tracey. 'About thirty years ago?'

'Yeah, that's right. 1959, it says here. And for ages after that, anyone who went anywhere near the castle got really sick and died.'

'Died?' echoed Tracey, appalled.

'*And* saw ghosts!' added Gary, stabbing his finger at the words on the page. 'You see? There *must* be something in there. The meteors must have woken something up, or set it free or something. We've definitely got to investigate this!'

'But we've never fought any ghosts that *killed* people before,' said Tim uncertainly.

'Oh, that was all ages ago!' scoffed Gary. 'Nothing's happened since then, has it?'

'Well, this book was written in 1973 . . .'

'But if anything'd happened since then, we'd know about it, wouldn't we?'

Tracey nodded thoughtfully, but the others looked uncertain.

'And what if we go waking something up again?' Michelle wanted to know.

Gary dismissed her caution with a wave of his hand. 'Don't be so daft,' he chastened her. 'Nothing like that's going to happen.'

'It'll just be an adventure, I suppose,' said Tracey. 'Like all the others.' And it was then that Gary Chambers spoke the most fatefully incorrect words of his entire young life.

'There's nothing for us to worry about,' he said. 'It's all perfectly safe.'

43

Getting into the police station had not been a problem. A fierce look in his eye, a snapped command and a quick flick of an Arcturian driving licence and the Doctor had been ushered quickly through from the tiny reception area into the equally tiny but much more private offices to the rear.

He found Police Sergeant Malcolm Blyth behind a precarious mountain of paper in the incident room – actually an interview room, now furnished with more chairs and people than it could comfortably hold – and greeted him cursorily. 'Morning sergeant, what's the situation? Any clues, suspects, evidence, theories?' He shrugged his jacket onto a paper-strewn chair, pretending not to notice that it slid immediately onto the equally untidy floor, and rolled up his shirt sleeves, ready to get to work. 'Well?'

Blyth was on his feet now, his cheeks flushing red as his initial surprise and confusion gave way to anger. 'Constables,' he blustered, 'arrest this man!'

'Oh, not again!' the Doctor groaned. He slipped neatly out of the way of two of Blyth's finest officers and produced a rolled-up piece of paper from his jacket pocket, which he pushed smartly beneath the sergeant's nose. 'Here. Read this!'

Blyth read it. 'A letter of authorization?'

'From the Commissioner of Police.'

He was still uncertain. 'Well, it *looks* authentic, I suppose.'

'And so it should, considering I spent almost ten minutes creating it last night.'

Blyth almost choked with frustration, struggling for words as he watched his control of the situation fly ever further away from him. 'You mean it's a forgery?' he finally managed.

'Of course it is,' said the Doctor, who was already busy rummaging through one of the mounds of paperwork, 'but you'll never get me to admit that – and by the time you've checked it out, I'll be long gone. Unless you co-operate with me now that is, in which case I'll stay around

44

long enough to solve your murder, catch the culprit and have a nice hot cup of tea and a chat about it afterwards. You've got the autopsy report on the first victim, I see.'

'I . . .'

'Stab wound to the stomach, followed by loss of too much blood to be solely attributed to said wound. Thank you, that's all I needed to know.'

'You . . .'

'And do you have any suspects yet?'

'We . . .'

'I didn't think so. Well never mind, I have a couple of ideas on that score myself. I'll check them out and get back to you. Thanks again for your help. Goodbye.'

And before Blyth's helpless eyes, the Doctor swung his jacket back over his shoulder and strode nonchalantly back out of the room, sending a dozen different reports flying as he closed the door behind him.

'Next time,' he finally announced, just for the sake of using his newly rediscovered voice, 'I'm going to nail that joker!'

From the outside, 'Rosemary Chambers' Mystic Emporium' looked every inch a tourist attraction. Unfortunately, it was of the type which usually made Ace want to steer very well clear.

'It's a bit tacky, isn't it?' she complained, casting her eyes distastefully over the highly inappropriate neon tubing in which the shop's name was picked out, and over the misspelt, handwritten sign in the window which enticed tourists into meeting 'Arandale's famus wich'. Behind the trappings, Ace could see what might have been quite a pleasant old building; Edwardian construction, she figured, just like the Black Cat, obviously built originally as a dwelling place. The conversion of the front room into a shop unit had been carried out within the last twenty years.

'To be honest,' said Karen, 'I don't really see what the attraction is. I think it's just fascination with witches and

45

black magic and all that rubbish – and Rosemary certainly plays on all that as best she can.'

'She's managed to get herself quite a bit of coverage in the press,' Mel added.

'So I gather,' said Ace, peering at a row of tubs in the grimy shop window. 'This is weird,' she commented. 'Is that really eye of newt? No, I don't suppose it can be.'

'Left-over semolina, the rumours say,' said Karen.

'And puppy-dogs' tails? This is ridiculous!'

'Disgusting, too.' commented Mel.

'But how can she make a living out of all this? I mean, people might like to have a look round, but they can't seriously think of buying anything!'

'The stuff inside's a bit more normal,' said Mel. 'You know, tarot cards, magic sets, books, that sort of thing. Mostly though, I think she gets her money from fortune-telling.' He pointed out a notice written in felt-tip pen on a piece of card in the door. 'Tarot Reedings, till 8pm. Ring for asistanse when closed.'

'Well,' said Ace, reaching for the door, 'we've seen the outside. Let's have a look at the rest.'

The Adventure Kids had read, a long time ago, about the vast cellars which sprawled intact beneath the ruins of Arandale Keep. They had all spent sleepless nights wondering what treasures lay within them and what mysteries they held for the intrepid explorer. But rumours about 'Vampire Castle' and the deaths in the sixties had led any reasonable parents in the village to ban their offspring from going anywhere near the place. So the secrets of the past were lost to them forever – or at least until they were old enough to search for them behind their parents' backs.

For twenty long and frustrating minutes, it seemed that the castle would deny them still; the iron ring set in the hard stone floor symbolized a classic route to adventure and excitement, but it seemed too stiff and too heavy for the children to lift it. Eventually perseverance paid off, and the ancient block rose hesitantly from its housing and crashed deafeningly onto the floor beside. After that, things became a little less clear-cut, as the musty black pit which led down into places unknown seemed just a little darker and just a little more frightening than any of the children had actually imagined.

Finally it was Gary who took the initiative, announcing with a confidence he didn't quite feel that it was time they did what they'd come here for. He lowered himself unsteadily onto the top rung of the precarious metal ladder and slowly, uncertainly, began to feel his way downwards into the darkness.

Tracey went down next, followed by Tim and then finally Michelle who, despite her trepidation, was not prepared to let the others leave her behind. So finally all four stood together at the foot of the ladder, squinting myopically into the darkness and each wishing that they had had the foresight to bring along a torch.

'Looks like the stories were true,' said Tim, unsettled by the way his voice echoed eerily around passages and rooms both near and far. When, after a short pause, he continued his speech, it was in a much lower voice. 'These cellars could go on forever.'

'They might even stretch under the whole of Arandale!' enthused Tracey.

'That'd be something, wouldn't it?' agreed Gary. 'Our own little network of tunnels. We could find ways into them from all over the town and use them for getting around in secret.'

'Don't be stupid, you two.' Michelle admonished them. 'We're on the top of a hill, remember? We'd have to go a lot further down than this to get under the village.'

Gary scowled in the darkness, not exactly happy with having his illusions shattered, but unable to argue with such irrefutable logic.

'Well, come on then,' said Tim, presently. 'Since we're down here, we might as well have a look around.'

'Don't you think we should get some torches and come back later?' asked Michelle.

'We'll be all right,' said Tracey. 'I don't know about the rest of you, but my eyes are getting used to the dark already.' She took a few steps forward, her feet splashing uncomfortably in a shallow surface layer of water. 'Yes, there's a passage down here, look.'

'Okay,' said Gary, casting a smug grin in Michelle's direction even though it was too dark for her to see it. 'Let's get down there then, and do some *real* detective work.'

And that was when they heard someone sneeze.

Rosemary Chambers was a tired old woman, her thin face lined by worry and her prematurely grey hair pulled back and pinned into a severe bun. Her narrow eyes, however, were sharp and active, and Ace could not help but feel unsettled beneath their glare.

'We've just come in for a look, if that's all right,' she said, feeling that she had to explain their presence.

'Go ahead,' said Rosemary, her face softened by a slight smile. She seated herself on a creaking wooden rocking-chair in the corner of the shop, settling onto her knee the purring black cat which she had fetched with her from the back room. She made quite a sad spectacle, thought Ace, this dishevelled figure of a woman in her flower-patterned dress and woollen shawl; even at a charitable estimate, she thought, Rosemary was a good forty – six or seven years older than her husband. She looked more like a hundred.

Ace turned her attention to the shop instead. Inside, as Mel had said, the merchandise was a little more conventional than the obvious publicity gimmicks which had been sited in the window. Despite Rosemary's unnerving stare, she felt that she could have spent hours in there, just hunting around the cluttered shelves and unearthing the myriad treasures they apparently held. Instead, she limited her perusal to about five minutes, aware that Mel and Karen had seen all this before and were more than ready to leave.

'I'll have this please,' she said, selecting a fairly interesting-looking book on witchcraft. It wasn't quite her field; she was far more interested, in fact, in the cat which dozed peacefully in the witch's lap.

'He's beautiful,' she said, pleased to see that neither Rosemary nor the cat objected to her reaching out and giving him a gentle stroke. 'What's he called?'

'He has no name,' said Rosemary with a warm, genuine smile. 'He's my familiar; we each know the other too well for mere appellations to be necessary.'

'Yes, of course,' said Ace tactfully.

'Oh yes,' continued Rosemary, unabated, 'my friend here has served me well over the years. He guides my magic, enables my second sight and acts as an extra pair of eyes and ears for me around the village. You wouldn't understand, of course. Not unless you're versed in the magical arts.'

'I see, yes.'

'Not unless you've been out there, soul out of body, dancing with the spiritual coven . . .'

'I imagine not.'

'. . . or battling the forces of the Dark, using the arcane powers they can bestow but keeping one step ahead of their evil clutches.'

'Right. Erm . . . sorry, how much did you say the book was?'

Norman might have lived in a nice house, but for a decade of neglect. Now the paintwork was flaking, the garden was overgrown and shoots of green were flourishing in the cracks between the bricks. It was all, thought Benny, a very pitiful sight; as was Norman himself, when he finally shuffled his way to the blistered front door in his carpet-slippers and his long, woolly cardigan.

'At last!' she exclaimed, forcing herself to exude cheerfulness as his watery eyes peered out at her from behind a silver door chain. It had taken him almost five minutes

49

to open the door to her, and Benny suspected that it was an action he had not practised for far too long a time.

'So?' she prompted. 'Are you going to let me in, or what?'

He did – and it was only a matter of moments before Bernice found herself sitting in a drawing room which was in every bit as bad a state as the house's exterior. Out of politeness she pretended not to notice the damp, peeling wallpaper and the threadbare carpet, as she sat on the worn sofa and sipped at a cup of coffee that tasted far too sweet.

'Why did you come here?' asked Norman presently.

'I wanted to see how you were.'

'You did?'

'We're friends, aren't we?' He looked at her blankly, so she added: 'And I'm your guardian angel, remember?'

Norman smiled, weakly. 'You shouldn't have bothered,' he said. 'No one else ever does.' He seemed faintly touched.

'Then maybe you should get out a bit more,' suggested Benny. 'You know, meet some new people, make some new friends. You can't just spend all your days moping around here and your nights sitting on bridges.'

'It's a little late for that,' said Norman, morosely.

'No it's not,' said Benny, firmly. 'It's never too late.'

'I had a friend, once. A real, lifelong companion. But she died.'

'Look Norman, it's no good your living in the past all the time. You've got to snap out of it, do something about your future!'

It was as if he hadn't heard her. 'The nearest I've had to a true friend since then was when you came along. And I suppose you'll be off soon, back to . . . the stars.' He whispered the words with reverence.

'Yes, well – I'm not so sure about that.' Benny spoke awkwardly, feeling even worse as her comment was greeted by a heavy silence and astonished eyes which spoke of the most brutal betrayal.

'You're not?' Norman could hardly believe what he was hearing.

'It's just not as simple as that.' Benny protested, feeling for reasons she didn't know that she had to justify her statement. Who was helping whom here, anyway? 'I travel in a group, you see, and the others and me, we . . . well, we just don't get on very well. Not any more. So that's why I'm not going back with them. I'm going to find myself a home and settle down here on Earth. Definitely!'

And though she didn't know quite where her sudden decisiveness had sprung from, it felt as if the weight of the world had been lifted from her shoulders.

'Hello again,' said Ace. 'Fancy running into you here.' she added, a little sarcastically.

'Good evening,' answered the Doctor. 'On your way back to the guest-house?'

'Back to the "Cat" actually. We're getting something to eat.'

'Have you been to Rosemary Chambers' shop yet?'

'Just come from there.'

'Good. I might pay her a visit myself.'

'She's closed now,' Karen informed him. 'Unless you want a tarot reading.'

'Thank you,' said the Doctor. 'I might just do that.' He smiled briefly at Karen and Mel, before continuing his leisurely meander along the darkening street.

'Friend of yours?' asked Mel of Ace.

'Not really.'

'Perhaps we should have warned him about Rosemary,' said Karen with a giggle.

'Yeah,' agreed Ace, glad of an opportunity to change the subject. 'Can you believe that woman, or what? I mean, all that mystical crap she was spouting – and she looked as if she really believed it, too.'

'Oh, she does,' Karen assured her as they turned the corner into Parker Street, the Black Cat now firmly in sight.

'You can't say we didn't warn you,' said Mel, gleefully.

'She's something of a local character is Rosemary,' added Karen. 'That shop of hers just packs the tourists in during the summer.'

'That's where old Alan Brown got the idea for the name of this place from,' said Mel as they arrived at the entrance to the Black Cat Inn. 'Something more to hook in the witch-lovers.'

'That and the rumours about the castle, right?' said Ace, who had picked up a thing or two since arriving in Arandale. 'You must get all sorts of weirdos traipsing through this place.' Father Sheridan for one, she thought.

'We have our share,' admitted Karen with a laugh, as the group disappeared into the welcoming interior of the public house.

A moment after they had done so, the street outside seemed to visibly darken and a pale-faced figure with a black coat and blacker eyes walked slowly past the Black Cat Tavern, regarding it with an intense level of interest. It was almost as if he could see through those red brick walls.

He didn't stop, however, nor did he deign to enter the premises. Matthew Shade simply carried on walking – and when he was eventually lost to sight, it seemed as though the whole of the street breathed a deep sigh of relief.

The significance of all this I don't yet know, but as we hadn't seen that particular character since chapter one, I thought I'd better remind you that he existed.

It had taken the Adventure Kids almost two and a half hours to make the climb up Fern Hill to Arandale Keep, to prise the stone block out of its housing and to make their way down into the castle cellars. It took them almost twenty minutes to carry out the whole procedure in reverse, arriving breathlessly back in Tim Mitchell's back yard with aching legs and sweating foreheads.

'I don't know what we ran away for,' gasped Gary, although he had voiced no objections along the way.

52

'Because it was true, of course,' protested Michelle. 'There *are* ghosts in Vampire Castle!'

'Oh come on Mish,' argued Tracey. 'Ghosts don't sneeze. They don't even have noses, I don't think.'

'Probably not,' agreed Tim, squatting down on an upturned bucket to get his breath back. 'But there's obviously something going on in that place, and we need to find out what it is.'

'Perhaps it's smugglers again,' suggested Gary, 'hiding out in the cellars and putting out rumours about ghosts and stuff to scare people off.'

'I doubt it,' said Michelle. 'There can't be any smugglers left in the country; not after the number we've had put away in the last few years.'

'Then there's nothing else for it,' said Gary, firmly. 'We'll have to go back to Vampire Castle and find out what's what.'

'Preferably,' added Michelle, 'when whatever it was down there has gone!'

'You can't do it!' Norman said it again.

'Norman,' protested Benny, 'we've been through all this. I've made up my mind.'

'But you can't! You'll regret it!'

'And how would you know?' Benny was, quite frankly, becoming very irritated by all this.

'Because it happened to me, that's why.'

She looked at him incredulously. 'What are you talking about?'

'When I was the White Knight, I mean.'

'Oh, yes.' She had almost forgotten about Norman's super-hero fantasies, and she wished he hadn't reminded her.

'I had the most wonderful gift in the world,' Norman continued. 'I had super-strength, invulnerability and heat vision – and best of all, I could fly. I could even go to other planets; my super-thick skin could easily protect me

53

out in space, and I could hold my breath for hours at a time.'

'Norman . . .'

'But then, when Sparky . . . when – well, I mean something happened and – I didn't want to go on any more.'

'Norman, please . . .'

'So when my old doctor friend Carol Pullen devised a way of ridding me of my powers forever, I – well, I accepted.'

'Look, Norman . . .'

'And thirty years later here I am, not a friend in the world, just a sad, lonely man who's wanted to end it all for years and never had the guts. I'd give anything for my powers back, Benny – anything to soar amongst the stars again. And I can't just watch and say nothing while you give it all up. Not when you're making exactly the same mistake that I did!'

Benny finally managed to get a word in. 'Norman,' she asked, 'would you please stop talking about your being a super-hero? It's not good for you.'

'Opening up old wounds, you mean? I suppose you're right.'

'No Norman, that is not what I mean. I think you know exactly what I'm getting at.' She sighed in despair when she saw his expression of consternation. She was obviously going to have to spell it out. 'It's this fantasy of yours,' she told him, at length. 'This fairy-tale world you're living in. Nothing's ever going to improve for you unless you forget about it and move on. Give it up! Please, for your own sake, start to live in the real world.'

For a full minute after Benny had spoken, the room was silent, and she wondered throughout that time if perhaps she hadn't gone a little bit over the top. She'd never forgive herself if her wanton destruction of this old man's fantasies led him to do something stupid.

'You don't believe me,' said Norman eventually, and his voice was a flat monotone.

'I'm sorry Norman, no I don't.'

'Then I can prove it,' he said.

Benny groaned. 'Please, no . . .'

'No,' he interrupted her. 'I insist.' And by now he was on his feet and heading purposefully towards a dusty bookshelf which covered one whole wall of the room. 'Here,' he called over his shoulder. 'Watch this.' Then he reached out, grabbed hold of an unremarkable blue hardback on a shelf just above his head, and gave it a sharp tug.

What followed was a loud mechanical click, the grating of unoiled gears and a sight such as Bernice Summerfield would never have expected to see in a million years.

Chapter 4

Past Lives

Now, at last, we're up to one of those bits I've really been waiting for. Time to ruffle our Ms Summerfield's feathers a bit!

The first thing that occurred to Benny was that, given time, she could probably have thought of a devastatingly witty comment to use in a situation such as the one in which she now found herself. The second was the realization that she had already spent rather more time than was polite just staring at what she had been shown, her mouth open and her brain knocked temporarily into neutral.

'You're joking,' she said, it being the only phrase which sprang readily to mind as a means of breaking the embarrassing silence.

'Not at all,' Norman assured her in a voice which suggested that he was offended by the very idea. 'Why? Is there something wrong?'

For once in her life, Benny was lost for words. Someone pinch me, she thought, but she knew that this was no dream. 'So let me get this straight,' she said slowly, moving hesitantly towards the spot which, just a moment ago, had been occupied by a perfectly innocuous bookcase. 'This is the route down to your secret headquarters?'

'The White Knight's secret headquarters,' Norman corrected her. 'I do like to keep the two personae distinct – especially now that the second no longer exists.'

'Yeah, right.' It looked like she had no choice, she told

herself. She'd have to accept the all-too-plain evidence of her own eyes. The bookcase really had slid smoothly to one side. It really had revealed a secret alcove in which a fireman's pole stretched downwards into depths unseen. Most difficult of all to believe, the pole really did bear a plastic tag, emblazoned in black with the legend 'DOWN TO SECRET HQ'. That's great, thought Benny, that's really, really wonderful. And all I have to do to make things irretrievably worse is to follow this lunatic down there!

'Well?' said Norman. 'You wanted proof. It's down this way. Coming?' Without waiting for an answer, he swung himself nimbly onto the pole, sliding down it with a practised ease which belied his advancing years. Benny watched agog as he disappeared into the darkness below. A moment later a light flickered on, providing a distant glow which, under the circumstances, was anything but welcoming.

Benny sighed as she reached out for the pole. 'It looks,' she said to nobody in particular, 'like I'm about to do something incredibly stupid.'

You certainly are, my dear.

For Ace, a quick meal in the 'Cat' had turned into an all-night drinking session, starting from about seven when the pub regulars had begun to replace the small collection of diners. The least she could do, her conscience decided, was to use the situation to pick up a bit of information.

'So,' she said, putting her empty glass down on the table next to her temporarily discarded shades, 'how long have you been living in Arandale?' Whatever Mel and Karen's answer to that, she thought, she should be able to steer the conversation round into a slightly more useful direction – hopefully learning a few things about the village and its inhabitants without arousing too much suspicion.

Karen cast her mind back. 'Oh, must be about four months now, do you think, Mel?'

Mel nodded. 'About that, yeah. At first it was just a

stopping point on our way up to Scotland, but now – well, we've got kind of used to the place.'

Karen laughed. 'You're just stopping here for that role-playing club you found!' Mel didn't deny it. 'Still,' she continued more seriously, 'there's certainly no chance of our families finding us here.'

'Your folks didn't approve, then?'

'You could say that,' said Mel with a grin. The two lovers shared a quick cuddle and Ace, turning her attention discreetly away, was given the perfect opportunity for a furtive glance around the room. She smiled inwardly as she immediately spotted Jack Corrigan propping up the far end of the bar and attempting in vain to pass himself off as an ordinary customer just scanning the evening paper. She had seen him enter about ten minutes before, head down, moving quickly and with his eyes darting from side to side as if expecting to be ambushed at any moment. If nothing else she thought, she could at least narrow down the list of people he could be interested in.

Phil Chambers had taken up his usual position, she saw next, slumped miserably against the bar with a pint of bitter in front of him. Over to his left and in front of the marble fireplace, Mason and Tina Grimshaw were sitting around a table with a couple who Ace didn't recognize. Tina was obviously getting excited about something and the shrillness of her voice, if not her actual words, carried across the bar as she stabbed her sharp fingers into the air emphatically. Passing by with a handful of empty glasses, landlord Alan Brown paused to speak to her.

Alone in the opposite corner sat Father Sheridan – and he, like Ace, was taking advantage of his solitude to inspect his surroundings. Their eyes met for an instant and Ace looked away uncomfortably.

'How about you, Ace?' asked Karen. 'How long are you staying here?'

Distracted from her contemplation, Ace tried to reorganize her thoughts and come up with a convincing answer. 'Oh, not long,' she managed. 'We – erm . . . travel a lot, you know? Hey, what do you think the landlord's doing talking to those two? They can't be mates, can they?'

If the others noticed her rather clumsy attempt to change the subject, they didn't show it. 'I doubt it,' Mel answered her. 'He's probably just telling Tina to shut her ugly face.'

'He knows the signs, I think,' Karen clarified. 'Once she starts getting excited, it's only a matter of time before the bottles are flying. Honestly, I don't know why he doesn't just bar the both of them.'

Mel laughed. 'The amount of beer old Mason puts away? He'd go bankrupt in a week!'

Her eyes following Alan Brown's passage back to the bar, Karen had now found herself gazing upon the sad spectacle that was Phil Chambers. 'It's him I feel sorry for,' she commented, directing Ace's attention with a nod of her head. 'Look at him, hunched over there.'

'Isn't he married to that daft old witch with the shop?'

'To his regret, I think. He's always in here moaning that she never even speaks to him – too busy with her occult mumbo-jumbo, he says.'

'I know how he feels.' Ace spoke distractedly, one eye on the suddenly silent Mel Joseph. She wondered just who had distracted him, but all she could see when she surreptitiously followed his line of sight was the table occupied by the Grimshaws and their two friends. Mason was on his feet now, stopping to make one last point to his wife before he set off unsteadily towards the toilets – and even as he did, Mel pushed back his chair and stood up.

'Got to go to the loo,' he muttered. 'Back in a sec.' Talk about making things obvious, thought Ace; perhaps Mel could get together with Corrigan and they could both enrol for a night-school class in subtlety.

That, of course, is the whole idea – but she'll have to work a bit harder than that to find out what's behind *this* little scene.

Karen carried on talking, outlining in some detail her first encounter with the infamous Rosemary Chambers. Ace's attention, however, was elsewhere, her mind shifting firmly into overdrive as her narrowed eyes followed Mel Joseph across the room.

The Doctor had found Rosemary's shop easily enough, along with its painted sign offering tarot readings until eight. He had pushed the bell obligingly, spoken his request into the intercom system and finally been admitted into the darkened building. Standing alone among the cluttered shelves, he had heard the sounds of Rosemary busying herself in the back room; closing the connecting door to the house, hurriedly tucking a half-eaten plate of sandwiches away into a drawer – she wanted nothing around that could spoil the rich occult atmosphere she hoped to convey. Finally she lit one large candle, switched off the overhead light and gathered her tarot cards together. Then, with a quick apology to the Doctor for having kept him waiting, she ushered him proudly through the shop and into her sanctum.

Silently he took the proffered seat, rolling his hat into his jacket pocket and watching as Rosemary drew up the chair opposite and began to carefully shuffle her exquisitely crafted deck of cards. 'I'm going to try a fairly simple reading to start with,' she told him. 'Just five cards.' She laid them out, face down in a horseshoe shape on the table between them, and began to indicate each one in turn as she explained their significance. 'These will just give us some broad ideas,' she said, 'about your present position, your hopes and expectations, as well as what is *not* expected, and then finally, what the future holds for you, both in the short term and the long.' The Doctor nodded, and knew that this whole part of the routine had been very well rehearsed.

'So, to start with the present . . .' Rosemary reached for the card on the far left side of the horseshoe, but the

Doctor intercepted her hand, pushing it gently to one side as he went instead for the two cards opposite.

'I'd rather start with the future,' he told her, and flipped the cards over.

The first, the long-term future, was the Ace of Wands: the symbol of a new creative venture.

The second was the Death card.

Benny pushed herself away from the pole, making a special effort to clear the crash mat at the bottom and to land deftly on both feet. The last thing she wanted to do in this situation was to give her host any indication that she might not be at the peak of her physical condition. She wondered as she made the landing, however, why she had bothered. Norman Power was certainly no threat to her; she was even beginning to feel, almost ludicrously, that he could be trusted with her very life.

Norman looked on expectantly as her eyes adjusted to the dim fluorescent lighting in the cave. 'What do you think?' he asked.

What did she think? She thought that this place couldn't possibly exist, that's what she thought! The cave was huge, stretching in some directions further than she could see, at least through the assortment of glass cases, computer banks and various paraphernalia. A few yards to her left was a sleek white car, open-topped and built for speed, lying ready for action before a craggy wall which, Benny knew instinctively, would swing easily upwards in response to a simple infra-red signal. A few feet to her right was a costume, white again, draped over a flimsy wire framework. A pair of eye-holes stared blankly out from the all-encompassing face mask and a stylized yellow sword was embroidered on the left breast. Somebody's been reading too many issues of 'Batman', she thought to herself, and she suppressed a shudder as she realized that Norman himself had been wearing the costume, sans mask, beneath his coat that morning.

Aloud, she said, 'I'm impressed.'

61

Norman smiled proudly. 'If you want impressive,' he said, 'you should have seen the other cave. The one I had in New York when I lived there.'

'You lived in New York?' asked Benny absently, as she wandered slowly inwards. Her eyes were roving the cavern, unsure which of its myriad treasures to settle on first.

'Well, I had to. There was little use for a super-hero here, after all. I stopped the odd pickpocket, got the school bully to give little Billy James his yo-yo back, that sort of thing, but I did sometimes think I was wasting my powers just a little.'

'I can imagine,' said Benny. 'What's this?' She had come to rest by a statue and was now craning her neck backwards to view it in full; a huge stone dragon, one sharpened claw poised ready to strike. She couldn't for the life of her imagine who might have sculpted something quite so monstrous, nor how the White Knight as was might have manoeuvred it into his secret lair without engaging help and thus compromising his once-treasured secret identity.

'It's a dragon,' said Norman.

'I can see that. I mean, who made it? How did it get here?'

'No, I mean it's a real dragon.'

Benny breathed sharply in and took an instinctive step back from the petrified leviathan. It remained frozen, and she cursed herself for believing his lies.

'Or at least it used to be,' Norman continued. 'Dragonella used it against me. Created it herself, I think – that was one of her powers. It put up quite a fight, too.'

'So what happened?' asked Benny, not entirely sure whether she should be encouraging him like this.

Norman smiled. 'Dragonella had teamed up with my old enemy the Medusa at the time . . .'

'Right. I get the message.' She moved past the dragon, casting her eyes over the objects behind it, very gratified to note that the back wall of the cave was approaching.

So it wasn't infinite, after all. Just ask about a couple more of his souvenirs, she thought, show a polite interest. Then get the hell out of here.

'What about this?' She had reached into a glass case and picked up what appeared to be a pistol, albeit a very unusual one. If she hadn't known better, she would have sworn it was made out of pure gold.

'Be careful with that,' Norman cautioned her. 'It's extremely dangerous.'

She put it hurriedly back on its stand, wondering as she did why she kept on reacting to his ridiculous assertions.

'It fires gold energy,' Norman explained casually.

'What?'

'It's true. I don't understand it myself, but I took it from the Glitterbug, the last time I fought him. I even used it once. Silver Fist had tracked me to my cave in New York, and he attacked me there one evening. I thought I was beaten, but he knocked me against one of the display cases and the gun just fell into my hand. It worked, too. In fact, it killed him. I was devastated – at least, until I found out that he was only some sort of robot anyway. But I certainly never used the gun again!'

One more, thought Benny, just one more.

She eventually found it in the furthest corner of the cavern, a little apart from the rest of the trophies, and it instantly aroused the archaeologist's spirit in her. 'This could be worth something you know,' she said, carefully lifting the ornate vase to the light. Then she remembered what century she was in, and thought that the vase probably wasn't worth very much at all – and while she was still trying to think of a way around that little mistake, she realized with dread that it was the smaller of the two she'd made.

It was Norman's face that gave the game away; all the colour had drained suddenly from his cheeks and his eyes were wide as he stared with horror at the artefact she was holding. Inside it something shifted, and for a moment, neither of them spoke. Benny put the vase gingerly back into place, her mind casting about for anything she could say just to change the subject. By the time she had thought of something, it was too late.

'That,' said Norman quietly, 'is what's left of my partner.'

'My round,' said Ace, jumping to her feet almost as soon as the last drops of liquid had passed Karen's lips.

Karen nodded in acknowledgement and Ace headed for the bar, slipping her mirrored glasses back on and taking advantage of their concealment to have another good look around.

'It's the chalk circle again tonight,' Phil Chambers was complaining, mumbling into his half-empty beer glass. 'You ought to see her, Alan; she'll have shut up the shop now and she'll be sat there with her candles, muttering on about Lucifer and all his little demons or some other load of nonsense.' He fell into silence as the landlord politely excused himself and attended to Ace.

'You bitch!' came a scream from across the room, and she didn't need to look to know that it had come from Tina Grimshaw. She was on her feet, staring lividly at the woman she had been talking to. Alan tensed, hoping that the argument would go no further, but ready for action if it did.

The man was talking quietly to Tina now and, calming down a little, she retook her seat. Her husband was still nowhere to be seen, Ace noticed, and nor was Mel. She checked her watch; they had been in the toilets for over ten minutes. Much as the idea of spying on her friends repelled her, she had to admit that she was dying to know what was going on in there. She briefly wondered if she could persuade Corrigan to go and take a look for her.

'Any news of young Eileen?' asked a polite voice at her shoulder. Ace suppressed an inexplicable shiver when she realized that it came from Father Sheridan.

'I'm afraid not,' said Alan, placing Ace's last drink on the bar and holding out his hand for payment. 'I'm getting a bit worried actually,' he confided. 'She was due in over an hour ago, and when I phone her I just keep getting that stupid answering machine playing "No Place Like Home" at me. If she doesn't show soon, I'm going to have to go out looking.'

'Indeed you should!' agreed Sheridan, his eyes unnaturally wide. 'There is Evil at loose in Arandale this season – 'tis hardly safe for a young girl to be walking the streets alone.' His left hand jerked nervously at the crucifix on its chain and his voice took on an eerie wailing tone which Ace found more amusing than anything else. 'The Devil's work is being done in this town!'

'Yes, Father,' said Alan, with a nervous smile, 'I'm sure it is. Another diet coke, is it?' He's worried, thought Ace, and he's trying to hide the fact beneath his usual 'genial host' act.

'Psssst!'

'Sorry?'

'Pssst!' Jack Corrigan was signalling to her frantically, his shoulders hunched and his collar pulled up around his ears as if to avoid detection.

'You mean you want *me*?' shouted Ace along the bar, quite pleased with the sharp wince she managed to cause. 'I don't know why you're bothering to keep it quiet,' she added as she approached him. 'If it wasn't for all your stupid secret agent stuff, you probably would pass unnoticed.'

'Look,' snapped Corrigan, his voice still unnecessarily low, 'I've told you before – I'm just here on vacation. You got a problem with that?'

'Not at all,' said Ace. 'Are you sure that's your real accent?' she added.

'All right, all right, just forget about it!' Corrigan tried to wave her away, turning his attention back to his drink.

'Just forget what?' asked Ace, who had no intention of doing any such thing.

'I just wanted a quick pow-wow, that's all.'

'A quick what?'

'Talk!'

'Oh, I see. You mean you were going to pump me for a bit of information, just to help you, erm, "enjoy your vacation" a bit more?'

'Just zip it, can't you?'

'Or perhaps you're finally going to tell me who it is you're watching,' Ace continued. 'I'm narrowing it down, you know.' Corrigan didn't answer, so with a quick laugh calculated to cause maximum annoyance, she turned away and went to retrieve her drinks.

Instead, she found herself distracted by the squeak of the gents' toilet door as Mason Grimshaw emerged, his hair dishevelled and his expression dark as thunder. He strode straight past his table, much to the alarm of his wife, and out into the street, albeit not quite fast enough for Ace to miss seeing the cut on his cheek and the blood on his white jumper. She needed no further prompting. To Corrigan's evident surprise, she was across the room in seconds and shouting Mel's name as she banged urgently on the toilet door, uncomfortably aware that the customers nearby were somewhat amused by her efforts. There was no reply.

Oh, what the hell, thought Ace – and to the quite considerable delight of the pub's gossip-mongers, she pushed open the door and disappeared inside.

Norman had wanted to talk about it.

Benny had told him he didn't have to. In some suppressed corner of her mind, she had dearly hoped that he wouldn't. But after all these years, he was grateful just for the opportunity to sit down and actually talk to somebody. So they had pulled up two chairs and sat down, and Benny had listened sympathetically as Norman Power had recounted the events of almost three decades before.

They had been working together for five years, he had recalled. For almost two thirds of the White Knight's career, his name had been synonymous with that of his kid sidekick, the irrepressible Sparky. You'll remember

66

her, of course, from the stories I've told you in the past, so I'll make this resumé a quick one.

Sparky had been an orphan; her mother had died in childbirth and her father had been an innocent bystander, accidentally killed by falling debris as the White Knight brawled in Times Square with the villainous Doctor Nemesis. Norman Power had adopted the plucky young girl – and the White Knight, in a way, had adopted her too. He had helped to train her, building her already enviable fighting skills up to a new pinnacle. He had kitted her out with equipment, with ropes to climb, hooks to grapple and gas pellets to stun. Then he had given her a costume, all in black, which counterpointed his own white attire perfectly.

At first, she had simply gone out on patrols with him, often watching from the shadows as he trounced the bad guys and delivered them shackled to New York's finest. Then Doctor Nemesis had come back into town, and against the express instructions of her mentor, Sparky had struck out on her own. She had almost died in the process, but fortunately he had arrived just in time to bail her out – and in the final cataclysmic confrontation, *she* had actually managed to save *him*, bringing down his arch-foe once and for all.

Or so they had thought. In time, of course, he had returned, released from prison and looking for his revenge. His thugs had tracked the White Knight around town, learnt his secret identity and taken him in his sleep. A ransom note had led Sparky to a waterside warehouse – and as soon as she'd stepped inside, ten pounds of precariously wired explosives had gone right up in her face.

Even now, the recollection of that terrible night brought a lump to Norman's throat. 'I managed to escape of course,' he said quietly. 'I beat Nemesis and delivered him to the police. But it didn't bring Sparky back. Nothing ever could.' And then he lapsed into silence, his shoulders stooped and his head down as his imagination replayed the images of so long ago.

Sensing wisely that she could say nothing to make him feel better, Bernice kept silent. Her mind was in turmoil – and, strangely enough, the one thought which kept returning to it was of the comic books she used to read; the ones that the kids had abandoned, that she had salvaged to keep herself company on those long winter nights in the woods near the Academy. She couldn't help thinking how similar Sparky's story was to that of Batman's fifth Robin, and as she mulled Norman's words over in her mind, she wondered how much of his tale she could believe and how much he had merely fantasized or 'borrowed' from elsewhere. Then she remembered that this was the twentieth century and, absurdly, found herself wondering if the Doctor had any rules about revealing the plotlines of future comics. He probably did, she decided. He seemed to have rules for everything – for other people to follow, at least.

'Anyway,' said Norman, his voice suddenly cheerful as he jumped to his feet, 'thanks for listening.'

Bernice stood up too, uncertain what to say. 'Look,' she began. 'About Sparky . . .'

Norman smiled, gratefully. 'There's no need to say anything, honest. I'm sorry for burdening you with my problems – but I'm glad I've been able to get it off my chest. I don't get the chance to talk much these days, you know.'

Benny smiled back, realizing that somehow, despite all the incredible things he had told her, she had actually grown to very much like this ridiculous man. 'Look,' she said hesitantly, 'why don't you show me a few more of your mementoes? I was quite interested in the . . .' But the sentence was never completed. Suddenly aware of a strange heat on her back, Benny turned to look behind her, alarmed to find that one large section of the cave wall was glowing a fierce red colour. Rivulets of molten rock dripped to the floor, forming a hot scarlet pool where they hit.

'Get away from here,' yelled Norman. 'Quickly!' and Benny didn't need telling twice. She sprinted instinctively for the fireman's pole, immediately realizing that that was not such a bright idea. 'How do we get out?' she cried, but Norman didn't answer. A moment later she found out why, as he collapsed wheezing and coughing into her arms, the sudden exertion having proved too much for him.

It was then that the cave wall exploded.

'The Six of Swords!' announced Rosemary.

The Doctor's eyes sparkled kindly. 'Better?'

'Not at all bad,' she told him. 'Not,' she added quickly, 'that you've done badly so far. I mean, I explained about the Death card . . .'

'. . . not really meaning death, yes. Thank you.'

'And the Ace of Wands there is actually quite encouraging. You could have an exciting new career ahead of you.'

'Maybe,' mused the Doctor. His eyes narrowed, and Rosemary wondered not for the first time what glorious and terrible sights were reflected in those mysterious orbs. The Doctor's presence, she had to admit, was a little unnerving. Not in the same way as Shade's had been, of course (she shuddered as she remembered) but she found herself nevertheless a little wary of this strange little man who managed somehow to combine ages-old wisdom with an almost childlike curiosity.

The Fool, the tarot had said – and the tarot, of course, was never wrong. It depicted the Doctor, as he was now, in the position of the innocent traveller, charting the unknown and not afraid to face the dangers he may find there. And his expectations? The Three of Swords had laid those bare; a continuation of conflict, both physical and emotional. And most telling of all, the blood-red heart which the swords of the card were depicted as piercing. To the Doctor, it had seemed that the weapons represented the TARDIS crew, their lives forever in turmoil, their personalities forever in conflict, their hearts forever broken. And none more so than his own.

The Six of Swords, on the other hand, told of that which was not expected. 'A journey,' Rosemary explained to him, 'from times of turbulence to a much more serene environment. The voyage may be a physical one, or it may simply be on an inner level, the passage of your heart from a state of sorrow to a time of great peace and contentment. Of course, its placing in the reading shows that it is perhaps the last thing you would expect.'

'I think that's fair to say,' the Doctor said, wryly.

'And yet it links very nicely with the Ace of Wands,' Rosemary encouraged him. 'The happy new beginning in your long-term future.' She said nothing of the Death card in between. 'I think your dreams could soon be realized.'

The Doctor grinned, jamming his hat back into position as he got to his feet. 'Well,' he said, brightly, 'I can only hope so.'

'What the hell's happened to you?!' cried Ace. She could already guess most of the answer.

'Just leave me alone,' muttered Mel, weakly. He tensed his shoulders against the toilet bowl, trying to pull his bruised legs further into the cubicle away from her. The effort was in vain, as his lethargic body slid uncontrollably back into its original position.

'Not bloody likely,' returned Ace. She yanked a long strip of paper from the toilet roll, screwed it into a ball and tried to wipe some of the streaming blood from his face. 'Mason Grimshaw did this to you, didn't he?'

'Doesn't matter.'

'Yes it does. It was him, wasn't it?'

'No.'

'Don't give me that crap!' Ace retorted, her voice threatening. 'What did you follow him in here for?'

With a supreme effort, Mel forced himself to his feet, pushing past Ace and collapsing dizzily against the wall. 'I'll be all right!' he grumbled. 'Just stop hassling me, can't you?'

'You don't look all right to me,' Ace commented. 'You

70

look like you've just been knocked shitless by a six-foot, fifteen-stone gorilla. Which come to think of it, you have.'

Mel just grunted.

'He broke your glasses too,' she said, spotting the damaged spectacles on the floor. They had slid under the wash basins, one lens cracked and one arm detached. She scooped them up and placed them in Mel's weakened hand. Without even looking, he slipped them into his pocket. His eyes were closed and his breathing was deep and laboured. His right leg spasmed, involuntarily.

Ace regarded the pitiful sight for a moment longer before finally breathing a sigh of resignation and taking him by the shoulders. 'Come on then, Muscle Man,' she said. 'Let's get you home, shall we?' And as soon as he gets better, she thought, Karen's going to murder him.

Murder was on the Doctor's mind too, as he left Rosemary's shop, his head spinning with thoughts and ideas which . . . which . . . damn it, I can't see into them *again*!

In the mid-distance, the town hall clock was striking eight. The night had drawn in: another cold one, it seemed. And the Doctor knew that with the coming of evening, the lives of every man, woman and child in the town were once again at risk.

At some time in the next few hours, the mysterious killer would undoubtedly be claiming another victim.

Alan Brown trudged miserably through the slush, cursing the bitter cold which bit at his unprotected face. A neighbour of Eileen's had told him that his barmaid had been unexpectedly called out of town to see to an injured grandmother, and the very futility of his trip to her home only heightened his depression.

Still, he thought, it was good to have his fears assuaged, however groundless he might tell himself they had been. And as he turned into the alleyway which housed the back door of the 'Cat', he began to look forward again to

71

the comforting warmth and the cheerful company which it had always held for him.

The mahogany fireplace, more than anything, reminded him of his childhood; of Christmas Days spent in the closed bar, his parents smiling indulgently as the children gathered excitedly around the crackling flames to see what delights Santa Claus had brought them. The presents had never been too lavish, of course. The Lamb Hotel, as the pub had been called then, had never enjoyed any great profits, even in Arandale's tourist seasons. The 'witch' theme – Alan's own innovation upon taking up the reins of management – had helped for a while, capitalizing as it did upon Man's timeless fascination for all things occult. In the summer months, the Black Cat Inn was another quaint attraction to those who were drawn to Arandale by the rumours of its mystic past, and by Rosemary Chambers' ongoing efforts to keep that past alive. Still, the increased takings had been quickly swallowed up by equal rises in living costs, and with the onset of winter, it was time once again for belts to be tightened and pennies to be counted.

A sharp sound from nearby interrupted Alan's moment of introspection; the clatter of a dustbin lid, as a figure stepped out of hiding. For an instant his blood ran cold, his mind racing as his eyes shot nervously towards the thick wooden gate which led into his own back yard, and from there into the warm, comfortable safety of home. He could make it, he knew he could . . .

Only there was no need. The new arrival moved into view and a smile of pure relief washed over Alan Brown's face.

'Oh, it's you,' he said, as the figure drew closer. 'Thank God for that!'

They were the last words he ever spoke.

'I know you're in here, Power!' screamed the new arrival. 'Come out where I can kill you!' He moved slowly into the White Knight's cave, his majestic black cloak sweeping the dust from the ground and his armoured boots knocking fused lumps of rock out of his path. From beneath an impassive iron face-mask, blazing scarlet eyes swept the room with a malevolent glare.

'Don't answer,' croaked Norman in a breathless whisper. Like I needed him to tell me that, thought Benny. They huddled together in the dark shadows behind the dragon statue, grateful for the freak piece of shrapnel which had knocked out the cave's lighting system; equally grateful, for the time being, that the intruder was searching for them in the wrong direction. From the size of his blaster weapon and the way in which it was smoking profusely from its recent use, Benny was pretty sure she wanted to be elsewhere when he turned around. As if she had a choice.

'Who is it?' she hissed, hoping that the information might just in some way come complete with the very clue she needed to get them out of this situation.

'That's Doctor Nemesis,' came the ominous answer. 'I told you about him before.'

'Aaaaa-ha!' Benny pondered that for a moment. 'So just remind me will you, Norman? He's your personal physician, right?'

Norman looked at her as if she had gone mad. 'No, not my physician – my arch-enemy. He's the most evil, destructive force ever to walk this planet; an unstoppable megalomaniac with incredible powers, devastating weaponry and no conscience whatsoever! He killed my side-kick and now he's out to kill me – and anyone I associate with!'

Benny clicked her fingers in mock recollection. 'That's right,' she said. 'I remember now. Thank you, Norman.' She swallowed hard and tried to remember how, only that morning, the world had seemed to make some kind of logical sense.

Chapter 5

Down and Out

A quiet evening in the Black Cat Tavern had never been so exciting, and if the regulars thought it was all over yet, they were very much mistaken.

The particularly curious amongst them, who had been keeping watchful eyes on the door of the gents' toilets (whilst not actually daring to venture within), were not at all disappointed when Ace staggered back out through it, supporting the battered and bloody form of Mel Joseph with her own slightly less substantial frame. 'Look,' she shouted, responding to the communal gasp which arose from the pub's scandalized clientele, 'either help me out or shut the frag up – this is none of your bloody business!'

But it was the business of Karen Davies, who rushed forward now with a look of horror on her face. 'What's going on?' she cried out, trying to take the weight of Mel's body from Ace but finding herself not quite able to do so. 'What's happened to Mel?'

Left suddenly to the dubious support of his own legs, Mel limped across to the bar and collapsed against it. 'Just fell over,' he muttered. 'Out of breath. Be all right in a minute.'

Karen glared daggers at him, then turned to Ace with an expression which demanded an explanation. Ace shrugged helplessly and sidled out of the way. Best to leave them to it, she thought.

'Sorry about all this,' she muttered to the barmaid, suppressing the urge to lob a grenade into the middle of a nearby table where they were saying things like 'Well, I never . . .' and 'Young people today . . .'

'Does he need help?' the woman asked, concerned.

'I don't think so,' said Ace. 'He just needs to get out of here and sleep it off somewhere.' And think up some bloody good excuses for his fiancé, she added silently. Come to that, she'd be wanting to hear some of those excuses for herself.

'Right,' whispered Benny, 'so let's get a few of the more important ground rules established, shall we? Firstly, and perhaps most importantly: where the hell's the exit?'

'Right over there,' croaked Norman, his voice trembling as he pointed.

'Aha! Yes, but seriously Norman, I mean the other exit. You know, the one which your arch-enemy isn't standing directly in front of.'

'You think I'm making this up?'

Bernice sighed. 'No, no. Just mindless optimism, I suppose. So . . .' She turned her attention to the gleaming white automobile, by which the pacing super-villain had now come to a stop. 'I suppose we go for the car then.'

'I want you, Power!' screamed Nemesis again, and as if to underscore his words, he slammed both fists like atomic pile-drivers straight through the metal bonnet of the White Knight's transport. The car's suspension gave way beneath the onslaught and a wisp of smoke trailed out from the jagged hole the fists left behind.

'Because of course,' Benny continued, 'the engine's in the back, right?' She looked at Norman. He looked back at her. 'I know,' she muttered, 'mindless optimism again.'

'You have ten seconds to come out, Power!' shouted Nemesis, and Benny noticed the slight American twang in his accent. Well that made a strange sort of sense, she thought. If she could believe any of what Norman had told her, he had certainly made enough enemies in New York City. 'After that,' the villain continued, 'I'm going

75

to take this cave apart piece by piece – and you as well, when I find you! Ten.'

'What are we going to do?' hissed Norman, slightly louder than was necessary. Much to Benny's alarm, she saw that his eyes were beginning to fill up with tears.

'Nine.'

'Leave it to me, I'll think of something . . .'

'Eight.'

'. . . given time.'

'Seven.'

'We're both going to die!'

'Six.'

'A few hours ago, you weren't that bothered.'

'Five.'

'Now pass me that gun.'

'Four.'

'The gold gun, I mean. Pass it to me.'

'Three.'

'And make for the exit while I distract him.'

'Two.'

And it was there that the countdown ended as, feeling none of the confidence she was hoping to display, Bernice Summerfield stepped smartly out from behind the dragon statue and loudly cleared her throat.

Nemesis turned and regarded her as one might regard an insect; she could almost hear his brain ticking over as he considered how best to deal with this new arrival. Instead she took the initiative herself, taking a few steps across the cave with a smile on her face and a hand extended in greeting. 'Hi,' she said cheerfully – and Norman couldn't help thinking that, for someone who had promised to save both their lives, she had not made a very promising start.

'Looking for someone?' asked Ace.

The Doctor turned, showing no surprise at her arrival despite the fact that he had concealed himself as best he could in the darkness.

76

'Just watching,' he said.

'Watching what?' Ace peered round the side of the truck, but all she could see was the front of the Black Cat Tavern, bathed in a yellow glow from the street lighting outside it.

'I'm waiting for somebody,' the Doctor admitted. He was obviously not going to expand on that. As always, something inside Ace smouldered with resentment at his secrecy. 'Tell me something,' he added, almost as an after-thought. 'What made Mason Grimshaw attack your friend Mel Joseph in the toilets?'

Ace nodded, unfazed. 'You saw them both coming out injured, of course.' She had herself, only a moment ago, seen the battered Mel and the furious Karen into a taxi right outside the pub.

The Doctor smiled. 'That, for one. And believe it or not, the sight of a leather-clad young woman banging on the door of the gents' is enough to set a few people off talking.'

'I had noticed,' Ace commented drily, refusing to share his good humour. 'And to answer your question, I don't know what's going on but I'm going to find out. And I think I might start by keeping an eye on "my friend Mel Joseph".'

The Doctor nodded approvingly. 'Good idea. Just make sure you're . . .' The sentence tailed off as Ace shot him a black look. 'Okay,' he said finally. 'You do that.'

She nodded but didn't smile, and she soon disappeared into the shadows across the road. The Doctor sighed out loud, and reflected not for the first time on the problems of relating to this new, more difficult version of his one-time friend.

Then, with half a mind still dwelling on such domestic problems, he returned to his vigil.

It took Shade only thirty-three minutes to locate Alan Brown, his body dumped amongst the bins at the back of his own public house. As he had expected, there was no hope for the man. He was dead, a savage knife wound gaping dryly across the side of a body drained of all blood. There was only one slight difference this time, and Shade noted it with puzzled curiosity.

There was a phone booth outside the Black Cat, its interior walls almost invisible beneath an array of posters and stickers advertising the town's various taxi services. The cold wind found entrance through a broken pane of glass and someone had been all too recently sick on the floor. Ignoring such distractions, Shade tapped out the familiar number on the keypad and waited for a response..

'Police? Number Four. Directly behind the Black Cat.'

He replaced the receiver and stepped back onto the street. A short, dark-haired man barred his way, a polite smile illuminating his time-worn face.

'Good evening,' said the stranger. 'I'm the Doctor. And I think it's time we talked.'

'Looking for someone?' asked Benny in all innocence. Behind her, she clutched the gun nervously in her trembling hands, and prayed that she wouldn't have to use it.

Doctor Nemesis narrowed his blazing eyes and regarded her with suspicion, obviously surprised by her flippant attitude. He took two steps closer and she could almost feel the ground vibrating as his metal boots clanged against the hard stone surface. 'I have come in search of my arch-foe, Norman Power,' he rasped. 'The much-vaunted White Knight. And you, woman, would do well to tell me where the craven coward is hiding!'

'The White Knight?' echoed Benny, glancing around the cavern from the dragon statue to the costume to the shattered remains of the car. 'No one by that name here, love. Have you tried the cave next door?' Nemesis gave no reply; he merely regarded her with a stare that could have cut through ice. 'I might be able to do you a Pink Elephant, or a Black Adder . . . but no White Knight, I'm afraid, definitely not. Erm, have you tried the phone book, perhaps? Or the yellow pages? I'm terribly sorry, I'm rambling, aren't I? I do tend to do that when I'm being stared at by silent homicidal maniacs. You don't think you could perhaps say something, do you?' Norman had better be making damn good use of this distraction she thought, uncomfortably aware that her face was beginning to sweat.

'Don't play games with me!' snarled Nemesis, his voice low and threatening, then rising suddenly to an angry bellow. 'Where is he?'

Benny nodded slowly. 'Well, that's not quite what I had in mind,' she said, 'but it's a start, I suppose. So if that's the way you want it . . .' She produced the weapon from behind her back with a flourish. 'I think you'd better keep very silent and stay very, very still indeed. You see, this gun may look like a giveaway from a cornflakes packet . . .'

'Yes,' Nemesis agreed. 'It does.'

'. . . but it'll blow your insides right the way back to America if I have to use it.'

'Really?' There was a hint of amusement in the villain's eyes as he moved one confident step closer. Damn it, thought Benny. She had been hoping he wouldn't do that.

'I'm warning you!' she threatened, realizing as she did that backing nervously towards the cave wall was not the most ideal way of punctuating her threat. 'Back off! Get out of here!' She waved the gold gun somewhat feebly and wished it looked a little more like the lethal weapon of destruction it was reputed to be.

And then Nemesis was upon her – and the next thing she knew, his metallic arms had pinned her to the wall, his vice-like fingers pressing painfully into her throat.

'Tell – me – where – Power – is!' Bernice recoiled from his oily breath and felt the vaguely reassuring presence of the gun, now pressed directly into her aggressor's stomach. Her options, she realized, were fast diminishing. Speech was out; movement too. She hated using guns at the best of times – and at such close quarters, things were bound to get messy – but she had no choice. She couldn't even shout a warning.

79

With her eyes tightly closed and her fingers crossed, she pulled the trigger and braced herself for the consequences.

The first thing she noticed was that, thankfully, the merciless grip on her throat had been released. She coughed and spluttered as she fell uncontrollably to the ground, and her closed eyes dripped water onto her already flushed cheeks.

The second thing that sprang to mind was that nothing else seemed to have happened. No sound, no recoil, no cry of pain, not even the pungent smell of burning flesh which she had so been dreading. She didn't know quite what that meant, and the fact that she would soon have to find out was not a source of pleasure for her.

Wiping a sleeve across her face, she forced open her eyes and looked upwards – to where the imposing bulk of Doctor Nemesis stood over her crumpled form, his chest decorated with gold tinsel and a strangely bemused look on what could be seen of his face.

'Didn't work, huh?' she said weakly, her face muscles struggling to form what she hoped was an engaging smile as the gun clattered uselessly to the floor beside her. 'Shit!' she added.

It seemed the only appropriate thing to say.

'Four!' said the Doctor, pausing for dramatic effect but gleaning no reaction from those pitch-black eyes. 'You said four. Four what, I wonder?'

The impassive figure gave no response, not even an acknowledgement of the Doctor's question.

'Four victims?'

Still nothing.

'The police have only found two.'

Was that a twitch he saw?

'Plus our poor friend Mister Brown makes three.'

He was definitely getting somewhere.

'So where did you find the other one?'

The silence was long and heavy. For a moment the Doctor thought he would have to take another tack. Then

Shade spoke, his voice low and husky as if its very use brought pain to his throat.

'There is a fourth.'

'Where?' the Doctor asked, eagerly.

No answer again – but this time, he was at least able to interpret the silence.

'You haven't found it, have you? So how do you know? How do you know there's a fourth body?'

'I just know. That's all.'

The Doctor's head shifted inquisitively to one side, his eyes boring into the ebony depths of Shade's own. He wasn't letting things go at that.

'The slayings began on Sunday,' Shade explained finally. 'The thirty-first of October; All Hallows Eve. They will continue for six nights. I assumed that the police had located the first body themselves.'

'And what is your interest exactly?'

A tight, lipless smile. 'The same as yours, I would imagine.'

The Doctor was silent for a moment, then his face lit up in a broad grin. 'Thank you,' he said. 'You've been very helpful.' He stepped back with an extravagant gesture, allowing the other man to pass. Shade did so, with a gracious sweep of one white hand.

Without even realizing that he had had it passed to him, the Doctor found himself holding a small white business card. 'MATTHEW SHADE,' it read, in neat silver type. 'Psychic Investigations.' Then, with an almost inaudible *pop*, it disintegrated in his hand.

The Doctor watched in amusement for a second as the ashes of the card melted slowly away. When he looked up again, Shade had gone. He had melted away too, into the shadows.

In the distance, the Doctor could hear the approaching wail of sirens.

Bernice tensed, rolled and narrowly avoided ending up as

a smoking hole in the floor as a beam of pure energy sizzled deafeningly past her ear.

'Tell me where he is!' screamed Nemesis, and Benny was no longer in the mood for snappy backchat. The one thing on her mind now was escape and she could only hope that Norman had done as he was told and got the hell out of the cave whilst his foe was distracted.

'Oh no,' growled Nemesis. 'You don't get away from me like that.' He had already leapt sideways, once more interposing himself neatly between Benny and the cave's exit; the unremarkable wooden door which Norman had pointed out to her before. 'You're not getting past me until I find out what I need to know!'

'Okay,' said Benny, 'that suits me fine.' And without breaking her stride, she veered off to one side, dived beneath a second bolt of destructive energy and hurtled out of the cave through the entrance hole that Nemesis himself had created.

'At least there's one thing that armour of his can't do,' she muttered under her breath as she raced down what turned out to be part of the town's sewer system, 'and that's move fast. I hope!' But her armoured assailant was not exactly stationary either, and a third shot from his blaster weapon narrowly missed her as she flung herself round the nearest corner of the tunnel. 'Okay,' she asked herself, 'so what am I going to find first? A ladder up to the street, or a dead end? Only one way to find out, I suppose.'

She carried on running.

If there was one thing about his visit to Arandale that was really getting on Jack Corrigan's nerves, it was the number of times he had been snuck up on by Ace. This time she caught him in an alley-way, crouched in the shadows by one wall and listening intently to the police band on his portable radio. When she shouted to him, her mouth an inch from his ear, he almost leapt out of his skin.

'So come on then,' challenged Ace. 'What do you think you're doing down here?'

Corrigan reacted angrily. 'I'm having a stroll. Now buzz off!'

'A stroll? So are you touring all the back alleys in the town, or is there something special about this one? Honestly, Jack, if you're going to go sneaking round the place, you might at least do it quietly. I heard you banging around back here from a mile off!'

Corrigan said nothing, so Ace proceeded to march out of the alley-way back onto the street from which she had come. 'I can't see anyone,' she announced loudly, standing in the middle of the road and surveying the surrounding area. 'You must have lost them – whoever you're watching. Want to tell me who that is? I might be able to help.' Her mind was ticking over furiously; the building in which Rosemary Chambers both lived and worked was nearby, just visible in the artificial glow of the street lights. And hadn't Mason Grimshaw been heading this way when he'd almost run Ace over the previous night? Perhaps his home lay on this street, too?

'I'm not telling you squat, sister!' said Corrigan, pushing his way past her and heading off down the street.

'There you go again, with those ridiculous speech patterns of yours. I wish you'd get them seen to.'

'Look,' snapped Corrigan, 'if you want to be smart, then I suggest you start by moving your butt back to the Black Cat.'

'And why might you suggest that?'

'You're helping out your Doctor buddy with these homicides, yeah?'

'Might be,' said Ace, evasively. Corrigan wasn't quite the fool he looked, she thought; he'd obviously been doing his homework. And part of that homework, it seemed, consisted of listening in on the Arandale police.

Corrigan brandished his radio at her with authority. 'Well I hear they've just found another body,' he said.

By the time Bernice climbed finally up from the sewers, she was tired, wet, dirty and more than a little relieved to be out in the relative light of the street. She considered briefly the merits of bouncing a nearby car over the man-hole through which she had made her escape, but she had the uncomfortable suspicion that Nemesis would have lifted the cover, car and all, without breaking into a sweat. Best, she thought, just to get away from here as quickly as possible.

'You made it!' cried Norman, rushing up to her side before she could even brush the dirt from her overcoat. 'Thank goodness for that! Is he behind you, or did you deal with him properly?'

'He's behind me.'

'Oh.' Norman actually looked disappointed in her. 'Then come on,' he urged, after a significant pause. 'We've got to get out of here!'

'My thoughts exactly,' Bernice agreed. 'And how did you get here, by the way?'

'I used the stairs,' said Norman.

'You're home early, darling,' Rosemary greeted Phil. 'Shall I put the kettle on?'

'If you don't mind dear,' said Phil. 'There was some trouble at the pub. Another murder, I think. Everyone else was out at the back, looking, but I couldn't face it so I came away.'

'Oh, how horrible!' Rosemary sympathized. She held him in her arms and they kissed, long and lovingly. 'But you're all right,' she said softly, 'and that's the main thing. I love you, Philip Chambers,'

Yeah?

Some hope!

The image faded from Phil's mind as he pushed open the front door and stepped into the frigid, damp hallway. The smell of incense and candle smoke hit his nostrils, noxious grey fumes seeping out from under the door which led into his wife's study area, and through that to the hated shop. This, Phil reflected bitterly, was the cold reality of his marriage, and of his life.

Rosemary was in there of course, as she always was after doing her readings and seeing Gary and Michelle off to bed. The carpet had been rolled carefully back and she was sitting with legs crossed and eyes closed, in her circle of white chalk on the bare wooden floorboards. A dozen scented candles surrounded her and threw her harsh, pointed features into sharp relief as she quietly muttered her sacred incantations.

Phil watched her for a long, unhappy moment, her ritual undisturbed by the mournful creak of the room's heavy door as he entered. He was tempted to call out to her and announce his return, but he knew that his voice would have even less chance than the door of distracting her. She had never listened to him before; why start now?

Finally he turned to leave, glancing over his shoulder one last time as he did. He was unsurprised to see Rosemary's body lifting slightly into the air, hovering unsupported a few inches above the floor. Her mumblings continued unabated, but her tired white face had softened gently into a blissful smile.

'Are you sure this is all right?' asked Norman, as Bernice bundled him into her room at the guest-house.

'Well you can't stay at home, can you?' she answered reasonably. 'Not with an armoured psychopath after your blood.'

'I suppose not.'

'And you need to get some rest somewhere. You've been shaking like a leaf since we got away.'

'Okay.'

'So just you get in that bed, get to sleep – oh, and make sure you keep quiet. Mrs Shawcross doesn't exactly know that I've sneaked you in here. Right?'

'Yes, mother.'

They exchanged a smile, and Benny turned to leave the room.

'Oh, and mother?' Norman called after her.

'Yes?'

'Think again about leaving your friends, won't you?'

Ace accompanied Corrigan as far as the Black Cat Tavern, pulling away from him as they got closer and running to where the police car stood at the rear of the building. She got barely a glimpse of the latest corpse, arriving by the Doctor's side just as the police began to gain control of the situation and herd the curious public out of the alleyway. This time the Doctor complied with their request without argument, not least because he felt he should leave the scene before Sergeant Blyth arrived. He didn't want to push his luck a third time – not yet, at least.

Ace followed him across the street, past the small gatherings of the Cat's customers who were busy discussing the terrible state of the modern world in unnecessarily loud voices. Corrigan, she noticed, was standing silently in the crowd's midst, collecting information from drink-loosened lips whilst at the same time avoiding the ongoing investigation. Right now, though, he wasn't her concern.

'The body,' she said. 'That was Alan Brown, wasn't it? The pub landlord?'

The Doctor nodded silently.

'Murdered, like all the others.'

The Doctor nodded again. His eyes were elsewhere.

'And drained of blood.'

Again.

'And you knew it was going to happen? That's why you were waiting out here?'

There was the hint of an accusation in her voice and he turned to look at her, fixing her with that reassuring stare of his. 'I knew it *had* happened,' he said. 'I was waiting for something else.'

Ace thought about that for a moment and decided to accept what he was saying. This time. Besides, something else was bothering her more. 'Did you see his neck?' she asked.

The Doctor nodded, slowly. She told him anyway.

'Two marks. Two red points, right on the jugular.' She looked up at him again, but there was no way of reading his expression. 'Just like I was talking about yesterday,' she pressed on. 'Just like a vampire bite.'

Ah, yes – I was wondering if she'd notice that.

In the cellars beneath Arandale Keep, a man in a blood-stained white robe stood once again before a rough stone altar and addressed the expectant crowd which had gathered before him.

'The fourth sacrifice has been made,' he intoned, and his voice reverberated strongly throughout the underground complex. 'We should fall to our knees and give thanks and praise once more to the Master of All Things, that he may grant us the strength to conclude our glorious task here.'

'Thanks and praise,' chorused the crowd.

'For in just two more nights, with but two more sacrifices, *our Master will arise*!'

And the assembled throng took up the familiar chant once more. 'Thy will be done. Thy will be done. Thy will be done . . .'

Faced with a definite problem to discuss, the Doctor and Ace had actually managed a civil conversation on their way back to the guest-house. They had not, however, been able to reach many actual conclusions.

'I've fought vampires before of course,' the Doctor had said, 'and not just the Haemovores either.'

'But not the classical Earth fiction type of vampire,' said Ace, 'not the "sleeping in a coffin by day, getting up at night, turning into a bat and getting people in the neck" type, surely?'

'Admittedly, no.'

'But that's what we've got here, from the looks of things.'

'Or that's what someone wants us to think we've got here, perhaps.'

'But in that case,' reasoned Ace, 'why wait until the third victim? Why not put the bite on the first two?'

'Why not indeed?'

'You don't suppose the murderer heard me or something, do you? Last night, when we saw that other body, I mean?' The Doctor shrugged. 'It's just that it seems so weird,' Ace continued. 'Almost as if my mentioning vampires made it all happen.'

Hmmmm. Well, I didn't mean it to be quite that obvious. Still, no worries. I might have given them a bit of a clue, but I can't see they're going to work the whole thing out from that. Not that it'd change things very much if they did.

So anyway, where were we?

Ah, yes . . .

Bernice greeted the Doctor and Ace as they entered Mrs Shawcross's hallway. 'We've got a guest,' she said. 'A sort of friend of mine. He's staying in my room, so I'll have to move in with Ace.'

Ace bristled. 'You bloody well won't!'

'It's just for tonight,' Benny protested. 'Norman's got nowhere else to go – and besides, he's already up there asleep.'

'So you screw up all my arrangements, just to bring in one of your little orphans. You could at least have asked!'

'I'm asking now!'

'And I'm telling you to piss off!'

The Doctor stepped hurriedly between the two, raising his hands to quell the brewing argument. 'You can use my room,' he told Benny. 'I won't be needing it.'

'Why, what are you going to do all night?' asked Ace. 'No, don't tell me, let me guess: Look around, do some planning and make sure you've got everything here sewn up by morning.'

88

'Something like that.'

'It doesn't matter anyway. I'm not sleeping here tonight. I'm going back to the TARDIS.'

The Doctor was evidently not pleased about that. 'Why?' he asked, icily.

'Why not? It's a bloody sight more comfortable.' And besides, she could work on that door again; back in the TARDIS, the dark-haired woman in the red velvet dress might return to drop hints at the edges of Ace's dreams.

'Well, I'd rather you didn't.'

'Then that's all the more reason to go, isn't it?'

The Doctor sighed. 'You know my feelings on this,' he explained patiently. 'If you're seen going backwards and forwards to the TARDIS all the time, you'll just draw attention to it and to yourself, especially if people find out you're not sleeping in the town.'

'Well that's their problem,' Ace asserted, already halfway through the door.

'Could you, erm, do me a favour?' Benny called after her, hesitantly. She looked rather self-consciously down at her feet; she had been able to scrape more or less all of the dirt of the sewers off her shoes, but her trousers were still a clinging wet mess. 'Could you bring back my chinos? They're on my bed.'

'Okay,' said Ace gruffly. And with that, she was gone.

'It's not such a big deal, is it?' Benny asked the Doctor, breaking a short, uncomfortable silence.

'I suppose not,' he answered sulkily.

Benny rolled her eyes. 'All this petty squabbling is doing none of us any good.'

'No,' said the Doctor, but he wouldn't be drawn further.

Bernice sighed, and thought about leaving again. This wasn't the time to broach the subject, but it did remind her of Norman, and she thought that perhaps his problems might take the Doctor's mind off his own.

'Okay then Doctor,' she said, forcing herself to appear cheerful. 'I've got a little story to tell you.'

Ace was lost.

She didn't like to admit it, but it seemed there was no option. For almost twenty minutes now, she had been marching up and down in the hills by the small town, her only light coming from the intermittent flashes of early fireworks overhead, yet still she seemed completely unable to trace her way back to the TARDIS. It was times like this that made her especially glad of her combat suit, with its ability to regulate the body temperature of its wearer, but even so the cold bit at her unprotected face, and she wanted nothing more than to settle down into her own familiar bed.

She kept up the search for another ten minutes or so, and by that time she knew what must have happened. She had far too much experience and far too much justified faith in her own abilities to believe that she could possibly have got this badly lost without assistance, even in the dark of the night. She was sure too that the Doctor hadn't activated the Defence Indefinite Timeloop Option, projecting the TARDIS a split second into the future – and likewise, he had made a point of switching off the chameleon circuit which might otherwise had cloaked the ship's presence. So she had to face it. The TARDIS was gone.

Well after all, I couldn't just let her get back into it, could I? Maybe now she'll go back to the bed and breakfast place, like a good little . . .

'I'm not having this!' muttered Ace beneath her breath and she broke suddenly into a run, heading – uh-oh! – in the only direction she had not yet covered; *outwards* from the town, bounding easily over the frozen grass, up hills, down dales, as far as . . .

'What the frag . . ?!'

. . . and then suddenly, she found herself at the very edge of the world itself – or at least, *at the edge of the world that I've created, damn it!* And before her, the frost and the earth and even the sky just came to one big full stop; a sharp, straight line which cut dead across the world

90

she had come to know here. And on the other side of that line . . ?

Well, actually, I haven't quite decided that yet.

Chapter 6

Flat Earth Theories

Okay, I know what you're thinking. So I shouldn't have let that happen, I know. I just wasn't expecting that stupid woman to go running out of the town like that, not till I'd decided what I was going to put outside it, anyway! So all right then, she's seen something she shouldn't have – but don't worry, I can handle it. It might spoil my continuity just a tad, but it's not going to change the outcome of the story, believe you me.

Anyway, it's not as bad as it seems. There are ways of dealing with problems like this. The power of 'meanwhile', for a start . . . oh yes, just by switching scenes I can leave our little Ace where she stands, not knowing yet even what it is she's discovered. By the time I get back to her, not a millisecond will have passed – but I'll have had plenty of time to work out a strategy while I'm writing the next scene. All happy now?

Good. So: *meanwhile* . . .

In the guest-house dining room, Bernice Summerfield had just finished telling the Doctor one of the most extraordinary tales that she, at least, had ever recounted, only to find that his reaction was exactly the opposite to the one she had expected. *I'd* anticipated something a little different, too!

'Logical?' echoed Benny, hardly able to believe what her companion had just said. 'What do you mean, logical? Doctor, we're talking about an old man who used to dress up in a skin-tight white jumpsuit and fly around New

York City catching super-villains! Don't you think there's something just a bit unusual about that?'

'Well, maybe the actual details are slightly far-fetched,' the Doctor admitted, 'and it does seem likely that your friend is a little prone to exaggeration . . .'

'In the same way that you're "a little prone" to understatement, obviously.'

'But it's certainly possible for him to have been given the abilities he claims to have had.'

'It is?'

It is?

'McAllerson's Radiation.' said the Doctor.

'McAllerson's . . ?'

'Discovered in 2542 – a little bit after your time – by Professor Bernadette McAllerson working at the New Scientific Central Trust on Earth.'

'But we're in 1993.'

'Which isn't to say that it doesn't exist yet, merely that it hasn't yet been discovered by Earth scientists. McAllerson's is a very rare form of energy, and one with some very strange properties indeed – particularly when it interacts with the human physionomy.'

'Like . . .' Benny could hardly bring herself to say it. 'Like turning people into super-heroes, you mean?'

The Doctor shrugged. 'It hasn't been known before, but it's certainly possible. Most people exposed to it are more prone to dropping down dead, which is probably why there are so many rumours about Arandale Keep.'

'The castle where the meteorites hit, right?' This is going to be easier than I thought! 'So what you're saying then, is that the meteor storm of 1959 . . .'

'. . . which demolished Arandale Keep, killed a number of the townspeople and altered Norman Power's DNA structure . . .'

'. . . actually did all that by bringing this – this McAllerson's Radiation to Earth?'

'Correct!' Can you believe all that? I can't make anything up – no matter how ridiculous it seems at the time

– without this idiot thinking he's got a rational scientific explanation for it.

'The trouble is,' said the Doctor, adopting a worried expression, 'if it really is McAllerson's that's causing all these problems, then they certainly aren't over yet.'

'No?'

'No.'

Okay then, he's convinced me – McAllerson's Radiation it is! And isn't it just so nice to be able to add that little touch of realism to the story?

'Just one little question, though,' said Benny, after mulling the concept over for a while.

'Yes?'

'You're not going to try telling me the Earth is flat next, are you?'

Which reminds me – about that other little problem . . .

A quick flick of the pen here (metaphorically speaking of course); suddenly, it's morning. A rather unpleasant one too, particularly if you were to wake and find yourself lying face-down in a patch of cold wet grass, frost settling over your jacket, and your throat feeling like it's just been sandpapered from the inside.

In case you hadn't guessed, that's how Ace had just greeted the pale morning sky, her head spinning and her chest aching as she struggled painfully to her unsteady feet. She sneezed twice, rubbed her fingers over her bleary red eyes, and tried to remember . . .

What?

She had been heading for the TARDIS, but had somehow managed to lose her way . . .

How?

. . . running across the icy green hills, heading away from . . .

Where?

. . . and waking here, sprawled on the ground, almost catching her death – having fainted, perhaps? It couldn't be possible, not her! And yet . . . yet . . . (and this is the main thing) her mind was a total blank, the last six and a half hours just erased from her head like chalk from a blackboard (you see? I told you I'd sort it!)

Right now she was in no state to even consider it. With a sneeze and a splutter, she lurched dizzily towards the suddenly very comforting sight of the town of Arandale. Maybe after a good few hours' sleep in a proper, decent bed, she'd be able to kick her brain into gear and think about just what had happened to her out here last night.

Yeah. Maybe.

The police found the first body at half past ten that morning; just a dirty old tramp, with no one to miss him or raise the alarm. Murdered on Sunday night, his body discovered on Thursday morning, hidden by the shadows where he slept and by the very rags which had once kept him alive through the cold winter nights.

The Doctor watched from a first-floor library window as the police returned wearily to their vehicles and the onlookers reluctantly dispersed. As the old metaphor goes, he was killing two birds with one stone; reading up on Arandale Keep (or Vampire Castle, as it was ghoulishly referred to on the spines of most of the reference books) whilst simultaneously keeping out of the sight of the temperamental Sergeant Blyth. Plenty of time to see *him* when he was next needed.

The Doctor felt the air shift almost imperceptibly. There was someone behind him. He spoke without turning.

'You were right. There was another victim.'

'Unfortunately,' answered the quiet, husky voice of Matthew Shade.

'You found the body yourself?'

'Yes.'

'Like all the others.'

Shade didn't answer that, and the Doctor smiled as he finally turned to face the newcomer. 'I don't mean to imply anything,' he assured him.

Shade smiled back – his own disconcerting, thin-lipped

smile. His deep black eyes seemed to swallow up the light; impossible to read, even for the Time Lord. 'You see why I don't make myself known to the police.'

The Doctor nodded. 'Too many questions.' He had been there himself, far too often, in too many places. 'Want to compare notes?'

'I doubt if you'd understand.'

'Perhaps not,' the Doctor agreed, after a moment's reflection. 'I was thinking the same thing about you.'

'There are occult powers at work in Arandale. Resourceful though you appear to be, I cannot allow you to get in the way of my crusade against them. Even if that were not the case, you could not possibly comprehend the Dark Forces with which I must struggle.'

'I see,' said the Doctor amiably. 'But share one thing with me, would you?'

Shade raised his eyebrows, non-committally.

'I assume, with my sadly limited comprehension, that we're looking for one person in the village who has become affected by the, shall we say, "mystical forces" around Arandale Keep. These forces have taken a hold on this person, forcing him or her to steal the blood of innocents to suit whatever their purposes might be. You said there would be six deaths, so presumably they will have all the blood they need by tomorrow night, November the fifth. At which point, I imagine something very unpleasant is scheduled to occur. Close?'

He paused, waiting for a reaction. Shade said nothing but his head was bowed in thought as he turned and walked slowly, ponderously, towards the exit door. When he looked back at the Doctor, it was with an uncommonly genuine smile on his face and an impossible twinkle in his dark eyes.

'Close enough,' he said – and then he turned and left, and the lights of the room seemed to brighten slightly upon his departure.

Ace was dreaming, and her dream went like this:

All aboard the good ship TARDIS, sailing out of Perivale Harbour on a voyage of discovery (but Perivale doesn't have a harbour, does it?) with Captain Ace at the helm, guiding that battered old ship and its mutinous crew through the rapids and whirlpools to the beckoning lights of the Isle of Svartos there in the middle distance (but Svartos wasn't an island, was it?) Land ahoy!

Then a bump, a creak, a sudden lurch forward; Svartos spinning out of reach into the blackness of space, not an isle at all but merely a passing planet ... and Ace was falling and the ship was falling around her, and the crows and the seagulls were pecking at her, chiselling away at the tough, hard cocoon she had wrapped herself in.

She fell down – down into the darkness, down past the stars, down off the edge ...

... off the very edge of ...

... of the world itself. But that couldn't be right either – because the world *isn't* flat.

Is it?

And that was the bit she really didn't understand.

Rosemary's dreams were, if anything, even more strange than Ace's – and rather more tenacious. They had started when she was six, that night of the Hallowe'en party when fresh-faced young Rosie was packed off to bed by seven o'clock so that she wouldn't see mummy drinking too much alcohol, smoking too many cigarettes and chatting up too many men. Mummy needn't have bothered; there was nothing going on that night that Rosie hadn't already seen too many times before.

The printed word was her refuge, her way of escape into the simple straightforward world of good versus evil, black versus white, where problems were easily solved and the virtuous live happily ever after. Night after night, poor neglected little Rosie would lie awake in the orange glow of the reading lamp, devouring book after book in her endless hunger for all things happy and unreal. She used to dream that she could travel through the looking glass, join the Secret Seven, *be* Cinderella or the Queen of Hearts. But still it wasn't enough.

On the night of the party, she took the Forbidden Book; the one her great-grandfather had written, which her mother had kept out of bounds on the shelf by her bedside until Rosie was 'old enough to read them sorta things!' Well she'd be too far gone to miss it tonight, Rosie decided, and who cared if she did anyway? So she carried the book lovingly back into her room, snuggled down beneath the bedclothes with her battery-powered torch and filled her mind with the incredible tales of ancestors she had never been told about.

Six year-old Rosie learnt something that night. She learnt that no matter how amazing the world of fiction, it was easily matched by the world of fact and by the real-life events of a history she had never known existed. That night she had the dream for the first time, and she was riding with her forebears on a broomstick high above the clouds, dancing with the Devil round a cauldron in the woods, choking and screaming as they burnt John Chambers at the stake. And they offered her a choice; pressed a pen into her hot, wet, clammy hands and told her to sign the Devil's Book if she wished their powers to be hers as well.

She screamed that first time, waking up hoarse and sweating – but her interest had been piqued, and from that moment forth, her weekly visits to the library were spent not amongst the shelves of the children's section, but rather in dedicated pursuit of any and all written knowledge on the subject of witchcraft.

The dream came again, and by the time she was seven, Rosie had made her choice. She made her mark in the Book that year and promised herself that no matter what their origin, she would use the powers she received to do only good. She would never succumb to the lure of the Darkness.

Almost thirty-two years later, she was proud to say that thus far, she never had. Phil had helped, of course;

immersed in her studies and surrounded by wicked rumours, she had never had much company – particularly not of the male kind. She had been quite taken by him, and him by her in a funny sort of way. More importantly, he had seemed to act as a positive influence on her, somehow sharpening her concentration, directing her powers, enabling her to make the breakthroughs she needed and to achieve new heights within her chosen sphere. She had been married at twenty-six (though Phil had been barely out of his teens), had the kids a few years later. They had all kept her name of course. 'Chambers' had a tradition, she had said: it was a name steeped in the wonderful history of the occult. If Phil was to marry her, then they would both have to use it.

And the dreams had continued – wonderful, magical dreams in which she walked the valleys of the Netherworld or flew high above the clouds on a broomstick of her own. And once every six months – at the festivals of Beltane and Hallowe'en – she signed the Devil's Book again, rejoicing in her powers and reaffirming without compunction her utmost dedication to the glorious path of witchcraft.

This year had been no exception. On Sunday night she had signed the Book once more, determined to replenish her mystical might more than ever now that her community needed her. The image of the Death card had swum before her eyes, and she had sworn in that dark and lonely place that she would learn of what dread circumstances it was warning her.

The following night the first body had been found, and Rosemary had known that she was running out of time.

She woke with a start, feeling somewhat embarrassed at having apparently dozed off during one of her sacred rituals. The crystal ball lay heavily on the table before her but its surface was still clouded and grey, and the illumination she had so desperately been seeking was not yet forthcoming.

Phil was standing bashfully in the doorway that led to the rest of the house, playing nervously with his hands as she turned to face him. 'Did I disturb you?'

'Yes,' she snapped, more annoyed with herself than at her husband.

'It's just that the kids, they want to know if it's all right to go out. To that club thing of theirs.'

'Oh yes, yes, let them go.' She waved a hand at him dismissively, already turning back to the crystal ball. 'As long as they keep out of trouble.'

Phil had left the room and eased the connecting door half-way closed behind him when her startled gasp halted him in his tracks.

He was by her side in seconds. 'What is it?!' he yelled.

'Quiet!' But it was already too late. The image had faded.

'What *was* it?!'

She was clearly shaken. 'I – I don't know. Some sort of priest . . . with a crucifix, on a chain. He was looking at me, Phil – *looking* at me . . . and he was looking *for* me!'

He put his arm around her shoulders, and for once she didn't shake it loose. 'Hey, come on now,' he coaxed her. 'It's just an image, that's all. Just a picture in the glass. It can't hurt you.'

'No,' whispered Rosemary, and her face was a deathly white mask. 'No, you never understand! He's real. He's coming after me. And when he finds me . . . he's going to kill me!'

'So what are you trying to tell me?' asked Norman, struggling to take in what the Doctor was saying. 'That the force which gave me my powers is still around? After all these years?'

'And it will be for a good time longer,' the Doctor confirmed.

'But I've been up there,' protested Norman. 'I've been up to the castle dozens of times. My whole reason for coming back to Arandale was to see if there was still anything there. But there never was!'

'Not that you can see, maybe,' said the Doctor. Infuriatingly, he took a long, slow sip of his coffee before continuing. 'What you have to understand is that the powers this energy gave to you were nothing more than an accidental side-effect.'

'No!' Norman was clearly affronted. 'There must be more to it than that! There has to be a purpose behind it all! I was given those abilities to do good, and they were taken from me because I lost the will to continue.'

The Doctor sighed and shook his head. 'The energy did – does – have a purpose,' he confirmed, 'but you are incidental to it. Like the people who died around the castle, you were just in the wrong place at the wrong time. It was only by chance, by the unique arrangement of your genes, that you were able to survive being irradiated at all.'

'This gets worse all the time,' commented Benny who, standing in the doorway of her room, had overheard this last snippet of conversation. She joined the others inside, sitting herself down on the bed next to Norman. 'I'm beginning to feel like I'm trapped in some sort of storybook,' she said. Which of course, she is – but there's no need to let her know that just yet!

'Did you look in on Ace?' asked the Doctor, genuinely concerned.

'Still asleep,' said Benny. 'Tossing and turning like anyone's business. I had half a mind to wake her, if only to ask what happened to my chinos.'

'I'm sure she'll tell us in her own time about last night,' said the Doctor, but his tone of voice betrayed his own doubts on the subject.

'And in the meantime,' said Bernice cheerfully, trying to lighten the atmosphere, 'you can explain again about this energy stuff.'

The Doctor sighed, and began the story for the third time.

'Sorry we're late,' said Gary Chambers, as he and his sister were ushered through the red wooden gate into Tim's back yard. 'Mum was doing a bit of crystal ball gazing, and Dad didn't like to disturb her.'

'Doesn't matter,' said Tim. 'Tracey's only just got here anyway.' He didn't particularly want to discuss the subject of Rosemary Chambers; the fact was, if she hadn't been Gary and Michelle's mother, she would doubtless have been the subject of one of the Adventure Kids' investigations long ago. Tracey shared his frustration: a real live witch living in the village, and they couldn't do anything about it because she had given birth to two-fifths of the team!

'Where's Carson today?' asked Michelle, disappointed that the loveable little pooch wasn't there to greet her.

'Gone to the vet's,' said Tim, 'with a stomach bug or something. Mum said if it was between him and the front-room carpet, it'd be Carson that'd have to go!'

'That's terrible!'

'But never mind that,' said Gary, impatiently. 'We came here to talk about Vampire Castle, didn't we?'

'We certainly did,' agreed Tracey. 'And now that I've had a good night's sleep and a chance to think about what happened, I vote we go straight back up there right away and sort it all out!'

'Hear, hear!' trumpeted Gary.

'Hey, now just a minute,' Michelle protested. 'It could be dangerous up there. We almost ran into someone last time, remember?'

'Well, of course we did!' said Gary, disdainfully. 'If the whole place was completely empty, there'd be no point in us investigating it, would there?'

'Look,' said Tim, diplomatically, 'I say we take a proper vote on it. Those for and those against going back up there. I'll do whatever the rest of the team decides.'

Michelle looked at Gary and Tracey, sighed heavily and prepared herself for a return visit to Vampire Castle.

The Doctor, thought Rosemary Chambers, was quite a different character by day to the man who had so unnerved her in the eerie candlelight of the previous evening. It was almost as if he knew exactly how to project whatever image of himself he desired, although she knew of course that that couldn't be the case.

All smiles and charm, he had arrived on her doorstep some ten minutes ago, and he was now sitting quietly in her living room and drinking tea appreciatively from her best china. 'We don't get many people round here these days,' said Rosemary, settling down into an easy chair opposite her visitor.

'Except for her coven,' grumbled Phil from behind his paper in the corner. She easily ignored him, through years of practice. Even so, Rosemary was glad of her husband's presence; after her terrifying glimpse into the future, she was none too keen to be left alone with her strange house guest, no matter how pleasant he seemed at the moment.

'I thought you might need help,' said the Doctor, simply.

Rosemary stiffened. 'You did?'

'You seemed rather worried when I saw you yesterday, and you look even more so now.'

'I've just . . . had a lot on my mind recently. What with these horrible deaths going on in the town, I mean. A lot of people come here to consult me about things like that.'

'But I think there's more to it than that,' said the Doctor, and Rosemary squirmed under his gaze. Friendly though he appeared, she really didn't want to disclose anything more to him than she already had – but she could see in his eyes that he was not prepared to let the subject drop.

Her anxiety was detected, as always, by her familiar; the door swung silently open and the beautiful black cat padded gently into the room. That, at least, was some sort of comfort.

'She's been trying to contact the victims,' Phil said, a hint of contempt in his voice and his eyes never leaving the morning news. Rosemary shot him a glance of pure hatred. She couldn't stand it when he was like this, all mocking comments and scathing put-downs.

When she turned back to her visitor, her expression changed to one of total surprise. 'I like your cat,' said the Doctor, scratching the approving feline affectionately behind its ears. 'What's his name?' Comfortably settled on the stranger's lap, the cat yawned, stretched and purred with contentment before turning its unblinking green eyes almost accusingly upon its dumbfounded mistress.

Rosemary sighed, and decided to tell the Doctor everything.

Karen wanted to talk to Mel. She had been making that perfectly plain all day, from the subtle hints of the morning through to the outright threats of the afternoon. But Mel was always too busy; he was putting the finishing touches to one board game, play-testing another, writing a campaign book for Dungeons and Dragons that he hoped to be able to sell . . . until finally, she could stand it no more.

She found Mel in his room, hunched intently over a computer screen as he guided Sonic the Hedgehog easily past the obstacles of the Scrap Brain Zone. Her first reaction was to flick the switch of the computer to 'off'. Her second, as Mel jumped angrily to his feet, was to knock the joypad flying from his hand.

'I'm still waiting for that explanation,' said Karen, icily.

'Just leave me alone, can't you?!' screamed Mel into her face. 'What the hell do you want me to say?'

Karen maintained a grip on her rising anger. 'I just want you to tell me how you ended up in such a . . .' she gestured in frustration at the bruises on his face, and at the thick wodge of sellotape which held together his wire-framed glasses '. . . such a *state* last night!'

'Well, that's none of your business.'

He turned away, but Karen seized him by the shoulder and spun him back round to face her. 'I think it is!' she answered, sharply.

Mel seemed to snap at that, screaming out in rage as

104

he lunged unexpectedly at her, propelling her backwards across the room and slamming her helplessly against the far wall. 'Just keep your nose out of it!' he bellowed at her, pinning her by the throat. He's not doing *that* for long, she thought; she brought her knee hard up into his groin, and the grip was suddenly released. Mel sank whining to the floor, affecting far more pain than the blow could possibly have caused him.

'It's the same every damn time, isn't it?' Karen berated him, profound disappointment in her eyes and her voice. 'The tiniest upset, the slightest problem, and all you can do is lash out, like some sort of animal. You're pathetic!'

Mel just groaned, painfully. He was well used by now to playing on Karen's feelings. The injured puppy act, a winner every time.

'Well this time . . .' (Here comes the threat again!) '. . . this time, you've gone too far! This time, you've screwed up for good!' (And she's never coming back, of course!) 'This time . . .' Karen swallowed hard, and tried to hold back the tears. 'This time, I've had enough. I'm going, Mel! And I'm never coming back, you hear me? I'm never coming back!' (Thud, thud, thud, thud, thud . . . *slam!*).

Mel sighed, picked himself up and lay casually back on his bed. How long this time, he wondered, before the rattle of the catch, her soft footsteps padding back up the stairs? A whispered apology, a lingering kiss, and we'll say no more about that business in the pub, it'll only come between us.

For almost fifteen minutes he waited, the furrow on his brow growing deeper and deeper as he started to think . . . maybe this time, for the first time . . . could she have actually meant what she said?

Eventually, Mel got slowly to his feet. He made his way quietly down the stairs (she couldn't be back already, could she? Couldn't have sneaked in, be waiting there in the main room?) looked cautiously, one by one, into every room of the house (Or maybe sitting on the doorstep, forgotten her keys, frightened to knock?) and then finally, desperately, yanked open the front door, afraid of what he might not see when he did.

There was somebody there, but it wasn't Karen. Karen didn't have tangled black hair and a thick black moustache. She didn't dress in worn old pullovers and tracksuit bottoms. Most of all, she wasn't built like a gorilla, with an attitude to match.

'Not so fast, sonny-boy!' snarled Mason Grimshaw, one heavy plimsolled foot preventing Mel from slamming the door in his face. 'I think it's time we had a few words, you and me!'

It was past three o'clock when Ace finally staggered out of bed, her throat much better for the rest but her head still sore and feeling packed with cotton wool. It was only through luck that Benny saw her sneaking out through the guest-house door; she was on her way back from the toilet at the time. With a quick instruction to Norman not to leave the building under any circumstances whatsoever, she pulled on her overcoat and hurried downstairs in pursuit.

She caught up with Ace outside the Black Cat, almost sobbing in frustration at the door which wouldn't open for her. 'It's closed,' she said gently, resting a steadying hand on her comrade's shoulder. 'They shut it down when the landlord died.'

'I know,' grumbled Ace, shaking her head but failing to clear it. 'I know that.' She punched the unyielding door, hard. 'What's *happening* to me? Bloody locked doors. I'm supposed to be stronger than this.'

'You're just a bit ill, that's all.' Benny smiled at her, kindly. 'Come on,' she said. 'Let's go somewhere we can get a drink.'

Ace accepted her proffered arm, and the two friends walked slowly away together.

'Something is going to happen,' said Rosemary quietly.

'Something terrible. And with all my powers, I still don't know what it is.'

'Something to do with Arandale Keep?' suggested the Doctor.

'It seems to be at the heart of the disturbance,' Rosemary admitted. 'I'm sure it's connected somehow with what's going on.'

'I think that's extremely likely.'

'And then there are the omens,' she continued. 'Strange things happening in the village; strange people arriving, as if to take up positions for some catastrophic final game. The private detective, the psychic investigator . . .'

'And me, I assume,' concluded the Doctor, his tone not unfriendly. 'Don't worry, I'm here to help. And so, I think, are our friends Corrigan and Shade – in one way or another.'

'And yet no one *can* help! Four murders now, four people cut down in the dark, and no one seems any nearer to uncovering the truth!'

'But you have tried to contact the victims?' The Doctor glanced over at Phil, but he remained steadfastly disinterested in the conversation.

'And had no success,' said Rosemary. 'Not with any of them.'

'Is that unusual?'

'Of course. It's as if this time, some . . . some force is frustrating my efforts. It's out there somewhere, blocking my powers, keeping the souls of the dead out of my reach.'

This comment seemed to bring Phil to life, flinging his paper to one side as he jumped angrily to his feet. 'Oh, there's some force in your way all right!' he scoffed. 'It's called Reality! And you,' he addressed the Doctor, 'would do well to get out of here before she fills your head up with any more of her mystical rubbish!' Without waiting for an answer he swept out of the room, and seconds later they heard the front door of the house slam shut behind him.

'More tea, Doctor?' Rosemary got to her feet, smiling

107

sweetly at her guest as she gathered his cup and saucer and headed off towards the kitchen with them. She paused in the doorway, looking back at him with a puzzled expression on her face.

'Is that a spoon in your pocket?' she asked.

Philip Chambers let out a sigh of relief as he stepped out of the house and onto the slushy, wet pavement. As always, leaving Rosemary behind was like slipping shackles off his arms and legs. He was free again, for the next few hours at least. Now, how to use that freedom? The Black Cat was closed, he knew – for once, he would have to actually think about where he was to go. It took him longer than he might have thought, but eventually, he remembered a few old friends of his who might well be in the Arandale Arms at this time of day. He set briskly off along the pavement, breathing deeply of the cold fresh air and blissfully unaware that he was being spied upon.

From his vantage point across the road, the figure in red watched Phil Chambers intently, and his hand jerked nervously as it held on tight to the crucifix around his neck. Finally, when he was sure that Phil was long gone, he let the crucifix fall. Then, with slow measured paces, each punctuated by a deep, nervous breath, he traversed the few yards around the corner to the front door of Rosemary Chambers' Mystic Emporium.

He stood for almost five minutes on the step, muttering prayers for forgiveness and gathering his God-given resolve. Then one of the local children asked what he was doing dressed as Santa Claus, and he decided it was time to get in off the pavement.

With his jaw set tight and his fists clenched in determination, Father Kenneth Michael Sheridan pushed open the door to Rosemary's shop.

Chapter 7

Bearing Crosses

The Pig and Whistle had nothing on the Black Cat, thought Bernice. No warmth, no feeling, no character; just a bare room full of smoke and two drinks slammed unceremoniously onto the bar top by a woman with a scowl that looked like it must be permanent. Still, there weren't many pubs still open past three o'clock, and in any case Ace didn't seem to mind where they ended up so long as she could sink into a chair and pour a pint of cider down her throat. So the Pig and Whistle it was, and best just to ignore the raucous laughter and vulgar comments from the table across the room. Ace really must be feeling ill, Benny decided, else she'd have been straight over there with a bottle in her hand after that crack about her combat suit.

'Feeling any better?' she asked, after a suitable length of time.

'A bit,' said Ace. 'Not much. Nice place you brought us to.'

Bernice smiled. 'Yeah. Well, beggars can't be choosers. And we can handle this lot, I'm sure.'

'Seen worse, I suppose.'

'Yes, I suppose you have.' End of conversation. Begin awkward silence, avoid each other's eyes, concentrate on the drinks.

'Why did you stay with us?' asked Ace, presently.

The question took Benny by surprise, not least because it was Ace who was asking. What had prompted this, she wondered? Had she made her thoughts about leaving so obvious?

'It must be a bit of a pain for you, that's all,' Ace clarified. 'I mean, everyone at each other's throats all the time.'

'It can get a bit frustrating,' admitted Benny, guardedly.

Ace smiled, just briefly, but her shades still masked her eyes in secrecy. 'I don't want it to be like this. I just . . .' She let the sentence tail off, and Benny wondered whether she was waiting for a prompt. She decided against delivering one, but instantly wished that she had. Ace changed the subject again.

'So go on then, why do you stay?'

Benny shrugged, not much more ready with an answer than she had been the first time. 'It's for the opportunities, I suppose.' She was thinking of Norman, of all that he had said to her. 'The chance to travel anywhere, anytime.' She hesitated. It wasn't fair; she thought she'd made her decision, now suddenly things seemed so terribly unclear again. 'I was going to leave,' she finally confessed. Ace raised one eyebrow in surprise. 'I was going to stay here, find somewhere to settle down – but I don't know if I can confine myself to one planet, one time.'

'Not here,' said Ace quickly.

'What?'

'Not here. Anywhere but here.' A pained expression flickered across the younger woman's features. 'I'm sorry. Just something I saw. Something bad. I don't know anything more.'

'Something last night?' Benny urged, concerned.

'Yes. No. I can't remember.' Ace screwed up her face in concentration, wracking her brain for that elusive final piece of the jigsaw in her mind (she was falling, falling through space, falling off the edge). She faltered, lost the image, and knew her chance was gone. She tried to smile again. 'Makes a change from dreaming about women in red dresses, I suppose.'

'Sorry?'

110

'Doesn't matter.'

There was another long silence.

Benny finished her vodka, turning thought after thought over in her mind. She was even starting to feel guilty, she realized with a start – guilty because none of the problems of Arandale, even those of Ace's missing memories, meant a thing to her right now. For here she was, on the verge of packing it all in, desperate to find something which would make things all right – and now here was Ace, for the first time in weeks actually talking to her, opening her shell just a little, just to let a few tiny feelings seep through. She wondered how far she could push it, and she agonized over what to say next, worried that the wrong thing might lose her this chance forever.

'Ace,' she asked, finally. 'Why do you stay with the Doctor? Why did you come back at all?'

I've blown it, she thought. My one big opportunity to start making things right, and I've gone and blown it!

For almost a full minute, Ace stared fixedly down at the remains of her cider, before finally getting to her feet and draining the glass in one swift movement. So Benny wants a heart to heart, does she? Ace thought. She really gets off on this soppy introspective stuff. Let's see which of us can handle what I've got to dish out.

'Let me get the next round in,' she said, 'and I'll tell you.'

'I don't like this,' moaned Michelle. 'I don't like this one bit!'

'Don't be soft!' Gary chastised her. 'There's nothing to be frightened of. We've even got torches this time!'

The Adventure Kids were standing once again at the foot of the iron ladder, an uncomfortably distant square of light above them marking the way to the bright, safe world outside. The stone block had lifted quite easily this time, allowing the children quicker access to the tunnels than had been the case previously. Michelle felt almost cheated; like she hadn't been given the time she expected to prepare herself for the horrors underground. As she was wont to do in such situations, she began to regret ever going along with her brother and her team mates. As always though, she was not going to turn back now.

'So where do we start?' asked Tim doubtfully, the weak beam of his torch flickering undecidedly about the cavern. 'There are half a dozen ways to go from here.'

'Well we need to find wherever that sneeze came from, don't we?' said Tracey, practically. 'So where was that?'

'One of these, I think,' answered Gary, hovering between two openings in the far wall. One of them had obviously led to a storage room of some sort. The wood of the door had all but rotted away, but its rusted hinges were still in place. The other was the beginning of a corridor, strewn with rubble and leading further than any of the torches could show them.

'So,' said Tim, 'it looks like this is the one. Agreed?' There were no arguments from the others.

'The question is,' said Tracey nervously, 'who's going to be the first one down there?'

The bells above the door jingled; a dull, tinny sound. Rosemary excused herself from the Doctor's company as she hurried to attend to her customer.

She felt a chill of fear as soon as she entered the shop. The man had his back to her, but his mode of dress was the first thing that rang alarm bells in her head; the deep red cloak brought instant images of thick flowing blood into her mind.

Her voice was hoarse as she called to him. 'Can I help you?' But then the man turned, and she caught her breath in panic as she finally saw his face, recognizing it from her earlier prediction. 'You!'

The next thing she knew, Sheridan was upon her, the sheer force of his leap slamming her back into the wall and knocking a shelf full of books to the floor by her side. She slid to the ground, her frail body shaking with fear, her arm suddenly aching though she knew not why.

'So you fear the emissary of the Lord, foul sorceress! As well you might! For I have come here this night to rid the fair township of Arandale of your heinous black magics!'

'No,' protested Rosemary, her voice now low and cracked. 'No!' But the priest's face was resolute, and her own blood dripped from his weapon of revenge – the glistening silver dagger which hovered above her chest and prepared to strike again.

'Let this holy weapon represent the Good which must exorcise the Evil within you! Let this instrument of Heaven . . .'

Sheridan flinched, albeit momentarily. He looked away and tried to forget the frightened, staring eyes of his prey, transfixed by the weapon as a rabbit is by the approaching headlights of its own doom. A nerve pulsed in his neck and he renewed his grip on the dagger – both hands now, let them drive this holy artefact downwards, vanquish the heathen witch and save a town from damnation.

He shuddered, clenched his eyes tightly closed, muttered a prayer to his god and drove the dagger towards Rosemary's heart.

Mel's head bounced hard off a thick wooden cabinet, and he went down for the third time. Grimshaw was atop him before he could so much as blink, one heavy knee slamming into the younger man's stomach and forcing the breath painfully from his body. Strong, thick hands clamped themselves around his throat and pressed for all they were worth, until Mel thought he was going to have the very life squeezed out of him. Black spots danced before his eyes and each breath seemed harder to draw than the last.

'Got the message yet, sunshine?' snarled Mason Grimshaw, unexpectedly relaxing his hold and climbing back to his feet.

Mel didn't move. He had lost his glasses again, his face

was bruised and a cut on his forehead was streaming blood down into his eyes.

'Thought you were pretty blasted clever, I suppose!' his attacker continued. 'Well you pushed it too far, mate! Grass on me now, and you're going down as well – always assuming I don't get to you myself first!' Mel tried to grunt a surrender, but his voice was lost and he was coughing up blood.

'No more warnings!' Mason told him, and to Mel's eternal gratitude, he seemed content to leave things there. For one brief moment after the front door slammed heavily shut behind his unwelcome visitor, Mel wondered what the hell he was going to tell Karen about this.

Then he remembered that Karen was gone.

It had taken a further three ciders, but Ace had finally opened up to Benny – perhaps more so than she had opened up to anyone in the past three years. Benny in turn had been equally forthright, filled with a warm glow of achievement that she had somehow managed finally to pierce the protective cocoon in which her companion had concealed herself. They had talked about the Daleks, about the battles they had shared and the people they had loved and lost; about space travel, and the wonders they had seen on dozens of far-off worlds. Finally, in a more sombre mood, they had talked about the Doctor and about the deaths he had caused on the world of the Silurians.

'I don't know if I can ever forget that,' said Benny. 'All those people, that entire world, just condemned to die like that.'

Ace nodded. 'He said there was no other way, though.'

'But we could have stayed there! We should have done something! We needn't have just left like we did, as if it all meant nothing!'

'But that's the whole point though, isn't it?' said Ace. 'To the Doctor, it *did* mean nothing. Just another of his games, another upset in the universe to be dealt with and then chucked.'

Benny took another swig of her drink. 'Like he did with the Althosian system. Seven planets, millions of people, and he just sat back and watched that Time Lord friend of his obliterate them. I don't think I'll ever look at him in the same way after that. Not after that, and not after the Silurians; not after seeing how cold and how callous he can really be.' For a moment the two women were lost in their own unhappy thoughts. Then, slightly more cheerfully, Benny asked: 'How did we get on to all this, anyway?'

'I was going to tell you why I stay with the Doctor,' said Ace, matter-of-factly.

This was it – what Bernice had been waiting for. 'And?'

'And it's hard to explain. I'm not even sure I understand it myself. It's just . . .' She gazed into the mid-distance, struggling for the words. 'It's just like a game, you know? Like through being dragged into the Doctor's life, I've managed to get hooked on the same sort of manipulation kick as him.'

'How do you mean?' Benny prompted.

'I'm not sure.' Ace rubbed her hand over her weary eyes, and her mirrored glasses dropped unchecked onto the table before her. 'It's like I'm playing his own game against him, like I can't come away from the board until I've beaten him once and for all.' She closed her eyes and concentrated on the bitter-sweet memories which were swimming into focus through the pain in her head. 'I trusted him, you know. Like I'd never trusted anyone else before. I never really had any parents, but he was the closest I ever came. He took me from Iceworld, showed me the universe, guided me, protected me. At least, that's what I thought at the time. But it was all just part of the game. *I* was just part of the game! Him versus Fenric, him versus the Daleks, him versus the Timewyrm. Whatever we did, wherever we went, it was him in control and me as his pawn, to be used, abused or damn well sacrificed whenever it suited him.'

'Like he did with Jan,' said Benny, quietly. She remembered only too well the events on the planet of Heaven; the ones which had introduced her to the Doctor, whilst splitting Ace from him seemingly for good.

'Like with Jan,' Ace confirmed. 'And with Robin before him. All like me, just pawns in the game. People I loved, but it didn't suit him for me to be with them. I mean, it's like with the Silurians; I know his motives are sometimes good, and I know he's saved a lot of lives. But what about the lives he's ruined? What about me?' She lapsed into silence for a moment, before forcing open the eyes she had rubbed red and slipping her shades back onto her face. 'I don't know why I'm telling you all this,' she said. 'I promised myself when I left, I was never going to trust anyone again. Not like I did with him. I was never going to give anyone the chance to use me like that.'

'Sometimes it's good to talk,' said Benny. 'It can help.'

'I used to talk to him. Told him everything, my hopes, my fears, my feelings. But he never gave anything back. He only told me lies. He was just a Time Lord he said, but I know that can't possibly be true. He was just a traveller, but he always knew what was going on, he was always ready to take things over, always ready to play the game again. I hated him for that. That's why I thought I could play the game against him, why I threw in with IMC when they wanted me to use him for a change. Only once we met up again, I knew I couldn't go along with that.' She faltered and looked up at Benny, seeing in her eyes the reassurance she needed to continue. 'It's like, as much as I hated the Doctor . . . I loved him too. And I couldn't do anything to hurt him.'

'So you came back.'

Ace nodded. 'To deal with the Doctor on his own terms. To prove that I'm no longer some sort of plaything he can just manipulate at will; that I've grown up now, become strong.' She sighed. 'Until today, I thought I was doing quite a good job of it.'

'But you are strong!' Benny insisted. 'Don't you see? But that doesn't mean you can't share your feelings, or let anyone into you life. Everyone needs someone to lean on, at some time or another.' A choked silence followed, and though she knew it would later be denied, Benny swore that Ace was holding back tears behind the protection of her shades.

'But there is one thing I'm not strong enough to do,' Ace said finally, her voice low. 'Whichever way I feel about him, however the game turns out in the end, I know I can't leave him. Not yet. Perhaps not ever. Because I can't let the Doctor out of my life.'

'I don't believe it,' whistled Tim.

'Things don't come much more obvious than this,' commented Tracey.

'But it's horrible!' protested Michelle, shying away from the children's find. 'I mean, that big stone block – it must have been used as an altar of some kind!'

'That's right,' said Gary eagerly, surveying the large, empty cavern with wonder. 'This whole place must be the underground headquarters of a secret group of devil worshippers! Isn't that exciting?'

'It'll be "exciting" all right if they come back here and find us,' said Tim, dryly. He gingerly lifted a dirty white robe from the floor by the altar's side. 'This thing's got dried blood all over it!'

'Is there only one of those?' asked Tracey.

'Dumped next to the altar,' Gary confirmed. 'It must be the coven leader's.'

'Yes,' agreed Michelle, shivering as she pointed down to where the garment had once lain. 'And it's not the only thing he's left behind either.'

They all saw it now, illuminated in the dim light of their torches: a knife, long and sharp, its painted metal handle flaking with use. And on the blade . . .

'It's horrible!' said Michelle again, and she turned away as her stomach began to churn uncontrollably.

'Blood!' whispered Tracey. 'On the knife as well!'

'You mean someone's actually been using it? On other people?'

'Don't be daft, Tim!' scoffed Gary. 'Of course they have! What did you think they'd been doing down here?'

'The murders in the village!' exclaimed Tracey. 'You know, I just bet we've gone and solved them!' The others stared at her, their eyes wide as the full import of her words sank slowly in. It was Tim who finally took the initiative.

'We've got to get out of here!' he said, and even Gary agreed wholeheartedly.

'Too late,' hissed Michelle. 'There's someone coming!' And suddenly they could all hear the footsteps, frighteningly close, approaching far too quickly. 'Come on!'

'No!' Gary pulled his sister back. 'I think they're coming from down there!' From the passage out to freedom.

'You're right,' said Tracey, already pushing Tim towards one of the other exits. 'Down here!'

'But we'll be trapped!' protested Michelle, as the others ran for cover. But as the footsteps drew closer, she knew that none of them had a choice in the matter.

Sheridan screamed and the dagger dropped to the floor as his hands went to his face . . . his *face*, where something was snarling and spitting and clawing and biting. Rosemary gasped, clutched at her injured arm and found the fresh resolve she needed to climb to her feet and run for it. She didn't get far.

The cat – her good old, faithful familiar – was hurled viciously to the ground, where it arched its back and stared threateningly at the man who had dared attack its mistress. But Sheridan had no further mind for it, other than to hastily wipe the blood from his face and turn his attention to the object of his hatred.

The Doctor barred his way. 'The First Commandment,'

he said. ' "Thou shalt not kill". Ah, but then, "Thou shalt not suffer a witch to live", either.' He peered at Sheridan questioningly. 'That is what you were about to say, yes?'

Sheridan nodded dumbly.

'So many contradictions. So many interpretations.' His voice hardened; his eyes did the same. 'Are you sure you have the right one? Sure enough to kill?'

'You . . . you have been sent to test me! To test my faith, my resolve, my loyalty . . .'

'No,' said the Doctor. 'I'm here to help. Both of you.'

Sheridan's hand closed tightly around his crucifix. He pulled it outwards, as far in front of him as the chain would allow, and he took a short, tentative step towards the stranger before him.

The Doctor didn't move.

Sheridan stepped forward again.

'You expect me to flinch? To cry out?'

The cross was only inches away from the Time Lord's face. 'Then . . . then you aren't a servant of the Devil?' The priest spoke with an almost childlike confusion.

The Doctor didn't answer. His eyes met Sheridan's own and for a full minute and more, the two remained locked in an impasse. Rosemary watched fearfully from the connecting door to the house, and she hardly dared breathe lest she break the thickening silence.

Then, his mind suddenly made up, Sheridan hurled himself forward and rammed his fist hard into the Doctor's skull. The two grappled for a moment, and it was the smaller man who crumpled, falling to the ground quite unconscious, a trickle of blood dripping hesitantly from his scalp.

'But I still can't allow you to obstruct my crusade,' whispered Sheridan, and he stared down at his fallen foe with genuine . . . regret? Despair?

'God help me!' he prayed.

By five o'clock the sky was growing wonderfully dark –

but the street lights had flicked on, and their yellow glow obscured the beauty of the firmament.

Norman looked wistfully up out of the guest-house window and his heart ached more than he had ever thought it could. Partly it was because of Benny and the Doctor, he realized – those living reminders of the life he had lost, with their outlandish ways and their maddeningly casual talk of travel amongst the stars. They would be leaving here soon, Benny had told him that. He wondered if they would take him with them.

Something else was adding to his pain. He had felt it for days now, more so with each sunset, with each fresh appearance of the glistening stars (he remembered the night on the bridge; the sudden tingle of energy, the following sense of loss). McAllerson's Radiation, the Doctor had called it. The energy which gave him his powers, which drew him back to Arandale when he lost them. It was out there somewhere, invisible in the night, calling out again ... only this time it was calling to somebody else, and he couldn't make it hear him no matter how he pleaded. He was on the outside looking in, his heart's desire a breath away yet totally unattainable.

He wanted to wear the suit. The White Knight's costume. It would comfort him, he thought, give him the strength to go out there and wrest back the powers that were rightfully his. But the costume was back in his cave, and Benny had told him in no uncertain terms that he was not to risk going there.

Damn it, he thought. The power was out there, ready for the taking ... in the robes of the White Knight, he could *make* it notice him, make it give back to him what he had once so foolishly given away.

By ten past five, the decision was made. Norman slipped quickly, quietly into the frosty night, and headed back to his home.

For one joyous moment, Rosemary had thought she was

free. He'd forgotten about her, he wasn't going to follow . . .

Then the door flew open behind her and the priest was there, more determined than ever, the body of the only man who could ever have stopped him lying helplessly in the dirt beyond.

'Keep away!' she warned him hoarsely, and she raised her arms in threat. 'Just keep away from me, or I swear I won't be responsible for what my magics do to you!'

Sheridan's only response was a twisted grin as he moved slowly around the table towards the cowering victim. 'Not when the symbol of the Lord can repulse you!' he hissed. 'Not when I wear the cross on which our Saviour died.' Rosemary's fear grew into panic as she realized that, somehow, he was actually right. No matter how much she willed it, how much she tried, the powers she was channelling refused to come to the fore, to repulse this attacker and give her time to flee. How could that be? They had worked before, those eldritch forces shaping themselves to the patterns of her will. So why not now? And Rosemary's panic turned to dread as she began to doubt even herself, to wonder if perhaps she *was* an unwitting instrument of all that was Evil, that the cross carried by this priest could so render her helpless. Was she really that corrupted?

It was then that Sheridan knew he had won – when he saw that terror and desperation and doubt, all mixed in her eyes. She was up against the wall now, at his mercy once again, and his dagger needed only to be thrust forward, up into her heart . . .

With renewed determination, Sheridan advanced.

The man in Norman's house was shivering, although his body was encased in metal and that metal draped with cloth. He was afraid, although his armoured form was reputed to be invincible. And for the past ten minutes (though it felt like an hour) since coming to his senses, he had stood unmoving, surveying with horror the carnage he had unwittingly caused. Furniture scattered, books shredded, television blasted, jagged holes punched through thin plaster walls. It had taken just ninety seconds and one furious outburst for Norman Power's drawing room to be rendered uninhabitable. It would probably take several days for the reverse to be achieved.

The Monster had been here again. The Monster which haunted his every waking hour, which had brought him to this country, to this village, so many years ago from his home in America. The Monster which had compelled him to track down his one-time foe and then begged him to squeeze the life out of the helpless, powerless White Knight. The Monster which had hidden when its request was refused, retreating to the depths of its host's tainted being. For five long years, he had thought the Monster dead. Five long years making a life for himself in Arandale, finding a job, a wife, forgetting all about his past career. Only he never tried to move away, did he? He never threw away the costume, did he? Or tried to forget Norman Power's address?

And the Monster was there, lurking deep within his soul, until the day he lost control again and the beast was freed by the furnace of his rage. Freed for good.

The Monster's name was Doctor Nemesis. The man . . . well, he was only a man. Weak and feeble, his body at the beck and call of the thing inside it. And in the evening half-light which filtered in through the broken window, the man removed the Monster's iron mask, buried his sweat-drenched face in his trembling hands, and cried for a mind which had once been his own.

Ace slept, and the dream came again. Bernice watched her restless thrashing from the doorway of her room, and her face was a picture of concern. It was hard for her now to believe that the pair had been so distant for so long; hard to believe that she had once mistrusted Ace so, seeing conspiracies in everything she did, worried that the cuckoo in the nest would destroy her life in the

TARDIS forever. With a bit of kindness and a bit of perseverance – helped admittedly by her companion's current state of confusion – Benny had finally chipped Ace's hardened exterior away from her, making it through to the bewildered little child underneath. And the child, she could identify with. She could relate to it, nurture it, help it through its difficulties. It felt good to be needed again.

Benny thought about the Doctor, and she wondered if he too had a child within him. She wondered if by talking to him, as she had to Ace, she could form a similar sort of understanding.

Perhaps then her own life would start to make sense too.

The ceremony was in full flow again, and the Master of the Coven laughed a shrill, maniacal laugh that mere human vocal chords could not possibly have produced.

'The penultimate sacrifice is nigh!' he screeched to an audience that packed the Sacred Cavern from wall to wall. 'With but two more offerings, the Power of Our Lords will be *mine*!' And he laughed again then and the crowd joined in, their feverish ecstasy almost matching his own and the echoes of their jubilation crashing gloriously around the tunnels in one grand symphony of obedience rewarded.

Through it all, the Adventure Kids were watching, crouched down in the shadows of a tunnel mouth nearby, all but one of them too terrified even to speak.

'Does anyone recognize him?' hissed Gary. 'I'm sure I've heard that voice before.'

'It's so hard to tell,' Tracey answered him, once it was obvious that nobody else was going to. 'In the dark, with that hood on, it could be anyone. But you're right, I think I might recognize the voice from somewhere – if only he'd stop all that wailing, and talk normally!'

'The question is,' whispered Gary, 'who does he think he's shouting to?' But there were no easy answers to that, and the children could only watch, transfixed, as the sepulchral figure at the altar wailed his litany alone. His words reverberated unaccompanied around the empty cavern, and his only response was the silence of the dead – and the fantasies of his own twisted mind.

Norman could feel it again; that thrill of energy, rushing through him, revitalizing him. He sought to keep hold of it, but it flowed in and out of his body with no regard for his own wishes in the matter.

He had reached the back door of his house now – his usual point of entrance. The key was in its accustomed position beneath the flowerpot, but he could hardly pick it up, his hands were shaking so with excitement. Just pop inside, slide down to the cave, pick up the costume and back out the door. What could be safer?

Barely a dozen feet away, an armoured figure was jerked suddenly out of his miserable train of thought. He leapt quickly to his feet – as quickly as his body suit would let him – and stared in panic at the door through to Norman's kitchen. From the other side of that, he had heard . . . yes, there it was again . . . the rattling of a key in the back door lock.

Then his tensed body relaxed and a sly, malicious smile spread slowly across his darkening face. The mask swung easily into position, locking shut with a satisfying clang, masking all but the fiery red eyes of the Monster beneath it.

Doctor Nemesis was ready.

Once again, it was an unexpected arrival which stopped Father Sheridan in his tracks. This time, it took the form not of a spitting ball of fur, but of one softly spoken word from the doorway behind him.

'No!' said the Doctor, and though his voice was low, his tone was hard and his expression would countenance no disobedience.

Sheridan paused, hating himself for doing so. What was

124

it about this man? He could barely even stand, still dizzy from the blow which had felled him, using the door frame to support his slight form. He was no threat to the mission; the witch would be dead before her would-be bodyguard could so much as cross the room. But Sheridan paused anyway, and he found himself listening and unable to turn his attention away.

'You're making a mistake,' the Doctor said.

'The woman is a witch!' returned the priest, but his voice was trembling.

'And you know that for sure?'

'She admits it herself!'

'Then she is very much mistaken.'

Rosemary's eyes widened and she shook her head in denial, stopping short of actually speaking as she realized she would be talking herself into the grave.

'Has she shown you any evidence of these powers she claims to have?'

'She cannot!' insisted Sheridan. 'No matter how she has tried. I wear the crucifix, the shield of protection which such as she can never pierce.'

'And without the crucifix, you'd be completely at her mercy?'

'Completely!'

'She could call up her magic and banish you from this place forever?'

'Indubitably.'

The Doctor smiled, and held up his hand. 'Then why hasn't she?' Sheridan's own hand flew up to his neck – but he could only confirm what the Doctor was showing him. His crucifix was dangling from the Time Lord's grasp, its golden chain wrapped casually around his hand.

'What price your protection now?'

'Then . . .' Sheridan could barely find the words. 'Then the witch has no powers at all? She is in truth naught more than a harmless eccentric?'

The Doctor threw the crucifix and chain across the room, and the dagger dropped unregarded from Sheridan's hands as he reached to catch it. 'Such were my mistaken beliefs, I might nearly have been responsible for the death of one who is innocent!' He held onto the image of the cross, and tears blinded his eyes as he turned it nervously in his twitching hands. 'Nearly responsible . . .'

Quietly, the Doctor stooped and removed the dagger from Sheridan's reach. He needed to do no more. His faith crushed, the priest had eyes only for the symbol cradled in his hands, and thoughts only for the evil he had done in the name of his God.

He didn't even stir when the police arrived, nor when they escorted him gently away to a waiting car. By that time, it just didn't seem to matter any more.

It was half past six by the town hall clock. Karen had been walking now for almost four hours, her mind buzzing round and round with thoughts and memories and recriminations.

Why did she do it, she asked herself? Why did she keep on going back to him? Why, when it was the same thing every time? Nice, happy, smiling Mel in public; irritable, secretive and downright nasty in the privacy of their own home. No one else had seen him like she had. The mood swings, the tantrums, the 'business trips' he wouldn't talk about – and always the attempt to turn it all around, to make her feel guilty for somehow mistreating him.

And always the refuge in violence. Say anything Mel doesn't like, anything Mel doesn't want to hear, and *smack*! Right away, no questions asked. Karen had seen battered wives and girlfriends before, weeping on television dramas and documentaries, their faces one big bruise but refusing to leave the bastard that had done it to them. She had always thought them stupid, found herself angered by their weaknesses – why didn't they just *go*? And yet here she was the same, forever walking out, always going back . . . and the only thing which stood between her and them was the fact that she could take *her* spineless fiancé down with both hands tied behind her

126

back. Sometimes, she could hardly stop herself from doing so.

Something rattled beside her, and Karen was shaken rudely out of her reverie. A sudden fear gripped her – how could she have forgotten? Allowed herself to get caught alone, in the dark, when a killer was on the loose?

'Wh-who's there?' she called, her voice lost in the inky void between buildings. Something had moved down there, she was sure of it. Her mind screamed 'run' but her legs had turned to jelly, and she was barely able even to stand.

A figure detached itself from the shadows, something glinting in its hand as it moved slowly out into the light of the street. Karen caught her breath, terrified . . . then let it out again in an immense sigh of relief.

'Oh, it's you,' she said, as the figure drew closer. 'Thank God for that!'

Chapter 8

Game Over

By the time the Doctor arrived back at his accommodation, the evening was drawing closely in. He had been held up for longer than he would have liked at the police station, comforting Rosemary as she made her statement and taking precious time out to fend off accusations from Sergeant Blyth. ('It seems that suddenly, I'm finding you at every crime scene I'm called to!' 'I could say the same about you. Similar motives, perhaps?')

He almost walked straight into Ace, running the other way through the guest-house door. 'Just got a few things to sort out,' she mumbled in response to his unvoiced question. She was still looking ill, he thought, but trying to disguise it. Pale in the face, obviously dizzy, probably still suffering memory loss . . . seemed a little drunk, too.

'Are you feeling up to it?' he called after her.

'I'm as well as I'll ever be,' she called back over her shoulder. Until all this is over anyway, she added to herself. She had been doing a lot of thinking since her return from the Pig and Whistle. She had decided that, above all else, it was time for her to get a grip on things, to put herself back in control. Okay, so she didn't know yet what had messed up her head, but there was one thing she had managed to work out and it was past time she put that knowledge to some sort of use.

All she had to do now was walk around the town for a few minutes until, hopefully, a certain private investigator managed to find her.

The Doctor almost ran into Bernice too as she rushed down the stairs to greet him. 'At last, you're back! Where have you been? You've been gone for nearly four hours!'

'Is there a problem?'

'It's Norman,' Benny told him, her words racing to get out. 'He's gone! I told him to stay here while I went after Ace, and he's gone. I need to go after him, but I didn't want to leave Ace here alone – she's asleep in her room.'

'Actually, I just passed her in the street.'

'Oh, great!' groaned Benny. 'Some guardian angel I am. Never mind,' she added, seeing the Doctor's look of puzzlement. 'We need to get out there and find Norman. He could be in all sorts of danger, especially if Nemesis has got to him.' She reached for the door, yanked it open, and was almost half-way through before she realized that someone was standing on the threshold.

'Help,' said Karen Davies plaintively, and then she collapsed helplessly forwards and bled rivers of scarlet onto Mrs Shawcross's carpet.

Norman was half-way through the door and into his kitchen before it hit him again; almost painfully this time, the energy resonating through his body, flowing over (but not into) that cold, lonely spot it had left behind three decades ago. There was no time to lose now. No time to go for the costume, just a symbol of the man he used to be. The power was out there. It was his to take. But he had to take it now, or he would be forever lost.

Without a moment's hesitation, Norman turned from the door, hurled the key to one side and set off at an uncustomary jog towards Fern Hill and the remains of Arandale Keep.

From behind the cracked and dirty pane of the drawing-room window, the man who was Nemesis watched him leave and sweated even more behind his heavy iron face-mask. 'So close,' he whined indistinctly, as the fire left his eyes. 'So very, very close. Another moment, and the treacherous Knight would have been mine!' He sank unsteadily onto the base of the upturned sofa, removing the mask again with almost feverish haste. When next he spoke, the American twang in his voice had been completely submerged.

'No, that's how the Monster talks,' he whispered, breathing deep, his voice unsteady. 'The Monster that won't let me forget the past! Only I'm not like that. Not any more. And the Monster won't control me. I won't let it!'

'Lost your quarry again?' asked Ace, with forced nonchalance. She stepped out from behind a parked van, joining the flustered Jack Corrigan in the middle of Crest Avenue.

'Not likely,' growled the detective in reply. 'I just dropped a nickel, that's all. It rolled down here somewhere.'

'Ah, I see. And that's why you ran out into the road panic-stricken and craned your neck to see into all the gardens down this side, is it?' Ace prided herself that, even feeling as bad as she was, she could still run rings around this fellow.

'Look, I've told you before, missy,' Corrigan blustered. 'Keep your hooter out of my business!'

'Ah, but it's my business as well, don't you think?' She could tell by the paling of his face that her guess had been right. 'You see,' she continued, enjoying the moment, 'I could never work out before who it was you were watching. I mean, I checked around every time you popped up to see who was nearby, but I could never see anyone obvious.' She shot Corrigan a pointed look. 'And you're nothing if not obvious. So I could only think of one solution: you're watching me, right?'

Corrigan considered that, thought over his options and finally gave a sigh of weary resignation. 'Right,' he confirmed.

'So,' said Ace, 'that just leaves the sixty-four thousand dollar question: why?'

130

'Come on, come on out! It's perfectly safe!'

Gary's shouts rang eerily around the cavern, and he began to wish just as fervently as the others that he'd kept his voice down a bit.

'Sssshh!' Michelle warned him fiercely. 'That weirdo might still be about for all you know.'

'I doubt it,' returned Gary. 'Not the amount of time we spent hiding after he'd gone.' He made the comment disdainfully, placing the blame for the team's inaction very much on its other members.

'So what do we do now?' asked Tim practically, once again heading off an argument between his comrades.

'Look for clues, I suppose,' suggested Tracey.

'What's the point?' asked Gary. 'We know what's going on down here now! Some loony's killing people as sacrifices to some sort of stupid power he believes in. What we should have done was jump him while he was still here.'

'Oh yeah,' scoffed Michelle, 'I didn't see you making a move!'

'So we'll have to come back here,' said Gary, 'and try again tomorrow!'

'Or we could always call the police,' suggested Tim.

'And let them take the whole thing away from us?' Tracey protested.

Michelle was looking at her watch. 'Either way, we'd better get home. It's almost eight o'clock! Dad was expecting me and Gary back for tea.'

Gary sighed and reluctantly agreed. Excited but weary, the Adventure Kids made their way swiftly back down the passage to where the steel-runged ladder led up to the outside world.

They were about half-way there when Michelle walked straight into someone in the dark.

Ace could hardly believe her ears. 'You're after Mel Joseph?'

'Keep it down, can't you?' Corrigan checked worriedly

around him, but could see no one who might be listening in on their conversation.

'Are we talking about the same guy here?' asked Ace. 'Tall, lanky, blond hair, glasses, couldn't punch his way through a slice of cheese?'

'Could be,' admitted Corrigan. 'I only got the monicker.'

'Aha!' Ace caught on quickly. 'And you're watching me because I mentioned Mel's name when I first saw you in the Black Cat. You don't know what he looks like or where he lives, so you're hoping I'll lead you to him.'

'Preferably without making too much use of that smart mouth of yours.'

'But surely you've seen him by now? I mean, you saw the fight in the pub, didn't you? And you must have followed me to his house yesterday?'

Corrigan pinched his lip as he thought about that. 'Tall and skinny, you say? Blond hair? The guy shacked up with the cute black doll?'

'That's him.' Though I don't think Karen would appreciate that description, she thought.

'Are you sending me up or what? You're telling me that that guy's the head honcho of the biggest illegal gambling operation in the States?'

'No,' said Ace. 'I think you're telling *me* that! You came here to find him, didn't you?'

Corrigan looked uncertain. 'Could be I've got the wrong Mel Joseph.'

'How many do you need?'

'Oh, swell! So now what?'

'Try checking him out, Mister Detective,' mocked Ace. 'Or better still, let *me* go and talk to him.'

'You? You're yanking my chain.'

'It makes sense,' said Ace. 'Firstly, I know him, and secondly, I know what "tact" means too. I'm not going to ever-so-slightly tip him off by dressing like Sam Spade and talking like an American comic-book stereotype. So what do you say, Jack?'

Given the strength of the evidence against him, Corrigan had little alternative but to agree.

The ambulance had arrived promptly. In a place like Arandale there were precious few emergencies and not much distance to traverse. Thus, only minutes after her collapse on Mrs Shawcross's doorstep, Karen Davies was in the hands of experts and on her speedy way to a hospital bed.

The Doctor joined Bernice now in the cold green corridor, pulling a metal-framed chair up by her side. 'She's lost a lot of blood,' he told her. 'More than she should have done; the slash wound is relatively minor.'

'The same as the others, then?'

The Doctor nodded.

'Any puncture marks in the neck this time?'

'No.'

'She must be strong,' said Benny. 'She must have put up a fight even while the killer was draining the blood right out of her.'

'She's been very lucky,' said the Doctor. 'But she's not safe yet. They're arranging a transfusion for her now.'

'Has she woken up?'

'Not yet, no.'

Benny considered. 'We'll have to keep an eye on her. She'll be able to identify the murderer. What if he comes after her again, to stop her talking?'

The Doctor shrugged. 'It's possible. Right now, I think he'll have other things on his mind.'

'Like?' Benny wasn't sure she wanted an answer to that.

'Like finding a replacement for tonight's victim,' said the Doctor.

If the masked killer had still been in the tunnels, then Michelle's terrified scream would certainly have brought him running. Fortunately for the children, he was not. The only people beneath Arandale Keep at that present time

133

were themselves and a man who now introduced himself as Norman. As he spoke to them, Tim's mind was ticking over like a computer, trying to work out just where he fit into their little adventure.

'I found the hole in the floor,' Norman told them, 'where someone took out the stone block. That was you, was it?' Gary acknowledged that it was. There was something almost pathetic about this strange man, he thought. What exactly was he after down here?

'What have you found?' asked Norman, almost breathlessly. He was straining to look past them, his eyes trying to pierce the gloom of the underground passage.

The children looked uneasily at each other, not sure whether they should be giving away their secrets like this. But one look into Norman's desperately hungry eyes persuaded Tim that they had to tell him the truth. Slowly, calmly, being sure not to miss anything out, he told of all that had happened since the Kids had entered the tunnels.

By the time he had finished, Norman was more excited than he had ever been in his life.

Much to Ace's disappointment, it was Mel rather than Karen who opened the door and invited her into the couple's shared home. Karen had just popped out to the off-licence for some food and drink, he explained, and perhaps Ace would care to join them as there would be plenty to go around.

This is ludicrous, she thought as he ushered her through into the game-filled front room and cleared a chair for her to sit down. Corrigan must have got it wrong. But she knew from experience not to judge too much from appearances, and her hand never strayed far from her concealed blaster weapon, just in case.

'Game of cards?' offered Mel.

'No thanks,' said Ace, politely. 'So how are you?'

'Oh, not so bad. So how about Monopoly then? Or Cluedo?'

'I've had quite enough mysteries for the time being,

thank you. And what I mean is, how are you feeling after being beaten senseless yesterday?'

'Fine, I said.'

'Not got your glasses fixed yet, I see.'

'No.'

Ace could see the spectacles resting on a box across the room. 'I thought you only cracked one lens,' she observed. 'The other one's gone now, too.'

'Yes.'

'Don't tell me you've been battered again!'

'No.'

Ace peered at him meaningfully over her shades. 'I seem to be doing all the talking.'

'I'll get us some coffee,' offered Mel. He turned to leave, but Ace's cutting voice stopped him.

'Have you told Karen how it happened yet?'

'Of course.'

'You gonna tell me, then?'

'No. But perhaps you can tell me something.'

'What?'

'Exactly what you've got on your mind. What have you heard about me?'

Ace frowned. She had intended to be a little more subtle than that. Her nagging headache and that annoying, ungraspable image in her mind were throwing her thoughts off, making her careless. Might as well just go for the big one, she thought. 'Did you know there's a private investigator trailing you?'

'Trailing you actually, and not being very subtle about it either. I imagine you've put him on to me by now.'

'You do?' Ace had not been expecting quite such a forthright response.

'Of course,' said Mel. 'It's that gambling business, I expect. Either that or old Mason Grimshaw's hired someone to get me off his back about the blackmail thing.'

'Blackmail?'

'Oh, hadn't you worked it out yet?' asked Mel, casually. 'I saw the drunken old git run a kid over a few months back. Drink-driving, as usual. He didn't even give a toss, just drove straight off home to that ugly dog he's married to, and the police never cottoned on to him. You can use that information yourself if you want. I won't be around for too much longer.'

'Hey!' Ace leapt to her feet, startled, as Mel scuttled quickly out of the room. She needed to get her head together, she berated herself. She had been too muzzy even to realize that he was standing in front of a connecting door – and now that door was locked firmly between them. 'All right mate,' she muttered as she rolled up her sleeve, 'if that's how you want to play it.' Her wrist computer would make short work of the door's electronic lock, and then . . .

Then? Ace thought again as the lock swam into view before her blurry eyes. Just one red button on a keypad, and a small digital screen which bore the words: 'LOCK PICKING: 65% – ROLL 1d20' Was this some sort of a joke?

She pressed the button, and the words were replaced by an image of a twenty-sided die spinning rapidly through three dimensions, coming finally to rest with the number eight facing upwards. 'FAILURE' said the screen, and refused to let her try again for twenty seconds.

On her second attempt, Ace scored a seventeen and the message 'WELL DONE – NOW ENTER CAREFULLY'. She did almost the opposite, kicking the door inwards as soon as the lock clicked open, and springing through it at knee level, her blaster drawn. It proved to be a complete waste of energy. Mel was standing at the far end of the room with his arms folded, apparently no threat to anybody. Between her and him, the floor was painted in a giant chessboard pattern and a set of finely sculptured marble chess pieces, a disconcerting four feet tall each, took up various positions as if in mid-game. Ace wondered as she got cautiously to her feet just what Mel Joseph was up to.

'Why are you doing this?' she called out to him, her gun still at the ready lest his answer be the wrong one.

'Doing what?' he asked her, quite innocently.

'Running away.'

'I'm not running anywhere.'

'Then come back here,' suggested Ace. 'Tell me about it. I might be able to help.'

'Oh, I doubt that, Ace. You see, you've only heard Jack Corrigan's side of the story. He's probably painted me as black as the King of Clubs; told you what an evil, despicable madman I am, how you can't trust me as far as you can throw me.'

'So tell me your side.'

Mel shrugged, and his face lit up with a mad, twisted grin. 'Nothing more to tell,' he said. 'Corrigan's got it just about right.' He scooped up a red-backed card from the floor – one of a number which, Ace noticed now, were scattered haphazardly around him. 'Staff car,' he announced to the door behind him, and it clicked easily open to allow him through.

'Wait!' cried Ace, but she was too late again – and as she set off in pursuit, she also set a series of alarm bells off in her own head. She stopped inches short of the chessboard, her every instinct screaming at her to go no further. A thrown coin revealed the inevitable truth, exploding into shards as she skimmed it onto the nearest square. There was no way around the board, so there had to be a way over it.

'Okay,' she shouted bitterly, positive that her foe would be listening from the next room. 'I'll play your bloody game for now – but you're gonna wish I hadn't when I get through that goddamned door!'

She turned her attention to the puzzle and tried to pretend that she wasn't at all riled by the sound of Mel Joseph's mocking laughter.

It didn't take long for Norman's hopes to be dashed. It

happened in but a moment, in the all too brief half-second it took for him to take in what he was seeing.

His voice was hollow as he spoke. 'So this is it?'

'Well . . . yes,' confirmed Tim. He had not been expecting quite this reaction. To him and his team, the stone altar in the hidden cave was the most exciting thing in the world right now. Exciting and, as Michelle had been quick to remind them, dangerous. They were risking their lives by coming back here, but Norman had insisted. He had seemed only too keen on sharing their adventure and viewing their find. And this was his reaction?

'I'm sorry,' said Norman, with a sigh. His footsteps echoed around the cave as he walked slowly up to the rough stone altar and leaned heavily against it. 'I'm not sure what I was expecting, really. Just something more than this.' He cast his eyes around the great dark cavern, looking for something, anything. He reached out and tried to feel for the power that had once tingled through him, that had called him finally back to this place at this time. There was nothing there.

'So can we go?' asked Michelle, peering nervously over her shoulder and wishing she had waited for the others outside. This place seemed to get scarier every time she entered it.

'Yes,' said Norman quietly. 'Yes, I suppose we can.'

Benny's conscience pricked at her as she left the hospital. 'I should have been out looking for Norman,' she said. 'I'll have to go now.'

The Doctor shook his head. 'You've had other things to do,' he told her. 'And I doubt he's in danger.'

'You do?'

The Doctor's expression was a reassuring one. It was times like this when Bernice felt, despite everything, that she could trust him with her life. 'There were no signs of a struggle,' he reminded her. 'Your friend obviously left of his own accord, and from what I've seen of him and what you've told me, I imagine there are very few places he could have gone to. Whichever one he's at, I'm sure he'll be safe – and I'm sure I can find him, if that's what you want.'

Benny nodded, but her mind was elsewhere again. She thought about her earlier talk with Ace, and she wondered if perhaps now was the time to start mending bridges with her other crewmate too. If only they had some common ground for discussion.

She moved in front of the Doctor, halting him in his path. 'But before you go, I'd like to talk to you.' She returned his inquisitive stare, and took a deep breath before continuing.

'It's about Ace.'

Ace was across the chessboard in just under ten minutes; not a bad time, she congratulated herself. In the process of doing so, she had even formulated a few theories on how to get through the far door.

She reached down and shuffled quickly through the scattered red cards until she found one that would do the trick. 'Chapel tunnel,' she announced loudly, smiling as the door clicked open for her as it had done for Mel. Too easy, she thought. Far too easy.

Mel was standing immediately on the far side, a gleam in his eye, a card in his hand and a revolver pointed at her chest.

'Tunnel detected,' he said.

'You're not going to shoot me with that thing.'

'You think so?'

'You can't!' said Ace. 'It isn't real, it won't fire.'

Mel smiled, and let the gun drop to the floor. 'A full-scale, cast-iron replica of the Cluedo weapon,' he confessed. 'Not fooled, eh?'

Ace shot him a look of pure contempt. 'Everything's got to be a bloody game with you, hasn't it? Well, I hate to disappoint you, but this thing is absolutely, one hundred per cent genuine.' Now it was her turn to be in charge, her blaster weapon trained squarely on Mel Joseph's chest. 'And I think it's about time you gave me some answers, don't you?'

Mel shrugged and backed slowly into the dark room behind him. 'What is there to tell?'

'Other than your complete change of personality, you mean?' Ace followed him warily, checking all around her for traps. She was careful to walk only in his footsteps. 'What about this house, then? Where did all these traps of yours come from?'

'Built them myself, of course.' Still backing away, further into the room . . . was she going to have to shoot him to stop him? She didn't want to, not even on 'stun'. Not until she had the answers she needed. She wished she knew what the questions were.

Mel moved quickly around a knee-high obstacle; a yellow tub of some sort, in a red frame from which a red trough ran, further than Ace could see. Not that that was difficult. The lighting was minimal at best, and although she'd removed her shades upon entering, it was taking quite some time for her eyes to adjust. She risked a quick glance around the room, taking in as much as she could see. That wasn't such a lot. Strange dark shapes rearing up all around her, the nearest ones looking like . . . yes, like they were made out of *plastic*. Red and yellow plastic! To her left, a red staircase led seemingly to nowhere, its steps tilting at odd angles to each other. By her side was a thin yellow pole, stretching high up into the rafters. She didn't dare crane her neck to see what it supported.

Mel was circling around her to the left, moving past the stairs and over to a strange, free standing wheel-like contraption. If she wasn't careful, there was a danger of him cutting her off from the door.

'Okay, that's far enough!' she said, waving the blaster gun as if she meant business. She wished the throbbing in her head would stop and let her start thinking clearly again.

'Oh poor Ace,' mocked Mel. 'All confused, are we?'

'How did you fit all this in here?' Ace blurted out. 'I've

been through three big rooms now, all in a row – where are they all coming from?' (Damn it, I hadn't realized that, I'll have to . . .)

'The house,' said Mel. 'Didn't I tell you? It's bigger on the inside than it is on the outside.'

'Don't be ridiculous!'

'It's only the same as your TARDIS.'

'How do you know about that?'

Mel thought for a moment. 'Sorry,' he said finally. 'Continuity error. You never did tell me that, did you?' This is getting just a little out of hand, I think. Best to end it all now.

'What are you doing?' cried Ace in alarm, as Mel suddenly ducked down behind the plastic wheel – a cog, of some sort – and began to crank it speedily round. Almost too close for comfort, she realized the answer to her own question. Above her, something whistled through the air, knocking a king-size silver ball down the rickety staircase, along the red plastic trough . . . something hurtled upwards, arced, landed smack in the yellow bath-tub . . . and Ace barely avoided the red plastic 'Mouse Trap' cage as it slid easily down the yellow pole and slammed hard into the floor by her trailing foot. By the time she was on her feet again, she was staring down the muzzle of a sleek black gun.

'I wouldn't consider going for your weapon,' Mel said pleasantly. Ace considered it anyway; the blaster had been dropped in mid-leap and was lying on the floor just a few short feet away from her. She wondered if she would be able to reach it before he blasted holes in her. She wondered as an afterthought if that was even possible. He was playing games with her again.

'That's just a Laser Quest light gun,' she pointed out, hardly daring to believe how stupid this was all getting. 'Just another bloody game!'

Mel smiled, cocked the gun and melted a square inch of molten plastic through the fallen cage. 'It's a fake,' he explained. And a manic grin spread wide across his face as he jammed the gun barrel hard against Ace's head.

'Game over, Ace!' he said to her quietly. 'Game over!'

'Get out!' screamed Rosemary.

'But . . .'

'*Get out of here this minute*!'

Phil went. He knew when he was beaten – he was used to it. But all of Rosemary's tantrums didn't change the facts. Gary and Michelle were gone. They had promised to be back by tea-time, and it was now a good two hours past. As time moved on, his nagging doubts had changed to concrete worries, through to outright fears. He needed to talk to his wife, needed to share his concerns, but all she was interested in was her stupid magic. She refused to even talk to him.

With a despairing sigh, he finally took the action he had hoped to avoid. No good leaving things to her, he thought bitterly. The kids could be gone for a week before she'd even notice. He could disappear himself (and don't think that hadn't occurred to him before).

He jabbed in frustration at the keys on the telephone, dialling out the number of the local police station and asking in a trembling voice to be put through to the sergeant. It was at the very moment that Blyth's gruff voice sounded in his ear that a key scrabbled in the door lock, and the wayward children finally returned.

'Sorry we're late,' said Michelle hurriedly, reading everything from her father's expression.

'But have we got a story to tell you!' said Gary.

'Wait!' cried Ace, on an impulse.

'Why?'

'Because you can't just shoot me in cold blood, that's why.'

Mel thought about that. 'Yes I can,' he decided.

'But it's not fair!' protested Ace. 'I mean, when did I ever get a chance? You picked the game, you chose the pitch, you stacked the cards and you went first. I haven't even had a go yet!'

Mel thought about that too, and this time his expression was a lot more serious. 'I suppose . . .' he began, uncertainly. Got him, thought Ace.

'So what about that game you offered me, then?' she continued, getting slowly and carefully to her feet. She didn't dare go for her blaster – not yet. 'I pick the game, we play once fair and square, and if I win I go free.'

'And if you lose, you die,' said Mel quickly. He took a few steps back and lowered the gun. 'Okay, it's a deal. Choose your game.' And at that moment, the world exploded into coloured sparks around him as Jack Corrigan wrapped a large plank of wood forcefully about his head.

'Good thing you managed to keep him shooting the breeze, Toots,' said the detective with a wry grin. 'I couldn't get that blasted back door open.'

'I'll forgive you,' offered Ace, 'as long as you don't ever call me "Toots" again. And as for you . . .' She stirred Mel's barely conscious body with the toe of her shoe. 'I think I'll choose pontoon. Jack and Ace win!'

Finally, as it always did, the village slept – and the Doctor paced its quiet streets that night, his eyes alert though his mind was far afield. He wandered aimlessly, lost in his thoughts, contemplating the mysteries of Arandale; worried at the same time about the secrets that Benny had confided in him. He passed Rosemary's shop and he passed the Black Cat Tavern, and he recalled as he did the words that Matthew Shade had spoken:

'The slayings began on Sunday. The thirty-first of October; All Hallows Eve. They will continue for six nights.'

Until the fifth of November.

Tomorrow.

Norman was by Arandale Keep, as the Doctor had predicted. Sitting alone on the grass, his tear-stained face buried in his knees.

'It doesn't know me,' he said as the Time Lord approached. 'The power is here, I can feel it. But it won't even acknowledge that I exist.'

The Doctor said nothing, but he sat quietly down by Norman's side, and until the dawn, the lonely pair watched the stars together.

Ace woke from a restless doze, flinching painfully from the early morning sun which, weak though it was, caught her full in the face. She felt the rough brick of the police station wall behind her, the hard concrete of the pavement beneath, and her mind did its best to fill her in on how she had ended up here.

'That's swell,' grumbled Jack Corrigan, sinking down into a heap beside her. 'Just swell!'

'What's going on?' She tried to remember ... the fight with Mel, Corrigan's timely arrival ... they had talked for a while after that, unsure what to do for the best. Ace had wondered about Karen, concerned about what her lunatic boyfriend might have done to her. When Corrigan had finally consented to calling the police, they had both endured long gruelling hours of questioning and more hours of waiting, down at the station. Malcolm Blyth, it seemed, would have been only too glad to see both of them in the cell next door to Mel's.

'They're throwing the blasted book at him in there,' said Corrigan, moodily. 'He's confessing to all sorts – blackmail, extortion, confidence tricks. My chances of getting him back to the States now are practically zilch. Which is what my fee's gonna be from the dumb jerks he owes money to.'

Ace struggled to her feet, brushing the frost off her pants and jamming her shades back into position. 'Never mind,' she said, with a new resolve creeping into her voice. 'None of this is real anyhow.'

'Say what?'

'I said none of it's real. It can't be!'

'What in Sam Hill are you jabbering about?' Corrigan was on his feet now too, but not quite in time to prevent Ace from getting past him.

'Even time doesn't move right here,' she said as he rushed to catch her up. 'You whacked Mel over the head about ten minutes ago, and suddenly it's morning and I don't know what happened in between.'

'We were at the station . . .'

'Bollocks we were! I don't remember any of that. I *know* it – but it's like I've just heard about it somewhere, like someone's just decided that that's happened and written it down in my memory or something. I never actually experienced any of it!'

'I don't know what you're on about!' They were half-way down Adelphi Street by now; heading, Corrigan realized, straight out of the town.

'And it doesn't stop there,' said Ace. 'I've spent the last twenty-four hours feeling like shit, walking round in a daze because some bastard messed with my mind, tried to stop me from remembering something important. But I'm starting to feel better now. I'm starting to feel better because I've started to work out what it was I must have seen.' (Uh-oh . . .) 'I mean, look at this place!' She took in the whole of Arandale with a sweep of one hand. 'Full of witches and super-heroes and characters who can't possibly exist outside of books and TV programmes! Look at Mel Joseph; a bloke who's supposed to have a full-size goddamned Mouse Trap game in his front room! For that matter, look at you! I don't know why I'm even still talking to you, you're too bloody clichéd to be real! I don't know what's going on here, but I do know I'm not on Earth, and I wouldn't mind betting I'm not even in the same dimension any more. So it's about time I found out once and for all exactly where I am, and what the hell's really going on!'

They were on the outskirts of the town now, and Corrigan almost jumped in alarm as Ace suddenly pushed

145

him to one side, racing out across the verdant hills beyond (okay, don't worry about it . . . so she's thrown off the mind-wipe – but I've got it under control).

By the time he caught her up, she was on the edge of the world itself – the place she had seen in her dreams. Where the landscape ended the blackness of space began, as if the whole of the village and the hills around it were just one big lump of matter floating unsupported through the cosmos. (You see? She won't go further than that in a hurry).

'So go on then,' said Ace. 'Tell me. Tell me I'm seeing things. Tell me you don't see what's in front of your own bloody eyes!'

Corrigan shrugged. 'I don't see it,' he said obligingly.

'Right,' said Ace – and with barely a pause to draw breath, she flung herself head-first . . . flying upwards, outwards, *off* . . . off the very edge of the world.

Which, on the whole, is not exactly what I'd hoped for.

Chapter 9

Ace of Swords

'There is Evil at work in the village; Evil which I know to be centred on the castle in the hills. Now my children have been caught up in the Web of Darkness, and I have to see what the future may hold – for all of us.'

Phil groaned and bit his lip. He knew there was no point in protesting, not when his wife was like this. His best bet was just to be patient, wait for her to get the whole charade over with so that they could get on with something more practical.

Rosemary, seated nervously at her desk in the inner sanctum between house and shop, took his silence as a sign of consent. Slowly, methodically, she shuffled the tarot pack and laid a dozen cards out before her.

She nodded sadly as she turned the first, gasped in astonishment as she turned the second – and again, as the third was revealed. By the time all twelve were lying face upwards, what little colour her cheeks once possessed had drained totally away.

Staring malignantly up at her were the white skull faces of an impossible six Death cards.

Ace woke up and it had all been a dream.

At least, that's what it felt like. Only so did reality . . . somehow blurred and indistinct, the soft lines of her bedroom folding horribly back on themselves and performing somersaults inside her head. She closed her eyes and the sensations seemed to ease. She looked deep into her memory but it was just a black hole, beginning only now to fill slowly with the information she needed.

She had been in an accident. That must be it. A young boy called Boyle, with an upraised brick . . . a blow to the head . . . or was it a time-storm? Ripping straight through the lab, lifting her upwards, spiriting her far across the universe in the blink of an eye.

No. That was a stupid idea.

Some dream she must have had. She rubbed her throbbing head ruefully as she climbed to her feet and looked for her reflection in the dressing-table mirror. She didn't possess one. She didn't even possess a body – or rather she did, but it had somehow managed not to get out of bed with her.

Poor, sweet young Dorry, there in her Care Bears nightie, resting gently on the soft pink sheets. Not moving. Not breathing. Ace wanted to be sick, only she lacked the necessary organs to do so. Her mind was almost back with her, but it had not bargained for the scenario that confronted it. Racing chaotically, jumping from thought to thought . . . *I'm only sixteen, I'm too blasted young to die!*

'I'm sorry,' said the Doctor, 'but that's what everyone thinks.'

The Doctor? No, that was just a nightmare. Just a stupid, childish . . . 'Didn't I dream about you?'

'Maybe,' said the skull-faced figure in the white suit and hat, and something sparkled in the empty black sockets of its eyes. Something that reminded her of the dream. 'Many people do. Premonitions, you know.'

'No,' said Ace. 'I don't know.'

'Well,' said the phantom with a shrug. 'That's life!' He laughed, and the eerie cackle sent a shiver running up the part of Ace where her spine should have been. 'Or rather not, as the case may be.'

She felt her face growing hot as her teenage temper boiled over. 'Are you going to tell me what's going on here, or what?'

'Nothing to tell. You're dead. End of story.'

'But . . .'

He raised an ivory hand to block her next question. 'Think carefully before you speak,' he said. 'I am empowered to answer only three of your questions.'

Ace's forehead wrinkled. 'Why?'

'Because when have I ever told you anything? Next question.'

'That wasn't a proper answer!'

'Ask me your second question.'

'Anything? And you'll answer me properly?'

'Yes. One question remaining.'

Ace scowled. She wanted to know what happened next, but she supposed she'd soon find out. Her mind cast around for another subject, but something still nagged at her. Something she should have known, but didn't.

'You wish to forego your final question?'

'No,' she said hurriedly. 'No. I just . . . I just want to know . . .' Anything? Any of the mysteries of life? She didn't know where to start, couldn't think of one thing which at this moment seemed even vaguely important to her. Then she realized what her mind was trying to tell her.

'I want to know,' she said finally, 'if any of this is real.'

'Of course not,' said the Doctor, 'but I think you've worked that one out for yourself.'

Norman looked up as Benny approached, and tried to hide the fact that he had been crying.

'The Doctor told me I could find you here.'

He nodded slowly, his gaze now back on the ruin that the meteorites of 1959 had made of Arandale Keep. 'I don't know why,' he confided. 'I know there's no point to it any more. I've kept hoping all this time – almost thirty years now – just hoping and praying that if I stayed near the castle and kept my eyes on the stars, then I might just be able to get back the powers I once gave up.' He took a deep sobbing breath as he turned to face her again. 'I've been wasting my time, haven't I?'

Benny slipped an arm round his shoulders and he seemed happy to be led away from this place of misery and down the hill back to the village. 'The Doctor said we should leave here,' she told him, deciding at least that she could take his mind off the loss he had suffered. 'Anyway, there's work to be done. There are still things going on that need sorting – not least of which is your friend from America.'

'Just let him kill me,' muttered Norman. 'I don't care.'

'I'll pretend I didn't hear that.'

'I don't care,' he reiterated. 'It's over.'

Benny stopped in her tracks and shook her friend with exasperation. 'Look, you're not finished yet, not while you're still alive, and if you pull yourself together, you might even be useful! This – this force thing under the castle – it's dangerous, right? And you're the only one of us who has any experience with it.'

Norman brightened a little. 'You mean I could help?'

'Maybe so, but not if you go sky-diving off bridges again. Now come on.'

'Where to?'

'First, to see a friend of ours in hospital: someone else who might be able to help. After that, we'll just take things as they come. Ready?'

'Ready,' confirmed Norman and they continued their journey downwards, oblivious to the fact that four pairs of youthful eyes were upon them.

Ace woke up and it had all been a dream.

At least, that's what it felt like . . . she was lying in the TARDIS library, blood trickling from a thin cut on her cheek, the Doctor's concerned face hovering over her.

The Doctor?

'Instant replay, or what? Forget it!'

She was on her feet now, and recoiled from her companion as he tried to rest a steadying hand on her shoulder. 'Easy, Ace – you've had a bit of a shock.'

'It won't work on me, scum-bucket!' she warned. 'You're just playing the old "confront-Ace-with-her-hopes-and-fears-and-memories-of-the- bloody-past" game again, and I've had it up to here with it, from you and from everyone else. So knock it off!'

'It's the real me this time,' the Doctor insisted, a note of pleading creeping into his voice.

'I don't believe it.'

'Trust me!'

'I wouldn't do that if you *were* real.'

'I need help,' he said, 'with this book.' He was suddenly rising above her on one of the library's gravity pads, his slight form receding into the shadows of the uppermost shelves. There was an indistinct thud, a flapping sound of paper, and a book shot down and past her ear, hurling itself almost desperately at the closed door behind her.

The Doctor was on the floor again and crying out to her in desperation: 'It's time-sensitive – the energies the Garvond threw around here have driven it wild. We've got to back it into a corner before it escapes!'

The book turned and shot past her again, the sharp edge of its pages drawing blood from Ace's cheek; a second paper-cut to match the first. She didn't even flinch.

'No,' she said. 'I'm not falling for stupid illusions and I'm not falling for stupid memories either. Show me reality. Now!'

I can deal with our intruder later. Right now, I'm more concerned with salvaging some sort of straightforward plot-line from the mess she's left me in.

Okay, so we're back in Arandale. It's getting on for noon and the Doctor has just received a pair of unexpected visitors at the guest-house; to whit, Philip and Rosemary Chambers. They have something rather important to discuss with him.

'We've never really had to be worried about Gary and

151

Michelle before,' confessed Phil, seated by his wife in Mrs Shawcross's dining room. 'We knew they were in some sort of kiddy detective group of course, but the first we ever heard about their adventures was when the police had been brought in and the smugglers or whatever had been caught.'

'Besides,' added Rosemary, 'my magics would have warned me of any danger to them.' Phil looked at her sharply.

'But they're in trouble now?' prompted the Doctor.

'Yesterday,' said Phil. 'they went out in the afternoon and didn't come back until almost nine o'clock. They'd been up to Arandale Keep – Vampire Castle, they call it.'

'Ah!'

'I did a tarot reading this morning,' said Rosemary with a shudder. 'I think the . . .' She hesitated, and a tear glistened in her eye. 'I think the mark of . . . D-Death is upon them.'

The Doctor leaned forward urgently. 'I think you'd better tell me the whole story,' he said.

For Tina Grimshaw, life was little more than just one recurring daily battle. From the moment she rolled out of bed, slapped on her make-up and flounced out into the street, she was forever beset by incompetents; forced into confrontation after confrontation, from the old man in the street who wouldn't get out of her way, to the shop assistant who passed her goods through the check-out too quickly for her to keep up, to the newsagent who'd put his prices up overnight and failed to forewarn her.

Usually the fighting ended when she got back to the flat. She would dig a box of chocolates out of her bag, drop the rest of the shopping in the hallway, kick off her shoes and flop down in front of the box to watch Australian soap operas for the rest of the afternoon. As the evening repeat of 'Home and Away' was finishing, her husband would return from his day's work at the builder's yard and she could start fighting all over again – at least until they went down to the Black Cat at seven, and teamed up against some of their friends.

She was not best pleased then, when today's routine was disrupted by the presence of Mason in her favourite armchair; though Tina was nothing if not adaptable, and was quite prepared to add an afternoon battle to her list of duties.

'What the hell are you doing home from work at this time?' she berated him. 'Have I got to do everything around here? Can you not just go out and earn some money like any decent husband? God knows you bring home little enough already, without you sloping off for days on end with no reason whatsoever . . .'

Mason said but two words. He told her to shut up – and for once in her life, Tina did. No screaming, no punching, no wrecking of furniture. 'S-say that again,' she stammered.

'I said "shut up".' he repeated quite calmly. He stood – one swift, powerful movement – and towered over her, his eyes afire. 'So do as you're told!'

'You've changed,' whispered Tina, and she was suddenly very afraid. She backed slowly away, one hand reaching out behind her for an ornament, a knife, anything she could use to defend herself. 'You said he wouldn't be back. You said it was all over now.'

Mason glared at the pitiful figure trembling before him, a small alarm clock clutched tightly in her hand. Unexpectedly, he smiled. 'Yes, I think I did say that,' he confirmed, and he spoke in the American drawl she had so come to dread. 'But he's back all the same.'

Then he sat back on the sofa and he turned back to the TV, leaving Tina shaking in the corner of the room. On the screen, Shane had just revealed that Paul was Marlene's husband's cousin's illegitimate son, and the whole neighbourhood was up in arms. Tina put the clock gently back down on the mantelpiece and made slowly for the door, keeping close to the wall, her eyes never leaving her silent husband.

153

'By the way,' called Mason, as her hand touched the doorknob. 'Don't think of leaving the house – or I'll kill you!'

The Monster within him smiled, and he promised it that revenge would soon be theirs.

'I don't know what we're all just sitting here for!' Phil exploded, jumping to his feet.

Rosemary tried to pull him back onto his chair, embarrassed by his outburst. 'The Doctor is the key to all this,' she insisted. 'The cards confirmed it.'

'Blow your cards!' Phil wrenched himself free of her grip. 'It's time we went straight round to the police station and told them what's going on around here, so they can get up to that castle and arrest that bloody maniac before he kills anyone else!'

'I don't think that would help,' advised the Doctor.

'Well why the hell not?'

'Because it's too big for them to deal with. The more I hear about Vampire Castle, the more dangerous I believe it to be. I think your children had a lucky escape there last night, but the powers behind all this are growing stronger by the minute. If Blyth takes his men up there now, they'll be killed like all the others.' He turned to Rosemary. 'What else did your tarot reading say?' he asked her. 'Apart from the six Death cards?'

Phil groaned and sank back down into his seat. This idiot actually believed her, he was actually giving credence to her lunatic notions. And he'd thought one of them was bad enough!

'The Fool was represented,' said Rosemary, 'as the one card that might have the power to change the future.' The Doctor remembered the reading she had done for him, and he nodded thoughtfully.

'The rest of the cards – ' she shuddered as she spoke ' – the rest were all Swords, the suit of combat and strife. Even the Ace appeared, in the dead centre of the spread.'

The Doctor smiled despite himself. 'That sounds like her all right,' he quipped.

Ace was at home now, stood in the living room. A fire blazed in the hearth and scorched the left side of her left leg. A voice blazed in her ear and sent a spring of fear and revulsion welling up inside her chest.

'Dorry? Dorry, is that you dear?'

She knew exactly what to expect as she turned.

'I might've known you'd turn up next,' she told her mother, 'and you can just piss off again right back where you came from. I've had enough of this one, too.'

Back to reality, then . . .

Ace was floating in the middle of nowhere. Or so it seemed at first – only the ground beneath her was solid and she still felt the pain of a landing which had come a lot sooner than expected.

'And this is it, is it?' she shouted into nowhere, but no answer was forthcoming. All around her was nothing but white, nothing but the endless, formless void. No sounds, no sights, no smells. This couldn't be real, she knew that with her head – but her gut told her that it was, that this was the first real thing she had seen since arriving in this maddening place.

She began to walk, picking a direction at random and moving uncertainly into the emptiness. 'You aren't fooling me, you know,' she shouted as she went. 'I knew there had to be something else out here – that space projection thing of yours was too fragging obvious. And it couldn't possibly have been there anyway without having sucked all the air out of that goddamned village of yours. You see, you aren't as clever as you think you are!'

Tough talk – but she's only saying it because she's so nervous inside. She won't be a threat.

'So what can we do?' asked Rosemary, ready to hang onto the Doctor's every word.

'Nothing for now,' he decided.

'Nothing?' exploded Phil.

'Nothing,' the Doctor confirmed. 'I have a few ideas of my own that I want to test out, and if the results are as I expect, then I doubt we'll be needing to find our murderer at all.'

'What?'

'Is there anything we can do, Doctor?' asked Rosemary, interrupting hurriedly.

'Just one thing, I suppose: make sure neither your children nor anyone else goes near Arandale Keep again.'

Phil nodded dismissively. 'I've made that quite clear to Gary and Michelle,' he said. 'And after last night, I'm sure they're in no hurry to go back there anyway.'

The Adventure Kids had waited patiently outside the hospital for longer than Gary thought was necessary. 'I'm telling you,' he complained, 'we'd be better off getting back up to the castle and sorting things out there than we are trailing a couple of folks just 'cos we saw them near the place!'

'Maybe,' agreed Tracey, 'but it looks like that old fellow stayed up there all night after we left him, and we don't know where the woman came from at all. I think it's worth checking out.'

'We'll wait here a bit longer anyway,' decided Tim. 'They might lead us to something interesting yet.'

Michelle sighed wistfully. 'If only we had Carson with us,' she said. 'We wouldn't have to bother with all this hiding – he could just track them wherever they went.' Notwithstanding the fact that her faith in Carson's abilities was vastly over-inflated, there was little chance of her wish coming true. Mrs Mitchell had said that Carson couldn't accompany them that afternoon – he was being kept indoors as punishment for attacking the postman – so once again, the team were short-handed.

'I just don't think there's any point,' said Gary, but he knew when he was defeated. 'Well, okay then,' he

156

grumbled, 'if this is what you all want to do. But if they don't do anything suspicious soon, I vote we just forget all about them and go back to the castle.'

'Well,' said Tim, uncertainly. 'I suppose that would make sense.'

The void again – where nothing made sense.

Somehow, this seemed like the only reality there was – like whatever else Ace was shown here, this was the only thing she could truly believe in. But then, there must be more to it than that, mustn't there? There must be somewhere other than this, where someone controlled all that she had seen? The question was, how to find it?

In the endless expanse of white, there was no way to navigate. She could walk a hundred miles and yet never know that she had simply been travelling in one enormous circle. If she could only see the village she had left, then she would at least have something from which to get her bearings. But there was nothing. Nothing at all.

'Well that suits me just fine,' said Ace, squatting almost casually down on the ground but with blaster in hand – just in case. 'In fact, I think I'll wait here a while until either you take the hint or you just plain run out of illusions to throw at me. Then you can come and show me what you're really made of.'

Okay. Time I sent the salvage team in.

Benny's heart went out to Karen as soon as she saw her – her soft, peaceful face framed by her thick black hair against the clinical white slip of her hospital pillow. How could anyone have done this to her?

She was still unconscious, still hooked up to a monitor and an intravenous drip. The nurse had suggested that Benny talk to her, say something familiar, something that might connect with her mind. The trouble was, she hardly even knew the poor kid. The person for that job would really be Ace, and there was no knowing where she was at the moment. As for Karen's boyfriend: well, the Doctor had done some checking that morning, only to find that Mel Joseph was being held in police custody for a number of crimes on which Sergeant Blyth wouldn't expound. Things seemed to keep happening, thought Benny – unfair things, cruel things, incomprehensible things. The sooner she or the Doctor could unravel just what was going on in this place and get back to the TARDIS, the happier she would feel. Happy? In the TARDIS? Maybe things were getting better after all!

Her thoughts were interrupted by a groan and the brief flutter of an eyelid.

'Nurse? Nurse! I think she's waking up!'

'Mel?' The word came out painfully, in a voice cracked and hoarse. It was not the right time for Benny to give her the news about her fiancé.

'It's Benny, Karen. Remember me? Ace's friend.'

'I . . . remember.'

The nurse was already by her side. 'You mustn't try to speak,' she urged her. 'You've had a terrible shock.'

'No, got to tell . . . snuck up on me . . . cut into me . . .'

'Who?' asked Benny, urgently. 'Who attacked you, Karen? Did you see them? Can you tell me?'

Karen screwed up her eyes, so tight that they watered. Her chest was heaving, her throat rasping, as she gulped in air and sweated in buckets.

'Can't . . . remember,' she wheezed finally, and her eyes filled up with water again. 'Can't . . .'

There was silence.

'She's passed out again,' the nurse reported, 'but I think she'll be fine now.'

Benny nodded. Fine as long as she didn't remember, she thought. Fine as long as the killer didn't get past that police guard on the door to finish off the job and silence the only prosecution witness for good.

Yeah, she thought. Strange definition of the word 'fine' they have here.

Cold hard bench. Cold hard bars. Sheridan wondered how

his life had led him to this place, this prison where lurked the deviants of society – and he a man of the cloth yet, just trying to follow the path to which his faith led him. He prayed for forgiveness for whatever sins he had committed, and he sobbed and clung tight to the crucifix like it was his last hold on life. In many ways, it was.

'You're no better than the rest of us, you know.'

The voice came from behind him, from the youth in the next cell, just one set of bars removed. He had disliked the boy at first sight, had wanted to stay out of his way – but Mel Joseph was not taking no for an answer.

'Just a quick game of chance,' he called to him. 'Anything you like. Any wager you like.' Sheridan tried to bury his head, tried to cut out the words, but Mel raised his voice and continued. 'I've got money, you know. Plenty of money. I can get it to you when you get out! A thousand pounds – more if you want it, if you win. And if you lose, there's just one little girl I want you to deal with for me. One little girl, who betrayed me and attacked me and landed me here.'

Before he could stop himself, Sheridan was on his feet and his terrible anger exploded outwards. 'I will hear no more of your words, you heathen devil! If you think to find me open to your dark temptations, you will be sorely disappointed!'

'It's talk like that that put you in here,' remarked Malcolm Blyth from the open cell door, not quite sure whether to be annoyed or amused. He settled on annoyed: this maniac was too dangerous to let his guard down with.

The priest's strong frame seemed to noticeably sag and he was quiet once more, the outburst over. Still, Blyth was sure to keep an eye on his prisoner as he escorted him from the cell. 'We've brought a solicitor in to see you, though God knows why we bothered.'

Sheridan looked down at his crucifix and smiled without humour. 'Yes,' he said. 'He probably does.'

Mel Joseph watched them go, his face pressed up against the bars which held him captive. When he was sure they were out of sight, he dropped his calm facade and punched his threadbare mattress until his arms ached with the effort.

The creatures took Ace by surprise, sneaking up on her in a way that she would have thought impossible. The first was barely five yards away when she caught sight of it, blending almost perfectly in with the flat white background as it approached. She jumped straight to her feet, immediately spotting another six of the things in a complete circle around her. More illusions? She doubted it. Like the void itself, these strange metallic beings seemed somehow only too real to be anything but more of her enemy's tricks.

'Who are you?' she asked, picking one as her target and aiming her blaster. 'Who sent you here?'

They didn't answer; just kept closing in, nearer and nearer, almost upon her now . . . She fired, but the blast was neatly absorbed, sinking into the robot's chest with barely a glow to show where it had hit. And then they were on her, pincer-like hands gripping her tight and dragging her back the way she had come (or was that forward? Or off to the right? It was so hard to tell.)

It was like she had blinked and was suddenly elsewhere. Back in the town – or rather on its outskirts, on a hill not too dissimilar to the one from which she had hurled herself just . . . just . . . minutes? hours? days? . . . ago.

Before her lay Arandale. Behind her? There no longer, the vista of space over the hills, the view replaced instead by a shell of some gleaming white substance, the like of which Ace had never set eyes on before.

She smiled. 'I know you can hear me,' she said. 'I don't know how and I don't know why, but I do know you're watching and I know you're aware of everything I say and do here. Well I just want you to know this – that I'm on to your little scheme now. You can put up your barrier, you can keep me in the town for just as long as it takes me to break out again, but you can't mess with my mind anymore. I'm together again. I know what's going on and I know what I'm gonna do about it – and you're gonna be bloody sorry when I do, believe you me!'

She let the threat hang in the air as she turned away, sinking her hands nonchalantly into her pockets and heading back to Arandale in a better mood than she had been for days. Her own person again. Back in control.

Then she remembered what she'd said to Benny.

'I see you managed to stay put this time, then,' Bernice spoke half-heartedly, and Norman flashed her only a brief smile as he turned to greet her.

'How's your friend?' he asked.

'Not good, but she might get better.'

They stepped out onto the hospital steps, flinching from the fierce wind which greeted them. 'So what's the plan now?'

'To fight back,' said Benny. 'I don't know how yet, but we've got to do something.'

'About the murders, or about Doctor Nemesis?'

Benny shrugged. 'About both, I suppose. I can't help thinking they're connected anyway. There's too much strangeness going on around here for it all to be coincidence.'

'You mean Nemesis might be responsible?'

'I didn't say that – but it is a possibility, yes.'

Norman groaned in despair and sank back against the nearest wall. (A little further down the street, four children hurled themselves into someone's front garden as their quarry came to an unexpected stop.) 'I should have known it would come to this. I should have known it all along.'

'How do you mean?'

'Destiny,' said Norman. 'My fate and that of Nemesis, linked together right up to the end.'

'You're not making much sense.'

He ignored the interruption. 'He was my greatest foe,

you know – almost from the start. Even when I defeated him, time and time again, he just said he'd be back. And he always was, always breaking out of prison, coming back from the dead, leaping out at me from around every corner. I think somehow it always had to come down to this. Thirty years later, all grown up and still fighting against each other, still slugging away and never mind the innocents who get harmed in the fall-out!' He thought of Sparky and a lump came to his throat. 'All of those battles . . . when he blackmailed the world with his nerve-gas bomb, when we found out each other's identities, when he shipped arms to the fourteenth century . . .'

'Whoa!' Benny broke into the train of memories. 'Just backtrack there a minute, will you? You said you "found out each other's identities"?'

Norman looked at her blankly, and just nodded.

'You mean you actually know his name?'

'Well, of course I do,' said Norman. 'I said I beat him, remember – I handed him over to the police a few times. You didn't think they threw him in prison with his mask on, did you?'

'I just can't believe you didn't tell me, that's all!'

Norman shrugged. 'No point,' he said. 'I told you, he's a clever one. He'd have to be to have given me all the problems he did when . . . well, when I was you-know-who!'

Benny sighed. 'I suppose you're right.'

'Oh, definitely!' he insisted. 'Well it makes sense, doesn't it? A murdering super-powered villain with a known identity, a prison record and probably a "wanted" tag to go with it, trying to track down his old foe and bait a trap for him in secret . . .'

'Yes, yes, okay – I get the point.'

'Well, he'd be mad to go around calling himself Mason Grimshaw, wouldn't he?'

It was only through tremendous force of effort that Benny managed to keep her mouth shut.

Chapter 10

Cat Fights

By now, it's about five o'clock in Arandale. Five o'clock on November the fifth; a winter Friday evening. The sky is turning rapidly black. The moon is out, but shrouded by the billowing grey clouds. The street lights have snapped into action and the snow has begun to fall again, melting into water as it hits the sludgy grey pavements of the town.

Time, I think, for the fireworks to begin.

Confrontation 1: Ace runs into the Doctor on her way back to the guest-house.

'I think I can guess what you've seen,' he said, interrupting her tale before she could even properly start.

Ace groaned and her expression blackened. 'Known it all from the start again, have you? Couldn't be bothered telling me, I suppose?'

'It's not like that, Ace.'

'No?'

The Doctor sighed. 'Bernice told me how you feel about me.'

It took a second for that to sink in – a second more before Ace could truly be sure that she'd understood things correctly. Bernice had failed the test. Never, ever, trust a civilian. Especially a civilian who's travelled with the Doctor.

'She told me what you said; that you couldn't decide how you felt about me, how you want to beat me at my own game . . .'

'She had no right!' Ace exploded, enjoying the almost-real anger.

'She was just trying to help,' the Doctor insisted, 'and I think she was right to talk to me.'

'Like hell!'

'We both know we've been having problems – ever since you came back on board the TARDIS. It's time we sorted them out. It's time we talked.'

Ace snorted derisively. She'd expected Bernice to swallow the story, but not the Doctor. Now she was stuck with two social workers. 'You can talk all you bloody well like, but leave me out of it!'

'I can understand how you feel . . .'

'Don't give me that crap – you don't even know what feelings are.'

'Ace . . .'

'Just get the hell out of my life, you bastard.' She pushed him roughly to the side, storming past without a backward glance. Satisfying, Ace thought, but not as satisfying as punching the nose of that patronising, stuck-up, busybody archaeologist was going to be.

The Doctor watched her for a few seconds. Then, with a Gallifreyan expletive muttered between firmly gritted teeth, he turned and headed purposefully in the opposite direction.

Bernice checked carefully around the empty guest-house before ushering Norman in from the street.

'Now this time,' she warned, 'I want you to promise me that you'll stay right here and not move for anything. We don't know where that costumed lunatic might be, and I don't want him killing you before I've had the chance to sort him out.'

'So where are you going?' asked Norman.

'To sort him out.'

'How?'

'Well, that's the tricky bit,' Benny admitted, 'but I'm sure I'll think of something.'

Norman sank down onto the bed with a despairing sigh. 'And I just sit here and wait, is that it? Like some useless fifth wheel waiting for you to come back and tell me it's safe to go out again?'

Already half-way through the door, Benny groaned inwardly at his words. She couldn't leave him like this.

'How long will it take to sink in?' She spoke kindly, sitting down by his side and laying a reassuring hand on his shoulder. 'Just because you don't have the sort of powers you had before doesn't make you any less of a hero, Norman. It's not the powers that matter. What counts is what you do with your life, with whatever attributes you're given – and from what I've heard, you've done a pretty good job on that score.'

Norman smiled weakly in acknowledgement of her praise.

'So now those powers have gone,' continued Benny, 'and now you can't go out there and take on a mass-murdering, supercharged armoured villain all by yourself anymore. So welcome to the human race, Norman – but don't think of yourself as any less of a hero, nor any less of a man. Inside, where it counts, you're still the brave, selfless warrior who went into battle as the White Knight three decades ago. Nothing important has changed. I want you to remember that. I want you to promise me you'll remember that.'

Norman nodded his head, but the tears were still in his eyes. That had to be good enough, she thought. For now, at least.

There was work to be done.

It was a long time after Benny had left before Norman stirred again. By then he had turned a lot of thoughts over in his head, and he had made one very important decision about the life he wished to live.

Benny would kill him, he thought, if she saw him sneaking out of the guest-house and heading back home like this. Still, that didn't really matter. What she had said about staying put seemed hardly to apply now.

He had made his choice. It was one she would be proud of.

He was going to be a hero again.

There were those in the small town who said the Black Cat Tavern shouldn't have reopened yet. They considered its closure a mark of respect to its former landlord, not yet even buried. There were others who insisted that Alan would prefer it that way; that he would like to see people getting on with their lives without him, and that he would have hated for the 'Cat' to take a nosedive in his absence. And then there was his next-of-kin, a cousin from across the town who didn't really give a toss what anyone thought as long as he could make a bit of cash.

Thus it was that, at five o'clock that evening, the Black Cat was open for business again, with its new – and probably temporary, though not if he could help it – landlord tending to the needs of the less offended of its old customers. It was the perfect place, thought Benny, for a confrontation with Mason Grimshaw. He'd be in there for sure, some time this evening, and he would almost certainly be bereft of his formidable armour. With a little bit of luck, he might even be frightened of tipping his hand by causing a scene in public, although she wouldn't count on that for sure.

By a quarter past five then, she was firmly ensconced in a seat in the corner, one wary eye on the door to the street as she nursed a glass of vodka and wondered what she might say to Mason Grimshaw when he did arrive. Maybe she could warn him off? The police were interested in him after all, and it was possible that he could still be reasoned with. She wondered why he had lived in the town for so long and yet waited until now to make a move against his enemy. Perhaps that information could give her a lever against him, too.

At twenty-six minutes past five the door of the tavern

swung slowly inwards, and Benny's eyes flicked up to meet those of the newcomer, filled as they did with a mixture of expectation and dread.

It wasn't Mason Grimshaw who entered the Black Cat Tavern.

It was the newly bailed Father Kenneth Sheridan.

'The old bloke's leaving now too,' whispered Tracey.

The Adventure Kids watched from across the street, taking care to remain out of sight behind a parked car, particularly as Norman kept throwing furtive glances across his shoulder.

'Do you think he knows we're watching?' asked Michelle.

'He can't do,' reasoned Tim. 'And if we stay careful, he'll never find out.'

'We were wrong though,' said Tracey. 'It doesn't look like he's going back to Vampire Castle either.' Indeed not. Norman had already turned the far corner and headed off up Moat House Hill, almost the opposite direction to the object of their concerns.

'I told you we should've followed the woman,' said Gary, sulkily.

'Well we've got to make a choice quick,' said Tim. 'Do we follow the man or not?'

Gary shook his head. 'No,' he decided. 'I think we're needed a lot more somewhere else.'

Michelle rolled her eyes. 'Don't tell me: you want to go back to the castle!'

'It's the only way to find out what's going on,' her brother insisted. 'Well? Isn't it?'

The children looked at each other and their minds raced with fear and excitement. Their next decision would be crucial.

I mentioned in Chapter One how quickly news travelled in Arandale. This was even more true when said news involved Rosemary Chambers! So it was that the few people in the 'Cat' who didn't already know of Sheridan's attack on the village witch the previous day were swiftly clued in by the hushed whispers of their drinking partners.

A murmur of discontent raced one circuit around the room. Someone asked the landlord not to serve the new arrival, but Alan Brown's cousin considered one man's money as good as the next. Bernice Summerfield rested her head in her hands and watched with furrowed brow. She was almost surprised when the priest was allowed to purchase his drink and take a corner seat without incident. By the time she thought to look back to the doorway, the Doctor had already crossed the room and was sitting down beside her.

'I spoke to Ace,' he said, matter-of-factly.

'Oh?'

'She's not happy.'

'Oh.'

'I came to tell you that I'm leaving.'

'Leaving what?'

'The town.'

'Now just a minute . . .'

'It's all right,' the Doctor assured her. 'I'll be back. At least, I hope so.'

'But where are you going to?'

'Nowhere you'll have heard of.'

Benny looked at him sharply. 'You know what's going on, don't you?'

'Most of it, yes.'

'And?'

'And remind me to tell you about it sometime.'

'Doctor!'

'I have to go.' The Doctor was already half-way across the room before Benny leapt after him and pulled him back round to face her.

'No more secrets, Doctor!' she said angrily.

'I'm sorry, there's no time for this.'

'Then just tell me, in words of one syllable: whodunnit?'

The Doctor shrugged.

'You said you knew everything!'

'The murders aren't important.'

Benny almost choked with disbelief, and the Doctor sighed as he lowered himself onto the nearest chair and pulled her down onto one next to it. 'Very briefly then,' he said. 'The murderer is someone we've met.'

'How do you . . .?'

'Because it has to be, for the plot of this book to make sense. And I think we can forget about Mel Joseph, Norman Power and Father Sheridan; we know what their secrets are already.'

'But . . .'

'And now I really have to go.' This time, Benny knew she couldn't stop him.

'Then I'll stick to you like glue!' she exclaimed. He ignored her, and the door slammed shut in her face. Angrily, she rushed out onto the street behind him, but her path was blocked by a new arrival.

It was Mason Grimshaw, and he was smiling.

'Going somewhere?' He spoke with a thick American accent, and this alone sent unaccountable shivers down Benny's spine.

She thought quickly, remembering that they had never been formally introduced. 'Do I know you?'

'I know you!'

'Erm . . . Bernice Summerfield. Nice to meet you.'

'Yes.' The smile had faded now, and Benny's attention was riveted to Grimshaw's fiery red eyes, skewering her to the spot with the intensity of their stare. He held his gaze for a disconcerting moment longer, then patted her hard on the back, almost knocking her over with the force of the ostensibly companionable gesture. 'I'll see you around,' he said meaningfully as he pushed past her to the bar.

Bernice shuddered as she watched him go.

And the evening drew ever onwards.

'I need to see Mel Joseph.'

169

'Are you a relative, sir?'

'I'm relative to everything,' said the Doctor. 'Relatively speaking anyway. Just show me through, there's a good chap.' The door through to the police station's main office was electronically locked, but the Doctor solved that problem by leaping nimbly across the reception desk and landing next to the startled duty officer.

'Now wait a moment . . .' the man protested, reaching out to bar his way.

'Time is relative too,' said the Doctor, popping his hat onto the officer's outstretched hand and breezing past him towards the door that he knew would lead to the holding area. 'Good day,' he called over his shoulder – and then walked straight into the portly figure of Malcolm Blyth, who was standing in the doorway watching the scene with a mixture of anger and resignation.

'It's all right, constable,' he said wearily. 'I know this clown.'

'Sergeant Blyth,' the Doctor greeted him, as if welcoming a long-lost friend. 'Do you work a twenty-four hour shift? Never mind, I need to see Mel Joseph. You can arrange that, can't you?'

'I can arrange for you to move in next door to him if you like,' Blyth commented sardonically.

'That's very kind, but just a few minutes will do.' The Doctor moved quickly, attempting to dive under Blyth's outstretched arm and down the corridor beyond. The police sergeant was too quick for him.

'I'll think about allowing your visit,' he said. '*if* you come along to the interview room with me first. I'd like to ask you a few questions.'

The Doctor clicked his tongue with exasperation. 'I really have no time for that, sergeant.'

'And if I was to place you under arrest?'

'That would be a very boring plot development. It's been done.'

Blyth's eyes narrowed. 'I'm not sure I understand you.'

170

'You don't have to understand. Just let me see Mel Joseph.'

Sergeant Blyth suddenly smiled, stepped to one side and handed a large set of keys to the Doctor. 'Go ahead,' he said, jerking his thumb to indicate the corridor behind him. 'He's down there.'

Just a minute . . . I didn't write that!

'No,' said the Doctor. '*I* did!'

The Adventure Kids had each bolted down their meals and rushed out of their houses, meeting promptly in Tim's back yard at half past six that evening. They were disappointed to find that they were down to four members again; Tim had returned home an hour before to discover that the loyal, lovable Carson had gone into a foaming rage and had had to be dragged off the throat of little Billy James Junior from down the road. The police had been called in, of course, and Carson had been hauled away to the vet where a small injection had curbed his temper for good. It had not done much for Tim's feelings though (nor Michelle's come to that), and the others were picking their words with care. The subject of recruiting a new fifth member, for example, had not yet even been broached.

'So,' said Gary, ignoring his sister's sobbing and getting straight to the matter at hand, 'now that Carson's snuffed it, what are the rest of us going to do?'

Tim shrugged, and tried to cast off his gloominess. 'I don't know,' he said. 'I mean, perhaps our parents were right. Perhaps it is time we handed things over to the police.'

'What, and let them just storm up there and take all the credit? Come on Tim, we've never given up like that before, no matter what the danger!'

'I suppose you're right,' said Tim reluctantly.

'I think we have to go back up there,' said Tracey, thoughtfully. 'Just for one last time, just to see what evidence we can get.' She produced a tape-recorder from her

171

pocket. 'If we can tape that fellow at it in the cavern, we might even be able to work out who he is.'

'That's three in favour then,' said Gary happily. 'Michelle?'

They turned to look at Michelle Chambers, but her mind was still on the dog and her tear-streaked face was dark and sullen. 'I don't care,' she said, quite to the surprise of the others. 'We'll go up there if you want!'

It was decided.

By now, the Black Cat Tavern was beginning to fill up again; not as much as might once have been expected on a Friday night, but a good thirty people wasn't bad under the circumstances. Benny recognized only a few of them – though, from Ace's description, she was sure that the rather obvious private detective drowning his sorrows at the bar had to be Jack Corrigan.

She recognized Phil Chambers too. He entered on the stroke of seven, walking with his characteristic slouch and unaware that his arrival had drawn the attention of almost all of the clientele. Some of them were actually concerned. Most, however, were just hoping for a cathartic display of violence. Bernice Summerfield tensed, hoping that her involvement would not be required, but ready for action if it was.

It was only after arriving at the bar and ordering his first pint of bitter that Phil registered Sheridan's presence. The priest was standing before him, a watery smile on his face, one hand extended timidly in a gesture of reconciliation.

'You must be Mister Philip Chambers,' said Sheridan, and the whole of the Black Cat Inn held its breath as Phil nodded slowly and took Sheridan's hand in a weak, uncertain grasp.

'Kenneth Sheridan,' the priest introduced himself. 'I had a little disagreement with your wife yesterday. I just wanted to apologize.'

Inside Phil Chambers' mind, little bits of information

172

were slowly coming together. A priest, a disagreement, his wife . . .

His eyes widened as comprehension dawned. The next thing anyone knew, Father Sheridan was hurtling backwards with blood flying from his face and Phil was howling and screaming like a maniac as he launched himself after the priest. Fists flew, glasses smashed, tables buckled, and suddenly almost everyone in the pub seemed involved in the scuffle, some of them trying to placate their suddenly wild friend or at least to drag him kicking and screaming from his defenceless foe, whilst others tried to get Sheridan to safety or in some cases just used the opportunity to get in a few sly punches of their own.

His fury spent, Phil collapsed against the bar and, shrugging off concerned hands, cried bitterly into his glass. Battered, bruised and exhausted, Sheridan collapsed onto one of the unbroken chairs and clutched at his crucifix as he muttered a quick prayer. A few people offered to show him off the premises, but the landlord was having none of it; he hadn't started the fight, after all.

'I just wanted to apologize,' Sheridan called out miserably. 'I made a mistake!' But, sitting with his back to the priest, Phil just shuddered and wept and refused to respond.

Benny relaxed a little and sipped at her drink. The landlord was still attempting to placate a few aggrieved customers, but it seemed the excitement was more or less over. She had not had to become involved in the brief skirmish and she was glad that such detachment had been possible. She frowned as she glanced up and met Mason Grimshaw's eyes. He was staring implacably at her from across the room, and she noted that he too had not stirred from his position. He was here to watch her, just as she was to watch him.

Benny had never been so glad to see a friendly face as when the pub door opened and Ace stepped over the threshold. 'Over here,' she called, and Ace came – but there was something wrong. Her face was grim and her fists were clenched.

'I want a word with you, you bitch!'

Mel Joseph didn't look up as the visitor entered his cell. He didn't even move until the Doctor pushed his legs off the bed, making way for the Travel Scrabble set which he yanked out of his inside jacket pocket. 'Fancy a game?' he asked politely.

'Why should I?' sneered Mel.

'Because you're a compulsive gamesman. Because not many people get the chance. Because I'll help you out of here if you win.'

'And what do you get out of this?'

'Information. Draw your letters and take the first turn.'

Much as Mel hated to admit it, the Doctor was right. Whatever the challenge, whatever the stakes, it was the thrill of the game itself that he couldn't resist. He took seven letters from the tray, inspected them briefly – then, with a smirk on his face, laid all seven out horizontally and symmetrically through the centre square of the board.

The letters spelt: PLAYING.

'I trusted you,' stormed Ace, waving a trembling finger in Benny's face. 'I trusted you, and you grassed me up to the bloody Doctor!'

'I don't know what . . .'

'Don't give me that rubbish, I've had enough of it! I've had enough of being lied to!'

'I thought we were friends,' protested Benny.

'So did I,' Ace hissed fiercely. 'That's why I let you take advantage of me, opened up my heart to you when I was too goddamned ill to even think straight. And you went and stabbed me in the back.' Her voice was growing steadily louder as she became ever more oblivious to her surroundings and to the curious customers who, one by one, were turning their attention towards this new source of entertainment. It was all too much for Benny, and anger boiled up within her.

'Don't you play the injured party with me!' she snapped, grabbing Ace's arm and pushing it roughly away from her. 'I've bent over backwards to accommodate you – I should have known from the start, you're nothing more than a selfish, two-faced, maladjusted killer!'

'*I'm* two-faced?' shrieked Ace. 'It's you who got me pissed, told me I could trust you, then went blabbing to my worst bloody enemy in the world!'

'I was trying to help you!' asserted Benny angrily. 'God knows, you need it – you're psychotic!'

'Bitch!' spat Ace, venomously. She swung her right arm out before her – more in a warding-off gesture than as an actual punch. Nevertheless she caught the infuriated Benny right across the face, and was rewarded by a swift elbow to the cheek.

By now, almost half the Cat's customers were on their feet, ready for their second fight of the evening. The landlord was between Ace and Benny an instant after the first blow had been struck, forcibly separating them and shouting something that neither woman paid very much attention to.

Walking ghost-like through the crowd, Father Sheridan held tight to his crucifix and his eyes were wide with horror. 'Tis the Devil's work that is done in Arandale this night.' Then his eyes popped even further out of his skull as Phil Chambers leapt onto his back and cut off his oxygen supply with an arm around his throat.

Someone tried to wrench Phil off Sheridan's back; someone else tried to help restrain the furiously spitting Ace. Suddenly the public bar was a battleground for anyone with any sort of grievance, or who just wanted a good fight for the sake of it. More chairs splintered, more glasses smashed . . . Ace snapped out of her rage with a cry of alarm as a Newcastle Brown bottle shattered on her chest. Only her combat suit had protected her from harm.

175

Benny tried to shelter behind the bar but the fight followed her round there. Blast it, she thought, why did things like this always have to happen? She tried to plough through to the door, but stopped short when she realized that that would mean passing Mason Grimshaw.

Ace found herself back to back with Jack Corrigan. 'Do scenes like this follow you around, or what?' he asked her wryly, and then they were separated as the burly form of Mason Grimshaw waded between them and sent Ace toppling off-balance into someone behind her. Her first impulse was to punch Grimshaw across the face, if only to relieve her frustration, but something in his eyes made her think again. She headed for the door instead, hoping to put as much distance as possible between herself and this madhouse.

Behind her, the pub's fire-alarm bell rang out, and the landlord's voice could just be heard above it, warning the brawlers that the police were on their way. A general surge towards the exit helped Ace on her way, and she was consequently one of the first people to spill out onto the street, as the Black Cat's fleeing customers sought refuge in their own comfortable homes.

Benny, conversely, was one of the last ones out – though not for want of trying. She left behind only those few people who were determined to fight until the end – ironically, none of them with any reason that she knew of. Phil Chambers and Kenneth Sheridan were long gone, as were both Mason Grimshaw and her own erstwhile companion, Ace.

The street outside the pub was now strangely deserted. Given the close proximity of the police station and the distinct absence of police, she could only assume that the landlord's threat had been a bluff – probably too worried about what they might think, being called out on his first night like this.

Bernice leant heavily against the side wall of the Cat, sucked in a lungful of air and coughed painfully at the smoke from a dozen bonfires and at her own blood in her mouth. In the distance, she could hear the bell of the village clock beating out one solitary note to mark the half-hour. Half past seven. She thought of five dead bodies, each person killed in the evening hours of the last five consecutive days. The Doctor had told her what Matthew Shade had said; that there would be six such murders, and the last would be tonight.

She wondered whose the final corpse would be.

The Doctor frowned, used five tiles to spell the word DEATHS through Mel's A and stared up at his opponent meaningfully.

Mel met his gaze and the ghost of a smile flashed across his face. Without even looking at the board, he played MURDERS through the new letter D.

Immediately, the Doctor used the last letter of DEATHS to start off a horizontal word, SUSPECT.

Mel smiled and played all seven again; the second R of MURDERS, the I out of PLAYING and the second S of SUSPECT helped him to form the ten-letter word DIVERSIONS.

The Doctor scowled. 'Now you're changing the subject,' he said.

Ace didn't know how long she'd been standing here on this wasteland, watching the preparations. There had been but a few bundles of sticks when she'd arrived, wandering aimlessly just to get away from the Black Cat and to be alone with her thoughts. Now the bonfire was almost built, the Guy was being lowered into place and the excitement of the children was mounting exponentially as they ran and laughed and played and thought of nothing but the night ahead.

Above her a firework whistled sharply through the air, and a sudden ferocious gust of wind hit her face and reminded her that time was still moving. She thought about Benny: the only person she'd opened up to in three years, and she'd gone straight to the Doctor – straight to him of all people – telling tales, betraying Ace's confidence. She felt like a fool, and she hated that feeling. Worse than that, she had gone and lost her rag again, like she'd promised herself she wouldn't, priding herself on her maturity and her coolness and her total self-control.

Smoke billowed finally into the already opaque night sky, and Ace lost all track of time again. The fire warmed her, gave her some sense of comfort, and she tried to pretend that she was no longer here; that she couldn't feel the wind which still whipped around her legs, that her ears weren't still red with anger and humiliation, and that it was only the cinders that were stinging her eyes.

STORIES was the Doctor's next word, turning SUSPECT into its own plural with the final S.

It was Mel's turn to look worried, as he played a tentative FACT through the only C on the board.

The Doctor shook his head patiently and used the first I of DIVERSIONS to help him form a horizontal FICTION.

Time froze for a moment ... then Mel picked up six tiles and placed them across the board from the R of STORIES – slowly, deliberately, as if he would stand for no arguments.

The word was REALITY.

The Doctor smiled.

'Hi honey, I'm home!'

The words were meant light-heartedly, but the underlying tone of menace set Tina Grimshaw shivering all the same.

She turned from the grimy window and rubbed a sleeve hastily across her face, hoping to disguise the fact that she had been crying. She was unsuccessful; her excessive layers of make-up were already streaked with black, and her eyes were red and swollen.

Mason's hefty bulk was framed in the doorway, and he was glaring at her threateningly. 'Where's my supper?'

he growled, nodding towards the unset table. She hated it when he was like this. She hated his words, hated his tantrums, hated her life.

'I-in the oven,' she managed to stammer out. 'I didn't know what time you'd be back.'

Mason nodded approvingly, as if the question had been merely a test of her obedience. 'I'm going out again,' he told her.

Tina heard him march heavily across the lobby, into the bedroom. She heard the cupboard door being wrenched open . . . no, not *that* cupboard! . . . and she was suddenly more cold and frightened than she had been since – since . . .

Since the last time.

By the time she dared to follow him, hovering nervously in the bedroom doorway, he was already in the armour. He was heaving the heavy metal boots onto his feet, fastening the flowing black cape around his neck, concealing his face beneath the mask even as he submerged his own personality beneath that of the Monster.

'No,' she whispered, more by impulse than by choice.

Mason's tone was dangerous as he turned and spoke to her. '*What* did you say?'

'I-I just don't want you to do this. You promised! You said you'd put it all behind you. You said he wouldn't come back!' Tina's voice trailed off weakly as the armoured man lumbered steadily, powerfully towards her. His eyes fixed on hers and his right fist was clenching and unclenching spasmodically.

'Please don't hit me,' she moaned, shrinking away and throwing up her hands in an ineffectual gesture of protection. Her pleas might have worked on her husband; but the thing which now confronted her no longer recalled who Mason Grimshaw even was.

This was the Monster, the creature within him. Shackled for years, thought of as dead . . . but now, Doctor Nemesis was free. Free for one final, fateful time.

Tina screamed as a set of iron-clad knuckles crashed

179

hard against her skull and she tumbled helplessly to the
floor in a blood-red daze. She felt his boot on her cheek,
heard his rasping voice as he looked disdainfully down at
her prostrated form.

'If you leave here,' he reminded her, 'I'll kill you.'

He was telling her the truth. She knew he would do it.

The Monster left her then. She heard the slam of the
flat door as it went in search of its prey – unmindful now
of who might see it, knowing that no one alive could
stop it.

She sobbed for a long time into the dirty bedroom
carpet. And she knew then, with a dreadful cold certainty,
that her life would never be the same again.

'Reality,' read the Doctor. 'That's a very interesting word.'

Mel smirked again. 'You mean you can't match it?'

'I mean it's physically impossible. On a fifteen by fifteen
square board, you just don't have the space to play it.'

Mel was somewhat taken aback. 'But . . . but it's there!'
he protested.

'I know,' said the Doctor. 'Interesting, isn't it?' In one
fluid movement, he folded the Scrabble board and tipped
the letter tiles back into their tray. 'You want to be more
careful what you write in future,' he remarked.

'I don't understand.'

'That's because I wasn't talking to you.'

'You weren't?'

The Doctor was on his feet now and his back was turned
to his confused opponent. 'No,' he said. 'I was talking to
you!'

To . . . me?

Father Kenneth Michael Sheridan had made the two biggest mistakes of his life.

The first, he already knew about. He knew it by the
humiliation of his arrest, and by the pain in his arms and
legs after the incident in the pub. As he walked the dark
streets home alone, his thoughts alternated between regret

at his ill-conceived actions in attacking Rosemary Chambers and anger at the lack of forgiveness he had encountered in this heathen town.

It was time to leave, he thought. Get away from here, maybe flee to a different country. He couldn't face the townspeople again, and he couldn't face the police either, and the ignominy of a term in prison simply for doing what he had felt to be right at the time.

His mind made up, he stopped and turned, intending to head back to his hotel and gather his belongings together. Two things then happened simultaneously.

Firstly, the priest noticed that he had wandered into a part of the town he had never seen before. He was lost.

Secondly, a figure stepped out of the darkness before him, and its eyes gleamed with insanity.

That was when Sheridan realized his second mistake.

This time, no knife was needed; just the sheer raw power with which the energy had infused him, giving him the strength he needed to snap his victim's neck, to draw the last drop of blood from his body and to feel the Force of which he was a servant feeding on the last of the lives it would need.

By the time it was all over, Kenneth Sheridan was lying dead on the ground – and the man who had killed him stood triumphantly over the corpse, as the power within and around him fairly shrieked its song of victory.

'You're not fooling anyone any more,' snapped the Doctor. 'It's time to give up this ridiculous charade.'

What do I do?

'Well? Are you going to let me come out there and talk to you? Or are you going to hide behind this fictional world of yours forever?'

What do I do?

The Doctor retook his seat, but he pulled it around so as not to face Mel Joseph again. 'I'm waiting,' he called. 'The next move is yours. But I know where I am, and I know what you want – and I won't be taking any further part in your story until I get what *I* want!'

His appeal received no answer, but his face was set and his body was unmoving. He meant what he said.

'I want to be let out of here,' he said in quiet, measured tones. 'I want to talk to you, face to face. You hear that? Whoever you might be this time, I want to see you.

'I want to speak to the Master of the Land of Fiction!'

Chapter 11

Writing Wrongs

The town of Arandale had moved, but the Doctor had not. It was as if the conurbation had shifted right out from under him, and he was suddenly standing alone in the empty white land outside. The sight was a familiar one.

'I'm here to meet you,' he reminded me finally. 'I won't wait forever for something to happen.' He needn't have worried on that score; the words were hardly out of his mouth when the world collapsed suddenly, sickeningly inwards. His senses went haywire – and the martyrs of the Althosian system welcomed him aboard a train ride headed straight for the depths of Hell.

'Revenge,' shrieked the spirits of long-buried people. 'Revenge for the games that you played with our lives!' and his carriage sped onwards and picked up momentum, and flames licked the sides as he sped into darkness. His sixth self attacked him and threatened to kill him – 'Revenge!' for a sacrifice made with no choice. The Valeyard's face mocked him and boasted of victory; their methods more similar than he might have wanted – and Adric and Sara and poor Katarina were shouting 'Revenge!' till the Doctor yelled . . .

'No! Stop this! Your mind games didn't work on Ace. They certainly won't work on me!' (Well, it was worth a try anyway.)

He was back where he had started from, whiteness on all sides. 'So?' he asked, his chin jutting outwards in a gesture of defiance. 'You've brought me this far, let me out of the village. I assume you're going to take me the rest of the way?'

His only answer was the silence of the void.

'I'm not moving until I get an answer!'

He won't, too – I can see it in his mind. Still, I don't suppose it can hurt . . .

The Doctor spotted my robots when they were still a good few hundred yards away. 'At last,' he breathed, and then he waited impatiently until the pair of automatons had closed the remaining distance and taken up their escort positions on each side of him.

Unexpectedly, the Doctor smiled. 'Reality at last!' he exclaimed. 'Of a sort, at least. I see you're still using the White Robots.' He tapped the nearest one smartly on its chestplate with the curved red handle of his umbrella.

'So,' he said, 'take me to your leader.'

Bernice stopped in her tracks.

One moment she had been staring down at nothing more than her own feet, crunching through the brown slush on the grimy pavement. The next, she was looking at the card: a perfect white, engraved with immaculate silver letters: MATTHEW SHADE, Psychic Investigations.

He stood beside her, his expression enigmatic and the black depths of his eyes unfathomable. 'There was a fight in the Black Cat Tavern,' he said.

'I know, I was there. I didn't see you.'

'I just know.'

'What do you want?'

'Your friend, the Doctor – he has left the area. I thought that was impossible.'

'Well, he tends to do the impossible every so often. You learn to put up with it.'

Shade nodded, knowingly. 'The final battle is approaching. The armies of the Dark are massing. Our own forces must be rallied against them.'

'I wasn't aware we had any forces,' commented Benny.

'We will need to join together,' said Shade, 'if we are not to be lost forever.'

Benny wanted him to say more, but somehow, as unhurried as his gait seemed, Shade managed to walk away from her before she could form her first question. He faded into the shadows, almost as if he had never existed – but Benny knew that he had. She had his business card to prove it.

She looked down at her hand, and her jaw dropped open in astonishment. It was empty. The card had vanished.

When she finally reached the guest-house, she found Rosemary Chambers waiting on the doorstep. 'My magics told me I would be needed here,' she explained. 'I think things are coming to a head. Tonight.'

'Yes,' said Benny thoughtfully. 'That's very much the impression I've been getting.'

The stone block came easily free this time, and the air which rose from the tunnels below seemed not quite so cold as before.

'I don't see why we can't just leave this till tomorrow,' complained Michelle, 'when it's light.'

'Because we don't have the time,' insisted Gary. 'Can't you feel it, in the air?' Michelle couldn't. Nor, he had to confess, could Tim. Gary clicked his tongue in exasperation. 'This is it! This is the night!'

'You mean something important's going to happen?' asked Tracey.

'What I mean,' said Gary, 'is that one way or another, I think this whole thing's going to blow up in the next couple of hours!'

In the nothingness which surrounded the town, neither time nor distance had any meaning. The Doctor could have been walking for minutes or days, traversing yards or miles – he had no way of knowing. All he did know was that he was finally nearing his destination. He knew that from the moment he encountered Aslan, the talking lion who bade him Godspeed on the final leg of his journey. From then on, his seemingly aimless path across the void was given direction, his pathway to destiny delineated by course markers of diverse and beautiful types.

Not once in his passage did the Doctor give any of these objects more than a cursory glance. His eyes were afire, his face was dark and his concentration was reserved solely for the journey and for the confrontation which he knew lay at its end. He showed no interest in the house of bread and cakes, nor in the tree from which hung such plump, delicious golden apples. The invitation to the Mad Hatter's tea party went unanswered, as did the entreaties of the irrepressible playing cards for him to 'join their pack'. Personally, I'd have wanted at least to sit on the famed Wishing Chair, but this too was ignored.

By now, the Doctor had seen the castle – larger than life and twice as grand, its fairy-tale splendour dominating the landscape and far outshining the myriad delights over which its benign shadow fell.

'At last!' he muttered, breaking away from his robot escorts and swiftly crossing the drawbridge to the castle doors. Even here, his haste was such that he would not pause to turn his attention upwards. The breath-taking majesty of the structure remained lost upon him.

'I might have been impressed,' he said, directing his words towards nobody that he could see, 'if it had been real.' I suppose he thinks that's clever.

Finally he turned and disappeared into the stronghold, slamming the doors closed behind him. By the time the White Robots caught him up, he was standing with his arms folded in the cavernous main hall, waiting impatiently for their arrival. 'So come on then,' he said irritably. 'Where's this leader of yours?'

With deliberate slowness the two mechanoids lumbered past him, taking up positions on each side of a set of double doors. Hitherto unseen, the words 'Throne Room' were etched on a gold plaque attached to their surface.

'Of course,' remarked the Doctor. 'I should have expected such conceit.'

He gripped his umbrella with renewed force, set his face in a mask of determination and strode purposefully towards the lair of the dragon ... only to pull back in surprise as the unexpected voice of a child shrilled out from behind him.

'Grandfather!' the voice cried.

Bernice tensed as Ace appeared at the dining room door. The last thing she wanted now was another fight. Fortunately Ace seemed to share that opinion, and she was certainly a lot calmer than when Benny had seen her last.

Ace avoided her crewmate's eyes as she moved into the room and took a seat next to Rosemary. Behind her, Benny saw for the first time that Phil Chambers was hovering in the doorway.

'I met your husband on the way in,' Ace told Rosemary. The town witch nodded in acknowledgement; she had left Phil a note in their hallway to tell him where she had gone. Even so, she was surprised that he had actually bothered to come after her.

'So what's going on?' Ace added conversationally.

'We don't know yet,' said Benny, with a sigh. 'That's half the problem.'

'The Forces of Evil are at work this night,' said Rosemary, ominously. 'Of that much we are certain.'

Ace didn't react to that, not wanting either to offend or to encourage the speaker. She settled back in a chair and turned her attention back towards Benny. She spoke naturally, but Benny still couldn't help feeling that she was being accused of something. She'd half preferred Ace when she was shouting and screaming – at least then she'd known where she stood.

'So what do we have?' asked Ace. 'A mass murderer, carrying out one last killing tonight to appease some power or other hiding under the castle on the hill.'

'After which something particularly unfortunate is due

to happen,' concluded Benny. 'Or at least, so everyone seems to think – from Rosemary here through to that Matthew Shade character. He even said something about massing our forces for the battle.'

'What forces?'

'That's what I said.'

'There's Jack Corrigan, I suppose – maybe Karen, if she's feeling any better yet. You don't suppose he meant that police sergeant jerk, do you?'

Benny sighed at the hopelessness of the situation. 'We really need the Doctor here. He seemed to know a lot more about this thing than he's told any of us.'

Ace rolled her eyes.

'But what about the killer?' chimed in Phil. 'Surely if we can catch him . . .'

'The Doctor had a few ideas on that too,' said Benny. 'For a start, he said it had to be someone we'd already met.'

'How could he possibly know that?'

'If you knew the Doctor . . .' muttered Ace sourly. She got to her feet, grabbed her backpack from the table and shrugged it over her shoulders. 'Well then, there's no point sitting around here. We know who our suspects are. Let's try making a few house calls and see what comes up.'

'Mason Grimshaw first,' suggested Benny, as she donned her overcoat.

For the briefest of instants, the electric light glinted off something shiny and metallic, and Ace's eyes widened. She was across the room in seconds, reaching around her companion's side and plucking a small, sticky object from her back.

'Some sort of transmitter,' she confirmed, placing the spider-like device in the palm of her hand and holding it out for inspection. 'It was stuck to your coat. You've been bugged!'

Benny was horrified. 'Mason Grimshaw – it must be!' She remembered their meeting in the Black Cat, how Grimshaw had patted her so theatrically on the back, how he had watched her thereafter, just waiting for her to leave the pub and . . . and what?

Go to where she had hidden Norman, that had to be it! She thanked her lucky stars that he had seen fit to totally disobey her and leave the guest-house alone.

'Stupid cow!' grumbled Ace, closing her fingers and crushing the bug beyond repair.

Benny ignored the insult, already half-way to the door. 'We have to get out of here.' Rosemary and Phil got uncertainly to their feet, but Ace was standing her ground.

'What's the problem? You wanted to go and see him, didn't you? So you've saved us a journey.'

'The problem,' said Benny, icily, 'is that he's super-strong, super-powerful and damn near invincible! Now come on, we have to leave here.'

She was, of course, far too late – and she couldn't help feeling a tremendous sense of *déjà vu* as the wall of the guest-house exploded suddenly inwards.

'There's nothing here!' exclaimed Tim, with disappointment.

Gary checked his watch. 'Well, it is only a quarter to nine. Perhaps things haven't got going yet?'

'Or perhaps we've missed it all already,' suggested Michelle, unable to disguise the note of hope in her voice. She hated being in this cavern, with its robes and its knife stained so horribly with blood.

'The knife isn't there,' Tracey pointed out suddenly. 'Someone's taken it.'

They looked at each other wide-eyed, the implications of that remark sinking slowly into each of their frightened minds.

'Can you feel anything?' asked Michelle, presently. 'Like this whole place is shaking or something?'

Gary groaned. 'You're just being soft again!'

'No,' Tim disagreed. 'I think I can feel it too. It's weird, like some sort of an earthquake.'

Michelle looked uneasy. 'Do you think we'd better get out of here?'

'Of course we shouldn't,' scoffed Gary. 'We're the Adventure Kids, aren't we? So we should investigate. It's probably some sort of a digging machine or something that's causing the shaking – probably someone tunnelling through to a bank vault, or making a secret passage to the town. If we can find where they are and what they're doing, we'll have cracked this mystery wide open.'

The others seemed uncertain, but they had to bow however reluctantly to Gary's logic.

After all, it had been that way so many times before.

'Where is Power?!' Doctor Nemesis ranted, framed dramatically against the dark night sky, visible through the large entrance hole he had made in the dining room wall. 'I want to see the White Knight!'

Same old record, thought Benny, played yet again. She hoped she could talk her way out of trouble this time. Too many lives depended on it; both Rosemary and Phil were trapped behind her, unable to reach either the door or the hole without somehow getting past this fearsome intruder. Benny was glad, for the first time, that Ace had arrived when she did.

'He's just nipped out for a moment,' she answered, trying to swallow her fear. 'Do you want to wait? Cup of coffee, perhaps?'

A plasma bolt ripped into the floor beside her and she hurled herself to one side, avoiding the blast by instinct alone. 'I'll wait,' growled Nemesis, 'on my own!' Ace was on his back in an instant, fighting for her life and those of her . . . her . . . well, whatever they were, she was going to save them.

Or perhaps not. Her stranglehold round the villain's neck proved useless as she realized that, like the rest of his body, it was sheathed with thick iron – and the fierce grip of her knees in his ribs was easily loosened with one

190

shrug from this armoured powerhouse. Benny hadn't been exaggerating about his strength.

'You want to die first?' Nemesis asked, taking point-blank aim at Ace's head. She stared down the end of his blaster – not the first time she'd done that recently, she thought ruefully.

'Oh, after you, I insist,' answered Benny with mock politeness, darting in from behind and breaking one of Mrs Shawcross's chairs over their attacker's head. The blow, as it happened, was completely ineffectual, but at least Ace had time to scramble out of the way and go for the weapons in her rucksack.

'Four o'clock, three feet,' she spoke urgently into her wrist unit, and a volley of explosive flechettes shot forward and bounced harmlessly off Nemesis's chest. For a moment she thought he hadn't even noticed; his attention was focused on Bernice, who he swatted casually away with one powerful backsweep of his gauntleted hand. She slammed heavily into the far wall and her nose began to bleed. Meanwhile, Nemesis had turned back to Ace, and while she still had the chance, she pulled her blaster from its hidden holster and hurled it deftly towards her companion. This was no time for rivalry.

Benny caught the weapon gratefully, letting loose a volley of shots at Mason Grimshaw's back. They had no effect – nor did a second and a third hail of flechettes from Ace's diminishing arsenal. Nemesis sprang forward and caught Ace a glancing blow as she tried to dive past him. She rolled onto her back, from there onto her feet, and shouted to Benny breathlessly: 'I'm gonna nuke the bastard!' Benny knew what that meant.

Two globes of nitro-nine-A rolled gently into the ample space between Grimshaw's legs. Ace had had no time to check their LEDs. Default setting, five seconds – she hoped Grimshaw's armour would shield the rest of them from the blast.

With one mind, Ace and Benny flung themselves in front of Rosemary and Phil, an extra line of human protection. It was all too much for Philip at least; with a whimper he fell back against the wall and sank slowly to the floor.

Right now, the others were more concerned with the fate of Doctor Nemesis, and as their ears stopped ringing from the tremendous explosion and the smoke began slowly to clear from before their eyes, they watched with baited breath to see how badly their enemy had been injured.

'I think we ripped his cape,' Benny observed finally, her voice trembling as the powerful frame of their aggressor was revealed in all its unscratched horror. 'That's something, at least.' She thought again, and added plaintively: 'I hope he's not too angry about that.'

'Oh shit!' was Ace's only comment on the situation.

And Rosemary just reached down and took a tight grip on the trembling hand of her husband. She needed his strength.

'Help me, Tim,' wailed Michelle, 'I'm frightened!'

So was Tim – and even Gary was starting to turn pale in the darkness. The ground was vibrating ever more ferociously now, and fragments of stone were beginning to shake themselves loose from the passage walls.

'I don't think it *is* some kind of machine,' said Tracey, already hurriedly retracing her steps back to the relative familiarity of the cavern from which they had come. 'I think this whole place is going to come crashing down around our ears, and we'd better get out of here before it does!'

If the others had ever had any objections, they were suddenly stifled by the large chunk of rock which plummeted from the ceiling and embedded itself in the ground directly in their midst.

'I think you're right,' muttered Gary, and the four children hurled themselves back down the passage as if they were running for their lives.

Which they were.

Ace tackled Doctor Nemesis low, Benny hit him high. It was like throwing themselves against a concrete wall, but at least they got him to take a pace backwards and to turn his attention away from their two terrified visitors. Bernice tried Ace's blaster again for good luck, but its effect, as before, was minimal. This time, the answering bolt of energy thumped heavily into the wall behind her, and a chunk of mortar ricocheted into the back of her head. She sank to her knees with a groan, and Nemesis crossed the distance between them with surprising speed, his booted foot finishing the job with a vicious kick to the chin.

Ace's next attack came too late to save her companion. She had no thoughts of victory now, only of escape; thus, the dining room table became an all-important barrier against the advance of the armoured aggressor. If she could only push him back against the wall, just long enough for Rosemary and Phil to make it out of here . . .

Beneath the iron mask, Mason Grimshaw's face twisted into a maniacal grin. Just one flex of his muscles, that's all it took – the slightest of shrugs, its force enhanced by both natural and mechanical strength, and the table splintered, cracking into two neat pieces which fell in opposite directions and hit the ground with concordant thuds.

Ace backed up against the wall and cast her eyes about for help. Bernice was still down, the others were still cowering in the corner and wishing that none of this was happening. She went for the wrist computer again, but even as she brought it up to her mouth and tried to work out what instructions she was going to give it, her left forearm was seized by the iron hand of her enemy, and the device shattered beneath his powerful grip.

She looked up into Nemesis's eyes, and they were alight with the thrill of battle. She swung her free hand into his stomach and suffered only bruised knuckles as a result.

Then, as casually as Ace might have tossed a coin, the cloaked super-villain sent her hurtling over his shoulder, her free flight stopping only when the far wall insisted on it doing so. She hit the floor hard, and quickly lost the fight to stay conscious.

Two down, thought Nemesis, with a great deal of satisfaction. It had been far too long since he had last put his powers to use. And indeed why stop now?

'K-keep away from us,' stammered Rosemary, her voice suddenly sounding very small and insignificant, even to herself. Her right hand still gripped, and was gripped by, that of her husband. Her left, she raised to ward off this evil assailant. But no spells would come to her mind, and all she could think of was her weakness in a similar situation, just one day before.

By the time Bernice opened her eyes, Nemesis had his hand firmly round Rosemary's throat. There was no time to lose, no matter how hurt her body was and how bad her head felt. She lurched to her feet, reached out towards the man who was even now choking the life out of someone she might call a friend – and then lights flashed in front of her eyes, her head spun round and she fell against the wall, unable to move, unable to even see.

'Hold it right there, Doctor Nemesis!'

The voice was loud and bold, and it seemed to cut through the chaos, reverberating solidly around what remained of the room. Benny couldn't place it at first. When finally she did, she could hardly believe she was hearing it. Then her vision cleared, and she knew for sure that the impossible had happened.

Standing in the entrance hole which Nemesis had made, framed as he had been against the black sky without, a man stood proudly and defiantly, his pose the epitome of confidence, his costume that of a warrior; a warrior of a different, better age.

The White Knight had returned.

'Grandfather!' cried the boy again, all smiles and curly hair as he skipped into sight through one of the great hall's doors. Lagging a short way behind him was a pretty, dark-haired girl, similarly overjoyed at the Doctor's arrival.

'We thought you were gone forever!' shrieked Gillian delightedly.

'You're regenerated again,' enthused John, pulling at the Doctor's jacket with fascination as he sized up the Time Lord's unfamiliar appearance.

'I . . .'

'Never mind that,' Gillian interrupted. 'Grandfather, you've got to help us. The Kleptons are here . . .'

'. . . and the Trods!' put in John.

'This whole castle is their creation.'

'This whole planet, even!'

'They captured us and kept us here . . .'

'. . . but we got free and came looking for you . . .'

'. . . and you've got to help us, before they use their megatomic nucleonic warhead bomb to blow up the entire universe!'

'So?'

Blessed silence all of a sudden, as two pairs of expectant round eyes awaited a decision.

'So what?' asked the Doctor, blankly.

'So what are you going to do about it?' cried John, seeming desperately hurt by this casual attitude.

The Doctor thought. 'Nothing,' he decided.

'Nothing?' Gillian was scandalized. 'But you can't just do nothing. You're *Dr Who*!'

'I can assure you, I'm not.'

'You've got to help!' John entreated him. 'Don't you remember? Don't you remember us?'

'No,' answered the Doctor, curtly. 'Goodbye.' And with that, he turned smartly and entered the throne room.

For a long tense moment, the White Knight's arrival was greeted only by a stunned silence. Even the self-styled Doctor Nemesis blanched at the blatantly symbolic imagery which the figure presented, and the memories of past defeats punched a savage hole through his previously

195

unassailable confidence. He dropped Rosemary and she edged out of his way, tears in her eyes and thick red finger-marks on her neck.

'I suggest you turn yourself in, you fiend!' the Knight threatened, and his voice was strong and confident, albeit somewhat muffled by his face-concealing mask. 'You know that you can never win against me. Evil can never stand against the forces of righteousness. I'm only sorry that it took me so long to remember that myself.'

For the man himself, it was as if time was suddenly running at quarter speed. Behind the mask, Norman Power breathed deep and evenly, at one with himself for the first time in too long a time. Only he was Norman Power no longer; that weak and feeble side of his character had gone, leaving only the hero ... all-knowing, all-powerful and ready once again to rid the world of Nemesis and all his ilk.

Even Benny's heart leapt when she saw him – for relief that her predicament was over, and for joy that Norman had somehow achieved his heart's desire, the return of his White Knight identity. Then she realized that the eyes behind the mask were just Norman's, and that the only thing which had truly returned was his own self-confidence. She wanted to shout out, wanted to stop him, but for her too, time was flowing like molasses, and it was all far too late ...

Benny was right, he thought, *she was right all along. The powers were just part – part of the whole. The important thing is that my heart is strong and my spirit is willing, and with all that behind me, how can I lose?*

The White Knight may have been dead, but for the first time in almost thirty years, Norman Power was truly alive. And so he leapt courageously into action, and the sounds of long-ago battles reverberated dully through the blood which rushed madly to his head. For once, this was no simple dream. For once, no insane hallucination dredged from the memories of days long past. For once, this was real; he was back there in the thick of things, facing down his mortal enemy in one final, glorious combat.

It felt right. It felt good. And it felt like the best moment of Norman Power's life.

An hour and a half later, Norman forced open his heavily bruised eyelids and looked painfully up at the spinning green walls of the local hospital's intensive care department.

He was one of the lucky ones.

Vampire Castle, Arandale Keep; call it what you will, it wasn't going to be around for much longer. The ground was trembling ferociously now, and the few crumbling walls which had escaped the meteor strike of '59 were beginning to break apart and to topple into growing heaps of rubble and powder.

In the tunnels below, it was getting hard to breathe. The Adventure Kids were running as hard and as fast as they could, but their lungs were filling with grit and they choked and spluttered as they staggered back into the cavern where the stone altar stood.

'Come on,' Tim urged them hoarsely, brushing the dust from his hair as he stumbled across the rock-strewn ground towards the exit passage. He needn't have bothered. His companions knew full well what the consequences of hesitation would be, and they had no intentions of suffering them.

They threw themselves forwards as one – and as one they toppled as a particularly vicious jolt surged through the tunnels seemingly wrenching the whole cavern to one side and sending a hail of rock thundering to the violently heaving ground.

'I think I've broken my ankle,' gasped Michelle, straining to regain her footing in the relative calm that followed the massive quake. She received no answer, and she screamed out loud as, through the dust, she saw her brother lying deathly still beside her. Gary's body was all

197

but buried, just one arm and a bruised, blackened head protruding from beneath the rubble. A huge gash ran the length of his forehead and was pumping thick black blood onto his closed eyelids.

'Oh my God,' whispered Tim, arriving by Michelle's side in response to her outburst. 'Gary!'

'What's happened?' they heard Tracey's voice cry from somewhere in the darkness.

'He's still alive,' confirmed Tim, feeling for a pulse in his friend's neck. His heart was beating hard against his ribcage, and his dirty face was streaked with cold sweat. 'He's still alive!' In all of their adventures, there had never been any such doubts before.

'This isn't fun any more,' moaned Michelle, falling back against the rocks, her aching ankle unwilling to let her stand. She wondered if it ever had been fun.

Tim had found his torch again, and he managed to locate Tracey in its beam. She limped carefully towards them, her left arm hanging uselessly and painfully by her side. 'Gary and Michelle are both down,' the team leader reported hollowly. 'We have to get them out of here, before . . .'

The ground shuddered again.

'Before . . .'

Tim didn't have time to finish.

For one short, breathless moment, nothing stirred. The ground was still, the birds fell quiet, the tumbling walls of the castle seemed to pause in their collapse. It was as if, in just this one small area, here on the top of Blood Hill, the whole of creation was holding its breath.

What followed was one almighty explosion. The earth was rent and the wind roared in pain as the sky turned a bright, blinding red and the Forces beneath Arandale Keep broke finally free of its decades-long imprisonment.

An outburst of satanic energy surged magnificently upwards, sending a brilliant spray of colours far and wide over the trembling hills. All across the town, faces turned and breaths were caught as the startled populace witnessed the terrifying beauty of a pyrotechnic display their fireworks could never hope to match. In the wake of that tremendous discharge, Vampire Castle, its immediate environs and most especially the tunnels beneath it were all completely, utterly and totally obliterated.

And after that, there was silence once again.

Chapter 12

Meeting the Maker

For the first time since leaving Arandale, the Doctor smiled. 'Just what I expected,' he commented, his eyes sparkling as they flitted around the room.

'Really, Doctor?' returned the other, his voice heavy with sarcasm. 'How extraordinarily intelligent of you.'

'Well, you were a little obvious,' the Doctor admonished him. 'The Scrabble game, for a start – and before that, the totally correct reading on the tarot cards. A little too coincidental to be real, I think. Oh, and if you were trying to trick me, then using twentieth-century England was not a good idea. Or did you think I wouldn't realize that the town of Arandale doesn't exist?'

This string of revelations provoked nothing more than a contemptuous sneer on the face of his opponent. So the Doctor continued: 'Of course, it was the TARDIS itself which gave me the biggest clue. You might have been able to fool the navigation instruments – and that was a very nice trick by the way, I'd very much like to know how it was done – but the chameleon circuit worked precisely as intended.' The Doctor's words were not just idle chatter. Throughout the time he was talking, his eyes were roving quickly and curiously around his surroundings, his mind storing any piece of information which may prove useful to him.

To his right, the whole of one wall was occupied by a computer bank, lights flashing, needles flickering and spools rotating as it quietly hummed and clicked its way through a multitude of complex operations. On the left, a row of monitor screens had gone suddenly blank upon the Doctor's arrival, although not quite fast enough to prevent his sharp eyes from detecting their purpose. This was one way in which the events occurring in Arandale – and indeed, throughout the Land of Fiction – were relayed back to their orchestrator. One of the screens had even shown the two White Robots waiting motionlessly outside this very chamber, although unfortunately the Doctor had been unable in the half-second available to him to ascertain the whereabouts and situations of his two companions.

At the far end of the room, an unremarkable door led to 'Places Unknown' – a fact confirmed by a simple white placard which hung from the wooden doorknob. Directly in front of that, and directly ahead of the Doctor, a wide strip of plush red carpet led to the throne itself, a magnificent object fashioned of what appeared to be pure gold, padded with the finest of velvet cushions and draped with silken robes of a very regal purple.

His ripped jeans and black 'Kiss' T-shirt incongruous against such glory, the youth lolled comfortably in his seat, his head rolling unsteadily against his left shoulder as his wild blue eyes regarded the visitor with excited anticipation from beneath a shock of bleached blond hair. He grinned lopsidedly and the grin turned into a laugh, high and penetrating. It was only then that the Doctor turned his attention fully upon his captor.

'Anyway, you must be the new Master of the Land of Fiction.' His distaste was obvious. 'I can't say it's an improvement.' He weighed his opponent with his eyes, wondering how much power resided in this unlikely form. With little surprise, he noticed that a thin black cable snaked across the back of the throne and into the base of the boy's skull, no doubt a direct link between his brain – and more importantly, his youthful imagination – and the busy circuits of the master computer.

'Say what you like, Doctor,' taunted the boy. 'None of it matters. I am the Writer here. You are nothing more than a character in my story. As long as I'm happy with you, then nothing else is important.'

The Doctor raised an inquisitive eyebrow. 'And are you?'

That laugh again. 'Happy? But of course I am. You wouldn't have been invited back here otherwise!'

'I'll bear that in mind in future.'

'Mind you, Doctor,' the youth continued, waving a stern finger, 'I have to pull you up on one or two points, I'm afraid. Your sense of humour, for a start. I mean, that other persona of yours was such a light-hearted fellow, always good for a laugh and a joke. I've watched your first adventure here hundreds of times, and I never tire of his clowning and his witticisms. I was so looking forward to having him back here, to using him in one of *my* stories, but all I got was you, with your moods and your tantrums and your oh-so-precious secrets. You're no fun any more, Doctor.'

'I play the game differently now,' said the Doctor solemnly, 'but one thing hasn't changed. I still play to win.'

'Then you're in for a shock, I'm afraid.'

'I really don't think so.'

'No one escapes from the Land of Fiction, Doctor. Not you, not anyone else. You might as well accept that now.'

The Doctor's eyes hardened. 'You've brought people here before?'

'Well of course,' answered the boy. 'As many as I possibly can. They stray into the wrong sector of space, and *zap*!' He punched his right fist into his open left palm to illustrate his point. 'They're mine. You see, it gets very boring controlling *all* the characters in a story. You always know what's going to happen next.'

The boy could tell that the Doctor hadn't expected that. He smiled, relishing his opponent's impotent fury. 'And I know that a bit of reality is appreciated by my audience,' he continued, his voice taking on a mocking tone. 'Of course, by the time their first story's over, my guests are turned into fiction themselves. That means I have to write

202

their actions for them, which is a bit of a bind – but I still think their presence adds something to my story-lines.'

'Just how many of your so-called characters are real people?' the Doctor spat, making no attempt to conceal his disdain for his opponent.

'Oh, one or two – three or four maybe – perhaps a dozen . . .' The boy wriggled in his seat, momentarily discomforted by the Doctor's penetrating stare. 'Could be as many as, ooh, about . . .' He plucked a figure from the air. 'Three thousand?'

'What?'

'I just don't know, it's so hard to remember the details. A lot of them were real once, I do know that – you've probably met some of them yourself – but others, I made up all on my own.' The twisted grin returned to his face as his head slipped back onto the throne, eyes staring blankly upwards and swimming with the unfamiliar but pleasant sensation of recollection. 'Norman was real, I remember that. Oh yes, my poor little Norman. He was in command of a passenger ship which went off course and came a little too close for its own good. That was one of my first ones, I think. I remember I had a bit of trouble bringing it down, killed almost everyone in the crash-landing. The White Robots had a terrible job cleaning it all up afterwards.'

The Doctor said nothing, but his eyes smouldered with contempt.

'But in the end, I got Norman out of it. Dear old Norman Power. I remember thinking what a ridiculous macho name he had, so I made him into a super-hero. It just seemed appropriate. He was very popular too, was my White Knight – and I got a big kick out of creating the super-villains he used to fight. Timewinder, Dragonella, the Purple Nasty, Silver Fist . . . come to think of it, that last one was real too; a Cyberman that got trapped here. I just gave him a domino mask and a cape and let him get on with it. Oh, and then there was Doctor Nemesis, of course. He was always my favourite, and the boss

203

seemed to like him as well. That's why I brought him back for one last battle.'

'And who else?'

'Alan Brown, I think.'

'The man you've just had killed!'

'So I did. Still, no great loss – he was hardly an interesting character. Too nice for his own good.'

'And what about you? Just where did you come from?'

The Writer's eyes hardened, not quite enough to match the Doctor's own. 'That is irrelevant,' he said finally, a sharp edge to his voice.

The Doctor smiled, and worked further on the nerve he had so obviously hit. 'Late twentieth-century Earth, judging by the influences. Possibly the very month you've set your story in. Certainly long before Man could fly this far out from his own planet. Someone must have worked very hard to get you here. The same person, I imagine, who rebuilt the Land of Fiction in the first place.'

'I said that is irrelevant!'

'Anything which threatens life is relevant to me!' spat the Doctor fiercely.

There was silence for a moment. Then suddenly, incredibly, the boy threw back his head and laughed out loud. 'Oh Doctor,' he said between chuckles, 'you are capable of a few jokes after all! I don't kill people, you know. I just turn them into fiction. Their lives are better this way!'

'I fail to see how,' the Doctor said pointedly, the furnace of his anger only stoked by the boy's carefree attitude.

'I've rescued them,' said the Writer. 'Rescued them from their normal, boring, humdrum lives. I've given them all the adventure and the excitement they could ever hope to have. Why, I've even given them immortality – I can't imagine a better deal than that.'

'Hollow words,' spat the Time Lord.

'But Doctor,' the boy said, 'fictional characters *are* immortal. The goblins never killed Bilbo Baggins, did they? Kirk always remained standing as his supporting

204

cast dropped around him. Enid Blyton's kids never found a poisonous cloud at the top of the Magic Far-Away Tree.'

'Yes, yes, yes, and they never age either.' The Doctor waved a hand dismissively as he completed his opponent's case for him. 'Else Dan Dare would be on his death bed, Spider-Man would be picking up his pension, et cetera, et cetera.'

'That's right,' cried the boy joyfully, the Doctor's mocking tone lost upon him. 'So you *do* see! You *do* understand!'

'I understand that your murdered Alan Brown! "Hardly an interesting character", I believe you said.'

'Some sacrifices must be made,' the Writer admitted, 'in the name of entertainment.'

'You could just let your characters leave,' suggested the Doctor.

'I could hardly do that, I'm afraid. Fictional characters cannot exist outside the Land, and the process which turns them into fiction is irreversible. Their real bodies die, and are disposed of by my maintenance squad, my beautiful White Robots.'

'Along with yourself and your control centre, the only real things in the Land of Fiction,' muttered the Doctor. His opponent nodded in confirmation.

'Except, that is, for myself and my companions.'

'For now, yes,' admitted the Writer, guardedly.

The Doctor moved closer, fixing the boy with a cold, piercing stare. The Writer could almost feel the Time Lord's eyes in his mind, straining to read his innermost secrets.

'So how does it happen?' he asked, in a low, threatening growl. 'Tell me how you expect to turn me into fiction – how you expect to trap me here.'

The boy tore his gaze away, looking fixedly downwards to avoid the Doctor's glare. 'The knowledge would do you no good,' he contended.

'Tell me!'

'There is no escape!' He was starting to shout now, frustrated by his foe's air of insufferable arrogance.

'So you say,' countered the Doctor, his voice even but fierce, 'but I'm taking my companions, and one way or another I'm leaving this place, whether you like it or not.'

Frustration gave way suddenly to anger. The boy's head snapped back up and he returned the Doctor's stare with a fury which more than matched the Time Lord's own. His voice was taut and barely controlled, and his body shook with rage as he spoke. 'Don't even think about that, Doctor! Don't think that you can ever leave here!'

For almost a full minute the two remained unmoving, each glaring into the depths of the other's eyes. It was the Doctor who gave way first, realizing that there was nothing more to be gained from this avenue of exploration. He recovered his composure with remarkable speed.

'There's just one thing you've overlooked,' he remarked, pushing his hands nonchalantly into his pockets and ambling back to the far side of the room to lean casually against the entrance doors. 'One mistake that you've made.'

The Writer's eyes narrowed and the Doctor could almost hear his brain whirring as it scanned worriedly down a check-list of possibilities. Finally he took the bait. 'And what is that, pray tell?' he asked, with exaggerated sweetness.

'You've allowed me to find your control centre, invited the enemy into your camp. From here, I can fight and defeat you a lot more easily than I ever could in your imaginary little town.'

'I doubt that, Doctor.' A cautious tone, this time.

The Doctor looked around him again with an air of casual interest. 'Of course, it might be easier just to destroy the lot.'

A smirk at that. 'Try it.'

'Maybe I will.' He beamed at the Writer disarmingly as he sauntered over to the computer. Not once did he actually turn to look at it. He trusted instead to touch as his right hand left his pocket and felt around behind him, finding a grip and yanking hard. To the surprise of no one present, a whole section of the apparatus simply swung outwards like a door. And inside ... nothing. Just an empty space where should have been an intricate tangle of circuit boards and wires. 'But I won't be starting here,' the Doctor concluded, and much to the annoyance of the other, his smile and his arrogance remained. He hadn't even looked! He had known beyond question what his actions would reveal. But how could that be?

The pretence over, the Writer slowly rose, the cable falling from his head and clattering against the back of the throne. He seemed somewhat unsteady on his feet, the Doctor noted, as if he were unused to using them. His thin arms hung limply by his scrawny body and his head retained its peculiar tilt, still tending towards his left side. 'So what now, Doctor?' he asked.

The Doctor looked around him, contemplating his options as a tourist might consider where to dine. 'Well,' he said cheerfully, 'now that you're up and about, I think it would be very gracious of you to escort me through ... *here*!'

And before the Writer could stop him, he had somehow reached the inner door.

'Places Unknown ...' quoted the Doctor, with some amusement. 'The Forest of Words, as I recall.'

'For the moment, yes.' The Writer had caught up to him now, and he viewed his restless captive with an affected air of cool detachment.

'A bit stale, isn't it?' The Doctor remembered this place from his previous visit to the Land of Fiction. Indeed, it had been the first part of it he had seen besides the featureless void itself.

'A creation of my predecessor,' the boy admitted, 'but nevertheless an apt setting for the rest of our scene together.'

The Doctor strolled up to the nearest 'tree', prodded it gently with his umbrella and gazed up into its branches with interest. It was shaped like the letter S.

'And different in some ways too, no doubt,' he mused. 'If I remember rightly, the trees spell out messages. Proverbs, mostly.' He gave the Writer a sharp look. 'Save me a climb. What do your letters spell?'

'That depends on how I feel when you reach the top.'

'Of course.'

'Remember, I am the Writer here. Nothing happens but that I will it, and whatever I will occurs immediately. Nothing is truly real here Doctor, and there is nothing I cannot control. You would do well to keep that in mind.'

'Maybe,' the Doctor consented, pinching his lower lip in thought. 'Still . . .' He paced distractedly in a tight circle before picking a seemingly random direction and heading off in it. His way was suddenly blocked.

'Grandfather!' Gillian greeted him, as she and her brother hopped out from behind a nearby letter J.

'I knew you'd find us again,' said John. 'And with our friend the Writer, too!'

'And all that stuff before,' put in Gillian, 'when you pretended not to recognize us – that was all part of your plan, wasn't it?'

The Doctor ignored them, turning instead to their creator. 'Ah yes,' he said mildly, 'I meant to ask you about these two. Friends of yours?'

'Friends of yours, actually – but creations of mine, yes.'

'So I believe. My grandchildren, apparently.'

'Oh yes,' boasted the Master of the Land, 'and this, Doctor, is why you can never defeat me. You see, this confrontation has been rehearsed a thousand times, from the moment I took control of this wonderful place.'

'How so?'

The Writer beamed at his own genius. 'I simply whipped up a fictional version of you – as you were when last you visited us, of course. I added a few of those companions you seem so inexplicably fond of, and hey presto, a whole

208

new series of adventures! A new source of entertainment for my audience, and wonderful practice for me, too. I think you'll agree that I've put it to good use.'

The Doctor sniffed loftily. 'I doubt if you've learnt a thing. For a start, you've got the formula all wrong. No corridors, no monsters and I haven't been imprisoned once!'

The Writer ignored that comment. 'I put together some stories with your other personae too,' he continued, 'once the boss man showed me his videos of those. I even used some of your real companions, just the ones I liked.'

'It sounds like you don't need me at all.'

The Writer smiled at that. Then he clicked his fingers twice, and John and Gillian vanished back into the nothingness from which they had sprung. 'The fictional replicas may have been entertaining, but I always prefer the real McCoy.'

The Doctor nodded. 'I'm rather partial to reality myself,' he agreed, 'which is why I'd like to see just what it is that my "grandchildren" were meant to keep me away from.' He pivoted on his heel, darting quickly through the trees towards a sound he had detected upon entering the forest. 'And here it is!' he shouted back triumphantly, as he came to rest by the rather incongruous sight of a chattering computer printer.

'Get away from there!' snapped the Writer, only now recovering his wits enough to pursue his opponent.

'An interesting little contraption,' the Doctor commented, noting with approval the reams of continuous paper which had piled up, concertina-fashion, beneath the device. 'And a real one too, I fancy. So what sort of things does it print, I wonder?'

He leant casually forward and scanned the latest line to be written, showing little surprise at what he read:

HE LEANT CASUALLY FORWARD AND SCANNED THE LATEST LINE TO BE WRITTEN, SHOWING LITTLE SURPRISE AT WHAT

HE READ: HE LEANT CASUALLY FORWARD
AND SCANNED THE LATEST LINE TO BE
WRITTEN, SHOWING LITTLE SURPRISE AT
WHAT HE READ: HE LEANT CASUALLY
FORWARD AND SCANNED THE LATEST
LINE TO BE WRITTEN, SHOWING LITTLE
SURPRISE AT WHAT HE READ: HE LEANT
CASUALLY FORWARD AND SCANNE

'Stop that!' The Writer grabbed him by the shoulder, pulling him away from the device. 'Just leave it alone, you interfering fool!'

The Doctor laughed infuriatingly. 'Spoiling your syntax, am I?'

'If I were you, Doctor,' the boy threatened, 'I would choose my words a little more carefully. I'm sure you realize by now that, if I willed it, I could dispose of you in any number of interesting ways.'

'So why don't you?' asked the Doctor, innocently. Even as he spoke, an ominous rumble of thunder sounded from above.

'Don't push me, Time Lord!' hissed the Writer. 'Do – not – push – me!'

The Doctor cast his eyes casually upwards at the gathering storm-clouds, allowing a long silence to elapse before speaking again.

'You must miss your home,' he said finally.

This comment was not, in all honesty, quite what the Master of the Land had been expecting.

'Earth, I mean,' the Doctor pressed the point. 'How long have you been here now? Months? Years? Centuries?'

'That is irrelevant!'

'Yes, I rather thought it might be. But you do miss your home, don't you? I mean, look at your creations; private eyes, murder mysteries, super-heroes, witches – all staples of twentieth-century Earth fiction.'

The Writer was on the defensive now. 'I prefer to work

with the things I know,' he admitted grudgingly, 'and why ever not, I ask you? After all, I have access to so many wonderful stories! I doubt you could appreciate it Doctor, but from here, I can decide how Dennis the Menace dies, how the Discoworld series ends – even what happens to Spike and Lynda!' His body inflated with pride as he began to warm to his theme. 'I can reach back to the earliest days of story-telling, the folk tales and myths, through to radio and films and television dramas. I can reconstruct the missing Christmas episode of 'Professor X', relive the '76 invasion and the dramatization of Danny Pain's 'Fight Against the Aliens'. Here, Doctor, in this place, in this beautiful Land of Fiction, I can do just *exactly whatever I damn well like!*'

The Writer's eyes gleamed fanatically now, as if challenging his opponent to dispute his assertions. The challenge wasn't taken. Instead, the Doctor just agreed.

'Yes. With power like yours,' he said quietly, 'you can do anything.'

The Writer's heart swelled with the words. 'Anything!'

'Anything!' Pause. 'Well, apart from *leave here*, of course.'

This time the thunder sounded closer, and it was accompanied by a vicious fork of lightning. Another nerve, thought the Doctor. The best one. But his only external reaction was an insufferably cheerful grin and a few pleasant words to his opponent, as he hurriedly unfurled his umbrella and opened it out above him.

'It looks like rain,' he said. 'Why don't we finish this inside?'

'So,' said the Doctor, as they re-entered the throne room, 'what do you expect me to do now?'

The Writer returned to his majestic seat, allowing his spindly frame to settle comfortably back against its cushion before he answered. 'I just want you to finish the story, Doctor. Provide me with a little amusement.'

'And how do I do that?'

'You return to Arandale,' said the boy, seeming almost weary of the game now. 'You unravel the mystery and you tell your friends and my characters which of them is the murderer.'

The Doctor thought about that. 'Colonel Mustard,' he said finally. 'In the kitchen. With the lead piping.'

'I'm being serious, Doctor.'

'So am I. I won't do it.'

The boy shrugged. 'It doesn't matter,' he said. 'Things are coming to a head in any case. We're into the last four chapters already. You can either solve the conundrum and end the story triumphant, or you can ignore it and end the story dead. Either way, the story will end, and the book will close on you and your companions, trapping you within its pages for evermore. That, Doctor, is when I win the game – and when you become nothing more than a character in my portfolio, to do with as I wish.'

The Doctor looked faintly amused. ' "End the story dead"? And just a few minutes ago you were extolling the virtues of immortality. You disappoint me.'

'Oh don't you worry about that, Doctor.' The Writer laughed again. 'Fiction is such a wonderful thing, you see – there are myriad ways of bringing good characters back from the grave, if needs be. Resurrection, time travel, an unexpected and hitherto unrevealed last-second save . . . you could even become a ghost, haunting the site of your demise for all eternity. I might enjoy casting you in that role. Alternatively, we need look no further than your own regenerative powers: a convenient *deus ex machina* if ever there was one. So no, Doctor, don't think that I won't simply kill you if I have to – for once you have been turned into fiction, it really will not matter to me one way or another.'

'So what happens then,' asked the Doctor with mock politeness, 'if I refuse to return to Arandale at all?'

'The same thing applies. Only I'd really rather you did, if only because I don't want my carefully plotted storyline

212

to be wasted. And I'm sure, Doctor, that I can persuade you.'

The Doctor raised his eyebrows inquisitively.

'After all, everything that happens in Arandale is controlled by me. With just a few little words – one tiny sentence in the ongoing narrative – I can cause a devastating earthquake to demolish the town and kill your lovely companions stone cold dead!'

'Which, you've just told me, will make no difference in the long run anyway.'

'Unless . . .'

'Unless you offer me a way of setting both of them free.'

The boy fell silent.

'That is what comes next, isn't it? I've been waiting a long time for you to come to the point.'

The Writer shifted nervously in the uncomfortable silence that followed.

'You want me to replace you,' the Doctor prompted him, finally.

Their eyes met then, and in those of his opponent, the Doctor could see nothing but pain and loneliness, and the longing for a simple life left far, far behind. His face was suddenly serious, the air of confidence replaced by deep lines of worry, and when he spoke it was with the voice of one a hundred years older.

'Will you do it?' he asked weakly.

'No.'

The boy's jaw dropped and his body collapsed, as if physically struck by the force of the Doctor's rebuff. 'But it's all arranged!' he protested, feebly. 'This is my last story, it has to be! I've tied up all my storylines, used up all my characters. I've no more ideas left!'

The Doctor shrugged. 'That isn't my problem.'

Then suddenly the Writer was upon him. His bony hands gripped the lapels of the Time Lord's jacket, his watery eyes stared pleadingly up into his face. 'You've got to do it, please say you will! It's the only way out for both of us!'

The Doctor seized his arms, removing the offending grip with ease. There was little strength in the boy's hands. 'So let's get this straight, shall we? Before I am, as you so quaintly put it, "turned into fiction", I'm to be offered an alternative. I will be kept alive and installed as the new Master of the Land. As such, I will be imprisoned here, creating my own characters and supplementing them with those, both real and imaginary, that I can draw from elsewhere. I will tell stories for the enjoyment of whoever is out there reading what your printer next door spews out, and will presumably suffer that person's terrible retribution if my attempts fail to entertain. Is that right?'

He could see by the look in the other's eyes that it was. 'But not forever,' he pleaded, and the tears in his eyes were beginning to spill out onto his face. 'Just until you can find someone else – someone with flair and imagination, who will be good enough to take over the Land from you. Then you'll be able to go, I promise!'

The Doctor released his grip and the boy staggered backwards, collapsing exhaustedly back into his seat. 'And I'm "good enough", I take it?'

'More than that.' The words came in breathless gasps. 'You'd be ideal – that's the whole point! You're the whole reason this place exists!'

'I should be flattered, but I'm not.'

'I'm ready to go, Doctor. You've got to let me do that. *Please* let me do that!'

The Time Lord didn't answer, and his face betrayed no emotion. For a long moment the only sound in the room was the fevered breathing of the Master of the Land, becoming gradually slower and calmer as he regained his composure. Then he spoke again, and the Doctor could see that he was back in control.

'So that is your choice,' he said. 'If you become the new Master of the Land, then your first act can be to allow your companions safe passage out of here. If not, then

214

both you and they will become fiction, to be used as I please. And I am unlikely to treat you with any great mercy.'

'Then I've no choice,' said the Doctor.

'No choice at all,' agreed the Writer, and hope shone in his eyes.

'I'll have to escape.'

'Impossible!'

'I doubt it.' The Doctor smiled, turned and clicked his fingers coolly in the direction of the monitors. As one they burst into life, their images of the fiction that was Arandale restored in all their technicolour glory.

'Off!' yelled the boy, directing his cry at the disobedient screens. '*Off*!' They flickered and died, and with a further nod of the youth's head, a steel shutter (one which, the Doctor suspected, had not hitherto existed at all) slid smartly across the wall in front of them, locking the knowledge they held firmly away from prying eyes.

'You see, Doctor?' the Writer gloated. 'You cannot defeat me on my home ground!'

'Just testing,' the Doctor said lightly.

'Don't ever forget that I am in charge here!'

'I won't.'

'I am the Writer of the Words, the Master of the Land, the Controller of all Fiction – and here, Doctor, everything *is* fiction.'

'There's no need to go on about it.'

'There is only room for one Writer here, Doctor. You'll jut have to wait your turn I'm afraid.' He laughed, briefly. 'And before you try anything else like that, I think there's something you should know.'

'Which is?'

'Oh, just that you're not where you think you are.' The boy's lopsided grin returned, and his eyes sparkled anew with the light of insanity as his tongue hung limply from his mouth and dribbled phlegm onto his black shirt. 'You see, Doctor, none of this is real.'

No reaction.

'Oh, it all exists somewhere, all right – most of it, at least. But what you've been standing in for the last half hour is nothing more than a fictional simulacrum. A prose description of the real thing.'

Although he tried not to show it, the Doctor's hearts sank as the room began to fade away around him, its existence supplanted by the whiteness of the void beyond.

'I want you to know, Doctor,' said the Master of the Land of Fiction, his voice now seeming to come from everywhere as his unreal body vanished along with its surroundings, 'that I'm not very pleased with you. Not very pleased at all. In order to deal with your interference, I've had to write myself into my own story – and I hate doing that.' The room was gone now, as was the castle; as were the intriguing items which had led the Doctor towards it. All that was left was the void and, almost invisible against it, the two White Robots, still standing sentry-like on the spot where the doors to the throne room had once been. He had even been wrong about the printer, the Doctor realized. Fiction, like everything else. All just a lure, an obvious trap that he had walked right into like some sort of idiot. He turned, scanning the landscape for anything which could help determine his next move.

'Of course,' the voice – *my* voice – continued to mock him, 'I needn't bother telling you any of that. You'll be able to experience it all for yourself, and sooner than you might think. Go back to Arandale, Doctor. Go back and finish your story. Then come to me with your decision. Only make sure that this time, it's the right one!'

The Doctor completed a three hundred and sixty degree turn, and found himself looking down a wide yellow pathway which stretched onwards for as far as the eye could see.

FOLLOW THE YELLOW BRICK ROAD said the rickety wooden sign at the pathway's start, and as he did, the Time Lord could hear the shrill and penetrating laugh of his captor, echoing malevolently into the emptiness.

Chapter 13

Tea and Symmetry

It had been just like the old days.

The villain had been before him, his expression of fear visible even through his thick metal mask. The White Knight had smiled and leapt into battle, cool and collected, his punches powerful and well-placed. Doctor Nemesis staggered, dropped to his knees and called out for mercy (and flash-bulbs exploded inside Norman Power's head, and why was that when he was doing so well?)

'You showed no mercy to your victims!' The Knight was on form now, and he knew that his arch-enemy could not be allowed to escape. He gripped Nemesis by the throat, glancing casually over his shoulder and calling upon the admiring crowd of onlookers to contact the police (but why was his stomach aching so, and making him feel sick?) as he growled to his foe that their lifelong battle was finally over (so why did his jaw hurt and his mouth taste the blood that rolled in thick rivulets down his face .. ?)

'He was hammered!' explained Ace unhappily. 'Norman Power got back into that stupid White Knight costume, took on his most powerful foe ever and got his head smashed in for his troubles!'

The police constable looked at her strangely. 'So you're saying that this damage was caused by some kind of, erm, super-hero battle then, miss?'

A look of annoyance flashed across Ace's face. 'You don't believe me, do you?' Then she glanced around the room, and her features softened. 'No, I don't suppose I can blame you.' She could scarcely believe it herself but the evidence was there, the jagged hole still looming large in the guest-house wall from where the self-styled Doctor Nemesis had smashed his way in. And that wasn't all.

Above and behind her, the lightbulb fizzed alarmingly, dripping a blob of congealed liquid onto the fire-blackened carpet. Ace saw the scorch marks on the walls, the melted and burnt remains of Mrs Shawcross's dining chairs, and she smelt fire and ozone on the air, recoiling from the dominant stench of badly burnt flesh.

Yet no one seemed to be hurt.

Well, except for Norman that was – the erstwhile hero, the fight knocked well and truly out of him by a beating that might yet prove to have been fatal. And then there was Nemesis, his attacker – and for him, 'hurt' was an understatement. Ace had been trying to avoid thinking about that, hoping maybe that she'd imagined what had happened in that terrible last flash-frame before the blackout; before the tremendous burst of energy which had slammed her helpless body back into the dining-room wall. She had seen death before, many times – but not often quite like this.

Of Mason Grimshaw there was less remaining than of the furniture. Just a scattering of ash in a vaguely human shape, its lines blurring in the wind which whipped through his own self-made entrance hole.

So this then was the aftermath: Norman stretchered off to hospital, an anxious Benny by his side; Rosemary and Phil huddled, frightened and miserable, together in the corner; Doctor Nemesis not just dead but practically atomized; and good old Ace, the only person left on her feet, stuck with explaining the whole damn mess to the police.

Something sparked on her wrist, and she realized that only the insulation of her combat suit had blocked a nasty shock from her shattered wrist computer. The bulb dripped something hot down onto her face. She tasted it,

218

and with a shudder of disgust knew it had to be Mason Grimshaw's melted body fat.

Outside, it was starting to rain.

'Oh, swell!' groaned Jack Corrigan as he dropped his bulging suitcase onto the pavement next to his wheel-clamped car. It burst open on impact, scattering his clothes into the road and only adding to his misery. After all he had been through! It had taken half a dozen phone calls to persuade the car rental company to agree to pay for repairs rather than attempting to send their own contractor up from Birmingham, and another half dozen to find someone that was willing to come out and do the work right away. And now the Arandale police – they who had kept him here this last day, giving him the run-around, ignoring his questions, fouling up his whole dumb case – now they had clamped his blasted wheels, like that wasn't the worst way to stop him from actually moving this clapped-out wreck!

He cursed under his breath as he stuffed his luggage haphazardly back into its case, and between expletives he speculated about what the town's train service was like, and whether it was yet operating normally after the severe weather conditions of the last few days. Specifically he wondered if he could get to the airport and out of this crummy wet country before the hire company caught up to him.

It was worth a try.

Matthew Shade awoke, lying face down in a dirty puddle in a back alley beside the pancake house. He struggled to his feet, clutched at his head and remembered with a wince the tremendous ball of pain which had coagulated inside his brain and exploded suddenly outwards.

The castle, he realized with a start. Vampire Castle, Arandale Keep . . . it was gone! And the Force had left with it; bursting out of captivity, streaking high across

Arandale, causing the tremendous psychic backlash which had knocked him insensate.

If only he had acted quicker!

But it was too late for that now. It was too late for anything. He could still sense the energy, inside the town now, easing into its new form, consolidating its control over the human whose actions it had directed for nigh on thirty-four years.

Matthew Shade wasn't used to defeat, but he knew that to stand the slightest chance of winning this time, he would need to find help.

And there was only one person who could provide that.

Police Sergeant Malcolm Blyth pushed himself uncomfortably out of his car, weary eyes watching the rain fall onto a mess of broken furniture and dislodged bricks. He was not, at this moment, one very happy man – called up out of bed again, out into the frozen night; more death, more destruction, more mysteries. At least this would be the last time – word had come through that, despite the still miserable weather in Arandale, the roads outside were now passable. A team of fully trained detectives would be trampling over the town by morning, and after that – well, for Blyth, that was it. He was too old for all this. He'd decided on early retirement, just as soon as he could arrange it. If he could just get through tonight . . .

His train of thought was derailed, his eyes widening in fury as he spotted a familiar figure picking her way through the debris. He folded his arms and fixed the bedraggled Ace with his sternest stare. 'Now why am I not surprised to find you here?'

'Don't try blaming me for all this!' she shot back, hotly.

'You and your friends do seem to have a knack of . . .'

'. . . being in the wrong place at the wrong time. Tell me about it!'

'So what happened this time?'

'You wouldn't believe me if I told you.'

'You're probably right. Just don't leave this house until

I've interviewed you properly.' Blyth turned to the constable who had questioned Ace before, and the pair moved off to one side so that she could no longer hear what was being said. She gathered though that it concerned Rosemary and Phil. The two men kept glancing towards them, and their expressions did not bode well for the couple.

They had barely moved in over an hour now; hunched in the corner, Rosemary's face pale and her eyes staring wide without sight, Phil crying on her shoulder and sounding like his world had just ended. They failed to register Blyth's arrival by their side, and a lump came to his throat as he tried to speak.

This too was a part of the job he wouldn't miss; being forever the bearer of bad tidings.

In this case, news of their children.

A streak of lightning cracked the sky wide, and the rain lashed down with renewed fervour.

The Doctor arrived back in Arandale without ever having felt that he was approaching it. The sky was pitch black now but for the intermittent flashes of lightning, and the village had fallen silent as the pounding rain effectively ended the Bonfire Night festivities. The only rumbling now came from the sky, and the only other sound was that of the town clock, its bell striking one hollow note across the beleaguered settlement.

Half past eleven.

The end was approaching.

His expression dark, the Doctor quickly unfurled his umbrella. Then, with teeth gritted, fists clenched and a renewed sense of purpose, he set off to gather his pieces for the final phase of the game.

'What happened?' he asked Ace as he stepped into the chaotic scene of the guest-house dining-room.

Ace sighed and leaned heavily against one of the remaining stretches of wall. This was no time to be antagonistic. 'The ashes on the floor, they're what's left of Mason Grimshaw, alias Doctor Nemesis, a super-villain from America. I know, just don't ask! He beat the rest of us and starting knocking the crap out of Norman Power – he's at the hospital with Benny now. Grimshaw would have killed him, only . . . well to be honest, I'm not sure what happened. I think it was the witch.'

'Rosemary Chambers?'

Ace shrugged, confused. 'It looked like it, but then it was all over in a flash anyway. She shouted something at Grimshaw, waved her hands about a bit and let loose with some sort of – some sort of bolt of power.' She thought about that for a moment. 'Looks like she really can do magic, after all.'

'No,' said the Doctor, shaking his head and thinking hard. 'No, she can't. Not unless there's been some sort of continuity error.'

Ace frowned. 'Mel Joseph said something like that. Are you going to tell me about it, or what?'

The Doctor parried the question with one of his own. 'Can you get away from here?'

'As long as Blyth doesn't see me.' She gestured over to the stout police sergeant, who was busy trying to comfort the distraught Chambers couple. Rosemary still hadn't moved, Ace noted – just sitting there staring, always straight ahead, like she had shut the rest of the world out of her life. Her husband was all wails and moans and floods of tears, and she wondered if he could ever truly recover from the events of this terrible day.

'Good,' said the Doctor, seemingly impervious to the devastation around him. 'We've work to do.'

They left quickly and quietly, and by the time anyone noticed their absence, it was far too late to care.

There was nothing more Bernice could do for Norman. She left him resting, her mind whirling as she miserably trod the stark corridors of the hospital. She should be getting back to Ace and the others, she thought – but first, there was one more thing to attend to.

Much to her surprise, Karen Davies was up and around, standing fully clothed by the bed and greeting her visitor with that disarmingly bright grin of hers. 'You're just in time,' she chirped. 'I'm all ready to go.'

Benny liked Karen, but she was suspicious none the less. 'You've made a quick recovery,' she commented.

'That's what the doctors said,' Karen answered, unabashed. 'They think I wasn't really hurt at all, just drained of energy. Left alone for a while, my body was able to regenerate itself back to full health.'

'And your memory?'

Karen's face fell. 'Not yet, I'm afraid. I can remember where I was, I remember walking down the street – I even remember a man stepping out in front of me, someone I knew. I spoke to him, said something about being glad it was him and not the murderer. He'd given me quite a fright.' She shuddered. 'But other than that, it's all blank. No matter how I try, I can't bring his face into focus.'

'That's very unfortunate,' came a voice from the door. It was the Doctor, and his expression was grim. 'Also very predictable.' He turned his attention to Bernice. 'Things are starting to happen. We need to move. Ace is outside.'

Benny nodded and joined him at the door. 'What about me?' Karen called after him.

'Do what you like,' said the Doctor, dismissively. 'I'm sure you will anyway.'

'So where are we heading?' the young black girl asked as she hurried out into the corridor behind them.

'Out of this world,' said the Doctor.

Norman shouldn't have been able to stand. He somehow managed it anyway, invigorated by the Force which crackled through the town, around the room, into his body. Elsewhere in the hospital an alarm bell sounded as he wrenched himself free from the equipment which maintained his life. Understaffed as they were, it took the nurses almost two minutes to respond to the alert. One minute too long.

The Force was out there, all around. Norman breathed deep of its sweet electricity as he teetered drunkenly towards the open window, beckoned forth by the energy without. He could feel it calling to him, rushing into him, filling him with the powers he had always known to be his birthright. Suddenly he could fly again. He knew that with an absolute certainty, just as he knew that it was time for the White Knight to return – this time, for real. This time, for good.

He smiled then, and the smile turned into a laugh, rich and heartfelt. It was the first time Norman Power had laughed in thirty years. But as he placed first one foot then the other onto the narrow ledge of the window, a sudden doubt gripped him. He looked down at the pavement, six storeys below, and worried about that distance. Six whole floors . . .

What if it wasn't far enough? What if, even in the dark, someone could still glance up and recognize him, leaping from the hospital window without his mask on?

Excitement overrode his fears. He had been waiting for this moment for too long – far too long to hesitate now. A team of nurses finally burst into the room, but they could only watch with horror as their supposedly bedridden patient flung himself the wrong way off the windowsill and out into the night.

For the first time in too long a time, Norman Power flew.

They had not previously seen the door on Sacha Terrace, just round the corner from the guest-house. It was new and white and trimmed with gold, incongruous against the battered bricks and mortar of the warehouse wall. A large plastic canopy extended outwards over it, and it was beneath this that the Doctor, Ace, Bernice and Karen finally came to a halt, grateful for the shelter it provided.

'This is ridiculous!' snapped Ace, the first of the group

to recover her breath. 'Are you going to tell me what's going on here, or what?'

'We're in the Land of Fiction,' the Doctor answered without argument. His voice was low, his eyes were elsewhere and he seemed uncommonly subdued. 'I've been here before. We're in very grave danger.'

'So what else is new?' groaned Benny.

'Then none of this is real,' announced Ace, with some satisfaction. 'Thought so!'

The Doctor scowled. 'It's real enough to be dangerous. As long as we stay here, we're just characters in someone else's book. The Writer can do whatever he wants with us.'

'You mean there's actually someone out there reading all this?'

The Doctor nodded. 'We've been under the closest scrutiny ever since we passed through what we thought was merely a time-storm.'

Benny considered that for a moment. 'But I was in the bath!' she protested finally.

The Doctor ignored that comment. 'I've never been overly keen on reading other people's versions of events,' he muttered distractedly. 'I prefer to create history for myself.' And the rain drove down ever harder as the distant bell of the town clock began to usher in the midnight hour.

The Doctor pushed open the door, and as the seventh chime rang out over Arandale, he led his companions out of the darkness and into a tea-room.

'You can't do this, Miss Ferguson!' a woman's voice wailed. Cue dramatic music, cut to commercial break . . .

Tina Grimshaw didn't care any more. The television was on out of habit, her usual diet of Australian soaps being pumped into the room as if everything was normal. Only it wasn't. Far from it. Tina was just as much a prisoner as any of the inmates of Wentworth Detention Centre; a prisoner in her own home, waiting for Mason and knowing that she could not leave. He might be gone for days, he might be gone for months, but she knew he would be coming back. Sometime, somehow, he would be coming back. And if she dared leave the house now, if she forced him to come in search of her, he would surely beat the very life from her fragile body.

She stared sightlessly out of the window now, as she had done since the Monster, in the body of her husband, had left her. Her tears of anguish had ruined the make-up on her face, but she no longer noticed. For all she cared, the town clock might as well have been sounding her own death-knell.

Norman flew, and the bells outside seemed to join the ones within, ringing out triumphantly in his mind and in his heart.

This was it, for the first time in decades, and the feelings he remembered so well were returning. He felt the air, more exhilarating than ever as it rushed against his unusually exposed face. He felt the lurch of his own stomach as his feet bade farewell to the ground, a crutch they no longer needed. He felt the power crackling within him, shielding him from gravity's sight. And he soared up there, high above it all, freed by the currents of the wind ... completely, totally, finally *free*!

And that was the best thing. He was free of this world; free of its chains. Free of his life.

Norman Power was flying – and this time, it was forever. This time, he wouldn't come down. This time, nothing could stop him.

Except for the ground.

And it did.

Pause there for a moment:

The tea-room was enormous; a flight of gold-trimmed stairs sweeping grandly down into a white-tiled portrait of elegance. The enormous French windows should, by rights, have been twelve feet underground but here, the norms of geography seemed to have little meaning. As did the laws of time. Through the clear sparkling glass the visitors could see an immaculately colourful garden, basking in the near-tropical heat of a midsummer's afternoon. Inside, the art treasures of a dozen worlds hung tastefully around the spotless walls. A white-suited figure played Bach's Toccata and Fugue in D Minor at an exquisite cream-coloured piano. Another hurried forth to escort the group to one of the beautiful marble tables, laying crisp white menus smartly before them.

Karen Davies, for one, was confused. 'Is your friend behind all this, or what?' she hissed to Ace, indicating the Doctor with a jerk of her head.

'He's not my – ' Ace began, then decided it wasn't worth the effort. The Doctor was making a point of ignoring Karen; a made-up character, Ace realized now – nothing more than a tool of their deadliest enemy (that's me, by the way).

The Doctor ordered a blend of tea fermented on a planet five galaxies distant. Ace scowled at his pretension and said that a cup of P G Tips would suit her fine. Then, sipping contentedly at his noxious-looking brew, the Doctor asked an unexpected question.

'Describe Mrs Shawcross,' he challenged his friends.

Bernice was puzzled, but she answered him anyway. 'Early forties, short blonde hair, dresses in casual slacks . . .'

'Come off it,' Ace interrupted, 'she's sixty years old if she's a day. And her hair's black, tied back in a bun, sort of a schoolmistress type.'

The Doctor smiled. 'You see?' he asked.

They didn't.

'We've never really met her,' the Doctor expounded. 'We've just been told that we have. And because she's just a minor character, little more than a creation of convenience, the Writer has never bothered to describe her.'

Ace nodded understandingly. 'I felt like that this morning,' she recalled. 'Like the whole night had passed away in a second and I hadn't really done anything, but I knew exactly what had happened. It was just like those memories had been planted in my mind.'

Benny groaned. ' "Just characters in someone else's book". That's what you said, isn't it?' The Doctor nodded, and Benny fixed him with a challenging stare. 'So what's the quickest way out the back cover?'

'That would be for me to take control of the narrative myself and to write us a happy ending. Hence this place.' The Doctor swept his hand across their plush surroundings. 'All my creation, my own little paragraph in the book. Like it?'

'You could have written us a few weapons or something,' said Ace sourly. 'They might have been a bit more use.'

'Against what, exactly?'

Bernice headed off the inevitable argument. 'Just what is the point of all this, Doctor?' she asked. 'Why have we been brought here?'

'As fuel for the Writer's imagination,' the Doctor told her. 'As the Master of the Land of Fiction, his job is to create stories that will entertain. If he can drag real people into those stories, to interact with his characters and react to his situations, then that job becomes very much easier.'

'Sort of like the difference between writing a novel and hosting a role-playing game,' guessed Benny.

'So he'll want to keep us here forever!' exclaimed Ace.

'Only until we're "turned into fiction", as he so euphemistically puts it. In actual fact, I suspect we will all die here – probably some fluke effect of the energies which make up the Land. The Master will no doubt write about us once we've gone. I think he considers that to be some type of consolation.'

'How long have we got?'

The Doctor shrugged. 'Hard to tell. There are too many ways for the Writer to distort time; words like "meanwhile", "eventually" and "later". We think we've been

228

here for three days, but it's probably been more like three hours. One thing I do know: the Writer told me that, when his book closes, we'll be trapped in its pages forever. I assume that when the story ends, the moment won't be too far off.'

Benny nodded. 'He's obviously making as much use of us as he can, before we die.'

'And keeping us too occupied to realize where we really are,' the Doctor added. 'It's almost too late already. The Writer's closing down his sub-plots, getting rid of his unwanted characters, introducing a little symmetry into the narrative structure. Norman Power, for instance, will doubtless have committed suicide by now.'

Benny winced at the casualness of his remark, but she made an effort to compose herself. 'So who's behind all this?' she asked. 'Apart from this Writer bloke, I mean. Who does he write *for*?'

'Originally, the Gods of Ragnarok,' said the Doctor, solemnly. 'Old enemies of mine, beings with phenomenal powers and rather perverse ideas on the subject of entertainment.'

'Scumbags,' muttered Ace under her breath. She remembered the Doctor's old foes from way back.

'Not that it really matters,' the Doctor continued. 'They are long since gone now. They became bored with their pet project even before my first visit here.'

'So now there's no one?'

'Oh no,' the Doctor corrected her, 'there's somebody out there all right. Someone who's dug up the Land from my own past and manipulated the timestream in order to reverse its destruction; someone who's brought the new Master of the Land here from twentieth-century Earth, with only one specific motive in mind – to ensnare me!'

The pattern was an increasingly familiar one. Once again, someone was interfering with time, and with the Doctor's own history in particular. Bernice remembered Mexico, and Oxford before that, and the false Earth controlled by the Silurians, and groaned inwardly. The traps had got harder each time. Was this the one they would finally fail to escape?

'Well then,' said Ace, jumping to her feet, 'write us a path back to the TARDIS, and we'll get right out of here and start tracking him down!'

'I'm afraid it's not quite as simple as that,' said the Doctor, and suddenly Ace saw the pain in the Time Lord's eyes and the sweat that beaded his forehead. His task was obviously more arduous than he had previously confessed, but he wasn't about to give up on it.

'I'm just about holding the Master of the Land back,' he grunted. 'I'm trying to defend this illusion against his onslaught. If I can manage it, then maybe . . .' He faltered, got a grip on himself. 'Maybe I will be able to write us out of this.'

There was a tense silence as the Doctor's mental struggle continued. Then, as quickly as his pain had begun, it seemed to subside. He straightened in his chair, dabbed at his hot sweaty face with a handkerchief and smiled broadly at his companions.

'Emergency over, I think,' he said cheerfully.

The waiter was hovering respectfully by his shoulder. 'Would you care to dine, sir?' The Doctor nodded gratefully, flipped his menu casually onto his lap and opened it up.

LOOK BEHIND YOU it said, in blood-red letters six inches high.

The Doctor did – and through the windows he had created, he saw a landscape that he had not. He saw the grimy street and the night sky and the rain, and he knew then that the Writer had too much control for him ever to usurp.

'Arandale,' he observed bitterly. 'Frozen in time, just waiting for our return.'

They could all see the truth of that statement. The raindrops themselves hung in eerie suspension, their movement halted until their story could continue. The white walls of the tea-room were already beginning to

230

melt as the whole illusion faded slowly into oblivion, like the remnants of a pleasant dream exposed to the bright morning sun. The Doctor had lost.

'So what are our choices?' asked Bernice practically.

'Just one,' said the Doctor. 'To go out and fight. If we don't, we'll be killed – and in the unlikely event that we're permitted to lose, we'll probably die anyway. If we win . . .' He paused, and sighed wearily. 'If we win, then at least the two of you will be able to leave.'

Despite their differences, Ace and Benny shared a worried look as the Doctor got slowly, painfully to his feet and pointed his umbrella in the direction of the French windows.

'Time to leave,' he said, and he tried to conceal the note of despair in his voice.

Remove pause, let time roll on and witness Arandale, a village under siege:

See the policemen, out there in the cold, sifting slowly through the remains of the castle on the hill – perhaps finding there a rag, a bone, a brand-new Adventure Kids club card, as charred and burnt as its owner, lying piteously in the wreckage.

Move further in now: there, Tina Grimshaw, standing at the window, tears on her cheeks, a cloud on her thoughts. As much a prisoner as Mel Joseph, alone in a police cell, waiting for revenge and knowing that it will not come. Their stories end here, in misery and defeat.

See Matthew Shade then, hurrying in search of allies and knowing that his quest will likely be in vain. See Philip and Rosemary Chambers, escorted home and pumped full of tea, still hopelessly confused and unable to comprehend the tragedies which have befallen them. And see private eye Jack Corrigan, cursing at the railway timetable that will keep him in the town until sunrise – or Malcolm Blyth, hunched disconsolately over his desk and praying that this terrible night will end, and with it the throbbing pain in the back of his head.

231

And somewhere in the town a murderer is loose, possessed now of the infinite powers which have lain for decades beneath Vampire Castle.

Once more, the stage is set. The Doctor is doomed.

The endgame begins.

The rain began to fall again as the Doctor stepped quietly out onto the dark wet street. The chimes of midnight rang in his ears and his face wrinkled with displeasure. The last five strokes; not a second had passed since his departure from the town.

The remaining players in the game were right behind him; Ace, Bernice, and finally, almost forgotten about in the confusion, my own pawn Karen Davies, about to draw attention back to herself. Hardly was the group through the door when she cried out in dreadful pain and wrapped her arms hard around the knife wound in her stomach.

The Doctor moved to her side, but his expression was coldly dispassionate and the tone of his voice was scornful. 'Let me guess: you've had a sudden flashback to the attack, and remembered exactly who tried to murder you.'

'You know, I think you're right,' said Karen, all innocence and sincerity. 'How could you tell?'

'Dramatic convention,' snapped the Doctor. 'This is the end of a chapter, no doubt. I assume we're due for a cliffhanger.' He turned quickly, and the others followed his line of sight.

It was as the Doctor had expected. The killer was there, and they all recognized him as such; recognizing also the identity of the man around whom the deadly McAllerson's Radiation now wildly coruscated.

It was Philip Chambers, and his eyes were like burning pools of ice in the shadows of his face.

Chapter 14

Backs to Reality

'Oh, I am sorry my friends,' said Phil Chambers with exaggerated politeness. His voice was far stronger now, and like his body it seemed to fairly crackle with the energy he possessed. 'Did I give you all a shock, just turning up like this?'

'Actually no,' said the Doctor. 'Not at all.'

Chambers ignored him. 'I suppose you'd all like to know what's been going on around here, then?'

'I imagine you're going to tell us,' the Doctor grumbled, checking his pocket watch impatiently. 'Just try to be succinct – exposition passages can be very trying.'

'Philip Chambers never really existed, you see,' said the energy being. 'Not as a whole person, not in his own right. When I came here to Arandale in the meteor storm of 1959, I sent my probes out towards the town for a suitable host body. Your fragile human forms were found to be inadequate and many were eliminated, but eventually I found what I was looking for. An unborn child, conceived but a few weeks before. A blank slate, ready for me to bend to my will. So I sent a sliver of myself into that child, and I worked on its mind, moulding its form and its personality – until eventually the child became a man, and the time became right for me to take total control of its body.'

The Doctor sighed. 'Just give us the edited highlights, can't you? You wanted a body, so you stole that of Philip Chambers. The process of consolidating your hold on him required a vast amount of blood, so you had to do it in stages, sending your dupe to collect more from the townspeople each time it was needed. The clue we should have seen was that Rosemary Chambers could only cast spells when her husband was present; she didn't possess any powers in her own right, but she could somehow draw on the ones which had taken over his body. All fairly logical albeit predictable, improbable and rather contrived. Now what do you do for an encore?'

'That's a very neat synopsis, Doctor,' said the thing that had been Chambers, a little disappointed perhaps that the Time Lord had stolen his thunder. 'And to answer your question – well obviously, now I revel in the joys of my new-found corporeity by going on a senseless rampage across this town and wiping out everyone who lives here.'

'Splendid. Well, we'd better leave you to it then.'

'Oh no, Doctor,' the creature said. 'I'm afraid you and your companions are to be my very first victims!'

'Ah yes,' said the Doctor. 'I had overlooked that possibility.' His eyes twinkled and he glanced casually at something over Chambers' shoulder. The killer caught his look, turned a moment too late, and took the full force of an impossibly proportioned male body hard in the midriff.

Suddenly the Doctor and Bernice were three streets away, and the Doctor hit the tarmac running. 'What did you do?' cried Benny, gathering her wits and setting off after him. 'More to the point, can you do it again?'

'I wrote Captain Millennium into the story,' the Doctor answered over his shoulders as he skidded round the corner into Vines Street. 'A character from the fiction of Earth's future. And no, I wouldn't count on it happening again.' He came to a halt outside the darkened windows of the second-hand bookshop.

'No one's ever challenged the Writer's control here before,' he explained. 'It caught him off guard at first, but he's learning to cope with it now. I'll have difficulty altering his story-line again.'

'Then he could just teleport Chambers onto this street

whenever he likes. We haven't gained anything by running from him!'

The Doctor shrugged. 'He won't do that yet. The Writer wants us to win this one, remember – he wants his book to end successfully. So he'll give us time to come up with a plan.'

'Well nothing springs to mind offhand. Any suggestions?'

The Doctor shrugged, as if none of this meant anything. 'Why don't we have a walk round the town and see what happens next?'

Benny brushed the wet hair back from her face. 'What happens next is that I catch my death of pneumonia and you're left without a companion!'

'Keep moving,' the Doctor suggested, 'and keep close.' They huddled under the scant protection of his umbrella and set off in a direction picked at random.

There were bodies in the streets. Burnt and blackened, victims of the deadly powers that Phil Chambers now wielded. The path of destruction was random, encompassing more of the town than Bernice would have dreamt possible in so short a time. Whenever she thought they'd escaped it, they would come across another one, leaning against a back door like yesterday's rubbish or lying facedown in the road, melted flesh merging with melted tarmac.

They passed the hospital, though she had not been aware of approaching it. Even here the corpses were left unattended, as if the police and the ambulancemen were simply long past caring or hoping. Bernice got her last glimpse of Norman there, spread across the pavement in a pool of dark red. But she kept right on walking, trying to feel nothing. She knew he wasn't real. She knew this wasn't happening. But why did things always have to be like this?

They rounded a corner, and the Doctor stopped so suddenly that Benny nearly walked into him. 'What's

235

wrong?' she asked as he rolled his umbrella and hooked it over one arm out of the way. He nodded towards the source of the problem. Through the driving rain, she could now see an outline; an indistinct shape becoming gradually clearer as something horrible drew closer. 'What is it?'

It was squat and grey, about four feet high, a powerful looking frame rolling steadily towards them on caterpillar tracks. Two metal arms protruded from its sides, ending in pincer-like claws. An eye-stalk protruded from its transparent domed head, and as it glided to a halt only yards away from them, Benny could see circuits clicking away in that dome, slotting into new configurations as a mechanical mind processed the input of its optical sensors.

The creature registered their presence and acted like lightning. A flexible tube attachment sprung up beside the dome, and an orange blast of energy rippled past Benny's arm. She flinched, moved for cover and felt the Doctor's restraining hand on her shoulder. A moment later, she saw why: there was another of the things behind her, a third to the left. That only left one escape route; a dark alley which, under other circumstances, Benny would not have dreamt of approaching. She looked to the Doctor, but he didn't seem worried. A deep frown creased his forehead. 'I thought this book was supposed to make sense from now on?'

One robot spoke, in a cold, flat voice. 'You are enemies of the Dredlox. You will be in-cin-er-at-ed! In-cin-er-ate!' And the chant was taken up, eerily, resoundingly.

All three fired, and the beams crackled as they crossed in the air above Benny's head. She ducked instinctively. 'Doctor . . .'

The Time Lord snapped out of his reverie. 'We'd better do something.'

'That would be rather nice, yes. May I suggest making a run for it, before we're both fried?'

'No need for that,' the Doctor told her. 'They aren't meant to pose a challenge. They're simply here to force me into taking a more active role in the narrative.' He reached into his pocket, seemingly ignorant of the deadly orange beam which flashed past his right ear. 'Any of the usual methods should do it – hypnotism, confronting evil with its own image, waving a sonic screwdriver at it . . .' From his capacious pockets he produced a small radio transmitter. 'Or this!' he concluded, with a flourish. He made a quick adjustment to the device, brandished it triumphantly in an arc before the three robots, and smiled in satisfaction as their weapons fell limply to their sides. Inside their glass domes, three mechanical brains whirled frantically, disoriented. One robot shot into an uncontrollable spin, whilst another simply exploded on the spot. Benny coughed as a cloud of acrid smoke drifted towards her.

'You see?' said the Doctor. 'I just scrambled their transmission frequencies. Childishly simple.' Then his eyes widened, and he pushed Benny to one side, hurtling to the ground himself as another volley of blasts shot out from behind them.

Benny rolled and scrambled to her feet. It was too late; she was staring down the blaster of a fourth robot, one which had trundled silently out from the alley-way where it had presumably lain in ambush. Something glowed red in its gun barrel as a metal synapse clicked in its brain, and it prepared to fire.

Benny's life was saved in the proverbial nick of time. It was saved by a dustbin lid, and by a strong pair of hands which drove the unlikely weapon hard down onto the robot's eyestalk. 'Stop!' it shrieked, its metallic voice tinged with panic. 'Stop!' But the new arrival meant to take full advantage of its blindness. The frantic creature was sent hurtling towards the nearest wall, where a sharp impact shattered its dome and snapped its blaster across the middle.

The Doctor was back on his feet, and using his hat to dust down his suit. 'Ah yes,' he said happily. 'One cliché I'd forgotten. The last-second save from behind – becoming quite your *modus operandi*, Mister Corrigan.'

237

The detective nodded his head in acknowledgement, not entirely sure whether he was being complimented or insulted. 'If I'd've been able to get my piece through Customs,' he grumbled, 'I'd've sorted the critter out sooner.'

Benny heard footsteps through the rain. She turned, alert for further action, but the new arrivals were friends: Karen Davies and Matthew Shade. She folded her arms and smiled tightly. 'Well then, the gang's all here.'

'Yes,' said the Doctor, but he hesitated before speaking. Something was wrong. Someone was missing.

Ace drifted, though she didn't know where. Blackness surrounded her, and she just wanted to sleep. Just close her eyes and forget about the world outside.

Rosemary woke, trembling and crying, and missed Phil immediately. She padded downstairs in her bare feet, but he wasn't there either. Alarm overtook her; she'd lost her children, was she now to lose her husband too? She took a hold of herself, counted to ten, tried to blot out the deaths from her mind. It seemed like they'd happened to someone else, not to her. She would try not to think about them now. There was plenty of time for grief later.

She turned on the dull electric light of her office-cum-sanctum. The cards were there, lying invitingly by the candle on the table. Almost by force of habit she reached for them, dealing out five face down before her. She had to know.

She didn't want to know.

She turned the cards anyway, keeping Phil uppermost in her thoughts. She forced herself to look at them, though she was prepared for anything. Even five Death images, she could have handled it.

But the cards were all blank.

The huge garage door was hoisted up with a shriek of

protesting metal, and the Doctor and his four companions stood on the threshold and stared at the machine.

'I thought your field was the occult,' remarked the Doctor to Shade.

'Why don't we discuss this inside?' suggested Benny, pushing past them. She was glad just to get out of the driving rain for a few minutes. 'As long as there's nothing else nasty in here,' she added, her eyes straying towards the darkest corners of the garage. 'I don't fancy running into those Mutant Ninja things again.' The Doctor glanced at her sharply, and she rolled her eyes as she realized why. 'Of course, just something else that never happened.' Another illusion, another event programmed into her memory. She wondered how much longer she could take this.

'The Force is exulting in its new-found freedom,' Shade explained. 'As it ripples across the town, it creates little packets of improbability. It is as we enter these that we encounter such things as the cartoon turtles and the Dredlok robots. Do not worry, my mystic runes have guarded this place from their influence.'

'So your field *is* the occult,' remarked the Doctor, with almost childlike satisfaction.

Shade shrugged. 'Our foe is an amalgam of both science and sorcery,' he said. 'A similar collusion is needed to bring about his downfall.'

'A collusion between you and me, you mean.'

'If you like.'

The Doctor knelt by the machine. Sitting incongruously in the centre of the bare stone floor, it quivered at his approach and threatened to topple ungracefully to its own destruction. All kinds of oddities had contributed to its composition; coat hangers, crisp packets, bus tickets, pens. The Doctor had often made things like this himself – in his third incarnation especially, it had delighted him to be able to build what looked like a random assemblage of junk, only to demonstrate that its true purpose was both practical and, in many cases, life-saving. Shade's device was neither of those things. 'It's rubbish,' the Doctor exclaimed. 'Total, unworkable rubbish!'

'Does the Tate Gallery know about this thing?' Benny asked.

'With the added power I command from the Netherworld, the machine will work,' Shade asserted, his voice hard-edged.

The Doctor looked at him quizzically. 'Without any help from me at all? And me the main character in the story. That would hardly fulfil dramatic requirements!'

Shade seethed inwardly, and spoke through clenched teeth. 'Your assistance would be invaluable – if you are prepared to give it, at last.' He thought for a moment. 'We need something to channel the voltage of the machine through the regulator. Something stiff and metal, say about six inches long.'

The Doctor smiled, nodded, and became aware that four pairs of eyes had fixed themselves expectantly onto the spoon in his jacket's breast pocket. 'I'm sorry,' he told them quietly. 'I have a special use in mind for this.'

'Will this do then?' asked Karen, flashing the group one of her special grins as she whipped a gleaming silver tablespoon from her inside pocket. 'I picked it up in the tea-room, before.'

The Doctor snatched the device from her before she could pass it to Shade. 'That's absolutely perfect, thank you.' To the astonishment of the others, he rested one foot on the machine, gripped the two spoons in the palm of one hand, and proceeded to beat out a rhythmic tattoo on his legs, chest and forearms. Finally, still oblivious to the stares of his companions, he slung both implements to one side and gave Shade's ramshackle creation a sharp kick which sent it toppling. The machine hit the ground, and its component parts were scattered.

'I don't like this ending,' the Doctor explained mildly. 'Too easy. Too pat. Let's find a better one.'

'So long as we do,' muttered Shade. 'So long as we do.'

Back on the streets, the buildings were moving. Benny hardly avoided a record shop which pounced unexpectedly. Karen screamed as a car reared up in front of her, teeth gnashing where once had been its radiator. The laundry and the Chinese restaurant were dancing a waltz in the courtyard by the laughing fountain, and the library sat and sulked, its head in its books.

The Doctor kept on going. Bernice wished she could share his casual attitude, but she followed at a cautious pace, eyes darting from side to side for the next danger. Corrigan and Shade fell into step behind her, Corrigan coaxing along the terrified Karen.

The Doctor stopped only once on their journey. A small electronics shop stood remarkably still in the dead centre of the road. Its display window had melted into slag, but the equipment within was unharmed. The Doctor scooped two portable hi-fi systems and a dictaphone into his arms. 'I wouldn't normally do this,' he said, 'but needs must.' Then he carried on walking.

Benny had to make a dive for the town hall door; no sooner had the Doctor passed within than the whole building seemed determined to stretch its foundations and find a home across the street. But there was no sensation of movement once the group were inside. Just empty corridors and the Doctor, hurrying on, always ten steps ahead.

'The reality disturbances are increasing,' noted Shade. 'We can't have too long now.' Benny had to agree; from one of the windows, she caught sight of a huge, hairy ape shinning its way up the wall. She decided not to mention it.

'You're cutting it mighty close, Doc,' Corrigan complained. 'I sure hope you know what you're doing.'

'I do,' said the Doctor, stopping at a large wooden door. It opened not without protest, and they found themselves in a small, dark, rubble-strewn area at the foot of a spiral flight of stairs. 'The clock tower.'

'And what can we do from here?' asked Shade.

The Doctor made for the stairs, the electrical equipment

still held tight to his chest. 'Stay here,' he ordered. 'I'm going to make a few adjustments to the mechanisms up there. If I can modify the pitch of the bells and set up an electronic speaker system at just the right frequency, I can make sure that when this clock next chimes, in just . . .' He checked his watch '. . . ten minutes' time, then those chimes themselves will vibrate our energy-driven friend into dust.'

'You mean you can really do that?' asked Karen, quite incredulous.

'Why not?' said the Doctor, breezily. 'It's only a story!' He vanished upwards into the darkness and for a long while after, there was silence.

Corrigan paced nervously, until finally his eyes alighted on a rotting plank lying in the corner. He hefted it and tapped it against his palm. 'What are we cooling our heels here for? I could go out there, get up behind that thing, and – !'

'No!' interrupted Benny, and there was no arguing with that tone of voice.

Karen collapsed wearily onto the bottom stair. 'I hope your Doctor friend knows what he's doing,' she addressed Bernice.

'He does,' the older woman confirmed. She was about to add: 'I hope!' Then she checked herself; they might have had their differences, but he'd never let her down before. He'd never failed to deliver the goods in a crisis situation. The thought made her feel better, so she repeated it to the others.

'How long have you been with him?' Karen asked.

Benny shrugged. 'A few months.'

'Just the two of you?'

'Just the two of us.' She thought about that. 'I think.' A thought crossed her mind, but she couldn't quite catch it.

The Doctor appeared on the stairway. 'All done!' he announced.

'And just in time,' announced Corrigan.

Half past midnight. They waited expectantly, each tensing as they heard the sound of machinery grinding into action.

Across the town of Arandale, a series of notes rang out. They sounded loud and clear, and resolved themselves into a tune.

The theme from 'The Magic Roundabout'.

The thing that had once been Philip Chambers paused, long enough for his latest victim to make a run for it. A brief reprieve, at best.

A smile spread slowly across the energy creature's face, and he headed slowly in the direction of the town clock.

Bernice was smiling too, though she tried to hide it from the others. 'Slight miscalculation,' the Doctor apologized, but there was no regret in his tone or expression. 'Let's try something else, shall we?' He headed back through the town hall and out onto the street. It was still raining, but at least the buildings were now still.

The others joined him, and Shade's expression was grim. 'I think it's time to stop playing games, Doctor.'

'And just when I was beginning to enjoy myself,' responded the Time Lord flippantly.

'Then perhaps you should learn to take this situation seriously,' growled Shade. 'Otherwise, you stand not a chance of rescuing yourself and your companions.'

The Doctor, already half-way across the street, halted in his tracks. 'Companions?' His lined face went suddenly pale, and his voice dropped to a breathless whisper. 'Ace! How could I have forgotten?'

Ace was running, though she didn't know why. The street lamps whipped by her, the rain stung her face and something terrible barked at her heels, urging her onwards, her panic increasing.

By the time she stopped to analyse those fears, she was in the town no longer. The buildings behind her had simply folded inwards, merging into a blank white wall.

She knew she hadn't teleported, yet somehow she was elsewhere. A phrase from her past occurred to her: 'Well wicked!' she breathed. Then before her, a light snapped on, shining straight into her eyes and hurting even through her shades.

From three sides, seven men faced her, safe behind their semi-circular oak table. Each one was tall and elegant, stuffed shirts with suits and umbrellas and black bowler hats. Ace took an instant dislike to them, to the central one especially. He sat directly ahead, straight-backed, staring down his nose, looking for all the world like her hated old English teacher.

She let them begin, still catching her breath. The teacher figure spoke first. ' "Wicked",' he intoned, all pomp and high-handedness. 'Sinful, iniquitous, vicious. Your understanding of this word is erroneous. Your use of the adverb form of "well" in this grammatical context is similarly unacceptable. Your application of the English language, young woman, is both aberrant and abhorrent; your dialogue is neither naturalistic nor of any particular literary value. You are in very serious trouble.'

He paused, and seemed to expect a reaction. Ace fixed him with her best stare, affected a casual pose and shot back: 'Yeah?'

A rolled umbrella was slammed petulantly onto the tabletop. 'You do realize,' scolded the man at the far left of the table, 'that you have already been suspended from the continuity? That you speak here for your very status as an active character? Your future circulation depends on the judgement reached this day.'

'And your future existence,' said the English teacher, his voice now a soft, threatening purr, 'lies in the hands of the Word Association.'

Ace grinned, and laughed derisively. 'An illusion. Another stupid illusion! Haven't you given up on all that crap yet?'

A shudder seemed to ripple round the room. 'Obscenities too,' hissed another of the bureaucrats, 'in a book deemed suitable for consumption by minors.'

'You seal the pages of your own existence,' warned the man in the centre.

'I'm not having this!' exclaimed Ace, almost amused by this madcap scenario. 'I'm no fictional character for you to muck around with as you like. I'm real, I'm me. I'm Ace!'

'Are you really?'

'Yes.'

'Then why,' came the question, in soft, honeyed tones, 'do you not possess a surname?'

A surname? Ace hesitated, and thought. She thought he might actually have a point.

'Do you have an answer?'

Ace grimaced. She'd had one that morning . . .

Her head started hurting. The chief bureaucrat got to his feet. 'You are now, were once, have always been, worthless. A mere supporting character, your inspiration plucked from a film, modified for your new genre, and granted with a limited potential that you have long since outlived.'

Dorothy . . . Dorothy . . . caught in a time-storm, swept over the rainbow (something beginning with M?). Landed on Iceworld, teamed with the Doctor, fought against Fenric (how could she not remember?).

'You are no longer of interest. Your audience are bored. Your continued existence in this series will not be countenanced.'

Ace's heart beat fast, panic drove thoughts in circles around her mind. This was stupid, this couldn't be real . . . but somehow, she couldn't get her head together, couldn't answer back, couldn't fight what they were doing to her.

She was yanked from her body, felt it tumble to the ground like the proverbial sack of potatoes. But when she looked down, it wasn't there; just a string of words, typed in black:

> *... a loner, with a self-protectively over-developed*
> *sense of individuality, personal morality, her own*
> *ideas of right and wrong ...*

This was her; her life, her times. Reduced now to words,
just paper and ink, her whole existence nothing more
than ... than ... *fiction!*

'You have been unable to account for yourself. The
sentence of this court is that your character, and any
mention of such, will be erased forthwith from all stories
in which you participated. Said erasure to be carried out
retrospectively. You will never have existed.'

Ace tried to ignore the words. She tried to close eyes
she didn't have, tighten fists she no long possessed. She
tried to block the illusion, to concentrate her mind ...

Concentrate ...

'What are you doing?' screamed the Doctor, at the sky.
'Why have you taken my friend? Why did you erase her
from my mind?'

'Doctor?' Shade beckoned him uncertainly, clutching
his hand to his forehead as he concentrated on something
a long way distant. 'I'm getting a message, something for
you. From the Spirit World. I don't quite understand ...'

'Just tell me!' snapped the Doctor angrily.

Shade stared at him for a moment, then straightened
up, his expression grim. 'I need only one of your friends
to make you do my bidding. Finish the story – or you will
never see Ace again!'

Concentrate!

Just think of one thing, something to grasp hold of,
something solid and comforting and real.

Ace was back in the library; an illusion again, but at
least one of her own making this time. She saw the shelves
and the books and the gravity pads, though her eyes were
screwed tightly shut – and she concentrated for all she
was worth, focusing her mind on the real her, and the real

246

life that she led. She wasn't going to let them just rub her out. Not without a fight!

Ace laughed then as she felt the sting of the twin paper cuts on her cheek, almost yelled out in triumph as her hand touched her face and came away warm and wet with blood. The rogue book fluttered by again, and in this dream – *her* dream – she caught it, pinning it victoriously against the nearest shelf with one smooth thrust of her arm muscles.

From the battered white cover, a face stared out at her. Her face.

She gasped, flinched away, and let the book drop unimpeded to the ground. It landed atop a mound of similar volumes, each emblazoned with the same futuristic logo, with a title beneath. Names like 'Dragonfire', 'Love and War', 'Deceit'. The story of her life, reduced to paperback form. And when her hand went to her face again, she felt not blood this time, but words – dripping impossibly, letter by letter, out through her cuts and down to the floor, where the greedy novels soaked her pain into their bloated pages.

The dream was no longer her own. She sank to the ground again and cried out in fear and revulsion. She had to ignore it, had to block it from her mind.

She had to keep control.

'All right!' yelled the Doctor, and his voice seemed to echo round the streets of the small town. 'All right,' he repeated quietly, crushed and dispirited. 'I'll give you what you want. I'll end it now.'

'And then?' asked Shade eagerly.

The Doctor sighed and shook his head. Ending the story wasn't his problem. He feared what lay beyond that; the decision that was his to make. His life for those of his companions.

'We'll see,' he said.

Shade smiled.

Ace was back with them then; all together once more. The Doctor, Ace, Bernice, Karen, Corrigan and Shade, grouped in a pathetic huddle at one end of the dark wet street, facing with trepidation the slowly advancing form of their Force-powered foe.

'This is it then?' muttered Benny.

'This is it,' confirmed the Doctor.

'End of the line,' hissed Chambers. 'Time that you all finally died!'

'Oh dear,' the Doctor sighed, although no hint of concern could be heard in his tone. 'And us without any type of defence against you whatsoever. Whatever will we do?'

His enemy's top lip curled back in an angry sneer, and the energies around him crackled ever more fiercely. Matthew Shade's black eyes widened and he tugged urgently at the Doctor's sleeve. 'The improbability packets are vanishing. Chambers is drawing the entirety of the Force back into his own body.'

The Doctor nodded but didn't reply. The slight form of Philip Chambers could hardly be seen now, engulfed as it was in a brilliant haze of spitting yellow fury. Soon, only the Doctor and Shade could bare to look directly at their blazing foe – and yet the light grew brighter still.

'I sure hope you've got something up your sleeve here, buddy!' whispered Corrigan. The Doctor merely shrugged, spread his arms wide, and showed not the slightest surprise as a small metal box dropped neatly into his outstretched palm.

'All-Purpose Energy Nullification Device,' he read. 'Simply press this button to eradicate any rampaging energy-powered monsters in the immediate vicinity. Instant results guaranteed, or your money back.'

'Wow,' breathed Corrigan. 'That was mighty convenient!'

'A present from one of the last improbability packets,' guessed Shade.

'Pathetic!' spat the Doctor. 'A ridiculous last-ditch attempt to write a happy ending to the story.'

248

'Well don't just stand there criticizing the plot-line!' exploded Ace, still confused and smarting from her dream sequence. 'Use the bloody thing, before the Writer has no choice *but* to wipe us all out!' By now, even the rain was unable to penetrate Philip Chambers' fiery aura. The heavy droplets of water were evaporating into steam before they could get close.

'It's time,' intoned the killer, portentiously. He pulled his right arm slowly back and braced himself to send his deadly energies surging towards his six helpless victims.

'He's going to do it!' shrieked Karen, shrinking back against Jack Corrigan's comfortingly large frame. 'He's going to kill us all!'

'Not,' announced Shade calmly, 'if the Doctor presses that button now.'

'He won't have time!' snarled Chambers. 'I'm going to murder you all!'

'Now!' repeated Shade, more forcefully this time.

'I really mean it you know,' said Chambers, with only a little hesitation. 'I really am going to kill you all. Stone cold dead. Without compunction.'

But the Doctor did nothing.

'And I'm going to do it any second now, unless you can find some way of stopping me.'

'Doctor . . .' murmured Benny, her voice tinged with panic.

'I really, really am not joking about this. You are all going to die, in just . . . one . . . more . . . second . . .'

The Doctor's expression didn't change. Nor did his eyes move from Chambers' own. But the device which might have saved them all slipped gently through his fingers and shattered into fragments on the hard pavement beneath him.

'I believe you,' he said solemnly. And for a moment, there was silence. 'But I've made my choice.'

All right then, that's *it*!

A look of anger flashed across Philip Chambers' face. His eyes darkened, his mouth opened wide in a piercing scream of rage and frustration – and before anyone could so much as flinch, he had gathered together the entirety of the McAllerson's Radiation within his body, hurling it all in one devastatingly potent blast of pure elemental force, directly at the six powerless forms before him. The tremendous bolt struck our heroes dead centre, and exploded in an apocalyptic tempest of fury from which there could be absolutely no possibility of escape – and no exaggerating here, I mean like, really, not one single chance whatsoever that the Doctor, Ace, Bernice, Karen, Corrigan or Shade might find the remotest conceivable hope of survival in any way, shape or form whatsoever; am I making all that clear?

Naturally, the Doctor, his two companions and his three fictional colleagues were all blasted into a billion tiny little

Chapter 15

The Last Word

, hurling himself at the TARDIS console and operating the controls with frantic desperation.

What the hell is going on?

'Doctor . . .' began Benny uncertainly, still out of breath from their headlong dash back to the ship.

'Not now,' he growled. 'The Land won't have been disrupted for long – its Master will be reasserting his control.'

Too damn right I will! Just let me get back . . . my breath . . .

The Doctor slammed the final switch into place, stepping back from the console with an expression which still betrayed his anxiety. The TARDIS was in transit now, the central rotor of its console rising and falling steadily as it fled through inter-dimensional space.

'Are we safe?' Benny asked, an eyebrow raised.

The Doctor shook his head. 'The Land's influence extends far beyond its own dimensions, otherwise it could never have ensnared us in the first place.'

'How long, then?'

'A couple of minutes,' he muttered tersely, staring at the time rotor as if seeking to propel his vessel forward by sheer force of will. 'Just a couple . . .'

Time to put a stop to this.

'Doctor!' cried Ace, the only one of the three who had had the foresight to operate the scanner controls.

They could all see it now; the hideous shape which loomed terrifyingly large on the monitor. A dragon, sleek and red, its leathern wings beating a path from out of the dimensional vortex, and directly towards the hapless vessel which was its prey.

Almost simultaneously the TARDIS jerked up and back, toppling its occupants and sending them hurtling into a twelve-limbed heap in one corner. The quiet hum of the console rose sharply in pitch and intensity as the engines tried to compensate for this new force, this gravitational pull, but all the power in the universe would not have been enough. The Land was reaching out to them, dragging them inexorably back, back down into its clutches – back down to their deaths. And the Land would not be denied.

'It's beginning,' whispered the Doctor, his face a deathly white mask. He had dragged himself free of the others and up on to his knees, his eyes tightly closed and his teeth fiercely gritted as he prepared to join in mental battle.

Ace acted quickly, leaping across his hunched body to the console. 'We need more power!' she cried to Benny, who nodded in acknowledgement and wished she could operate the Doctor's craft a lot better than she actually could.

'Isn't there anything else we can do?' she shouted over the increasing whine of the ship's engines.

'He's already set the controls,' answered Ace. 'There's no point messing with them. Just channel as much power as you can into the engines, and hope the Doctor can come through with his side of the deal. If he can't, we've had it!'

And out in the vortex, the dragon moved in for the kill, seizing the already stricken TARDIS in its razor claws and hurtling back across the dimensions to whence it came . . .

. . . only to be suddenly attacked by a far larger dragon, appearing seemingly from nowhere. The two beasts grappled, clawing, biting, breathing great plumes of fire – and

252

the TARDIS was forgotten, spinning back onto its original course as the leviathans fought on, oblivious . . .

. . . but oh no, Doctor, *I'm* writing the story here. And you'll have to do a lot better than that, I'm afraid, when I can whip up, say – say an asteroid storm, hurtling unstoppably through the dimensions, tons of rock hammering down on the ship's police box exterior and beating it back, carrying it down . . .

. . . until the ship was unexpectedly saved by the appearance of an enormous and powerful magnet which diverted the stream of highly metallic asteroids to where they could do no further harm. Free from the storm, it surged forwards once again . . .

. . . but came suddenly to a juddering halt as its escape route was blocked by a great silver barrier, stretching as far as the eye could see in all directions but one. There was only one way left for the ship to go, and that was straight back down . . .

. . . which is where it would have gone, but for the timely intervention of the battling dragons and a misdirected stream of fire which blew a gaping hole in the barrier before it. The TARDIS slipped easily through the gap, free at last . . .

. . . or rather, free for the moment . . .

'That's it!' announced Ace. 'I'm giving it all the power I can get.' There was no hint of panic in her voice, and Benny found herself grudgingly admiring the way she kept her cool under such tremendous pressure.

'It seems to be working,' she said hopefully, her eyes flicking between the console and the screen. 'We're getting away.'

'Yeah, but too bloody slowly!' Ace pointed out.

'Then it all depends on him,' said Benny, pretending not to notice Ace's momentary expression of distaste as she indicated the Doctor. He was writhing painfully on the floor now, concentrating all of his mind on the tremendous

253

effort of fighting me off. 'If he can't pull this one off, we'll end up right back where we started.'

Ace snorted derisively. 'We'll end up dead, you mean.'

Smart girl.

... and outside, the path of the TARDIS was suddenly blocked by the gaping maw of a deadly black hole. Either the craft turned back instantly, or it would be sucked irrevocably into the gulf, and ...

... and thrown unharmed to the other side of the universe. Far from instant destruction, this particular hole actually meant instant freedom – along with complete and total safety – for the ship and all aboard her ...

It meant *what*? I mean, it – it ... until it suddenly became apparent that the TARDIS was, in fact, going to bypass the swirling maelstrom altogether, and too late to change course as well ...

... although doing so was really not necessary, as the – as the – tremendous gravitational – forces within the hole – pulled the ship towards ...

... and past it, to where the next danger awaited. This time, it was a great mechanical monstrosity which stood between the TARDIS and its freedom. A ship of sorts, but a thousand miles deep and a thousand miles wide and screeching on an unstoppable course towards the Land of Fiction, giving the comparatively minute time vessel no alternative but to be propelled along by its tremendous bulk ...

... except that – except ...

... with no chance of diverting its course, no last-ditch attempts, no last-minute saves, no ...

... no power to the – to the propulsion engines, which – which – which cut out with a whine, leaving the gar – gargantuan vessel stranded and – and helpless, so that the TARDIS could just – slip around it ...

Oh, but I nearly had you that time, Doctor. You're weakening, I can feel it! ... and as if from nowhere, an enormous set of pincers materialized around the TARDIS, clamping themselves onto the ship and holding it fast in an unbreakable grip . . .

. . . but just – but just for a – moment, until the pincers – the pincers . . .

. . . held fast!

. . . began to – rust . . .

. . . held fast!

. . . and started – to – to break . . .

. . . *held fast! Permanently!*

. . .

Even Ace started involuntarily as the Doctor arched painfully backwards and a blood-curdling scream ripped itself from his tortured lungs. Bernice called his name and was by his side in an instant, but her concern was not a shared one.

'Never mind the bloody Doctor!' Ace snapped. 'He's left us all in it now!' She was desperately pushing buttons and pulling levers at the console, at the same time reaching out with her mind, trying to re-establish the link she had once had with the Time Lord's semi-sentient craft, urging it to go faster, pull harder, for the sake of them all. It couldn't, and such actions would have been to no avail in any case. There was no way of manoeuvring out of the trap I had set. The pincers were strong and solid and their grip was like that of a vice, holding the struggling little TARDIS helplessly frozen and at my mercy.

'He's botched it up!' spat Ace, with disgust. 'He gave in too soon!' And then they were knocked sideways once again, as the artificial gravity of the Land of Fiction took a renewed hold and began to drag them, enlarged surgical implements and all, back down into its embrace. Thought they could escape from *me*, did they?

'And there's nothing we can do?' Benny's voice was hollow and desolate. To die like this, with so much between them left unresolved . . . doesn't it just make your heart bleed?

But a sudden grin had crept over Ace's taut face as,

behind her mirrored shades, her eyes gleamed at some tremendous private joke. 'Well, I didn't say that exactly,' she replied – and with just a few deft flicks of the TARDIS controls, a familiar keyboard sprang willingly out of the console.

'The chameleon circuit?' Bernice was bewildered. 'What use is that going to be?'

'Watch.'

. . . and back outside, things were beginning to happen again – only this time, it was the TARDIS itself which was undergoing a change. Suddenly, it was smooth and sleek and spherical, and the clinging pincers could no more find a grip on its shining silver form than they could on a greased ball-bearing. With a snap, they slammed suddenly together, the very pressure they had exerted acting as the propulsive force which catapulted the Doctor's craft outwards and sent it hurtling, with ever increasing velocity, away from the Land . . .

. . . and out into space . . .

. . . and out of my influence . . .

NOOOOOOOOOOoooooooooooo . . .

'So,' said Ace finally, her voice low and controlled. 'All over?'

The Doctor nodded gratefully, still breathless from his exertions and relying for the present on the TARDIS console to support his battle-drained body. 'You found a physical way of altering reality – something I couldn't do with my mind. Thank you.'

Ace glared at him, her arms folded. He wasn't going to get off the hook that easily. 'What you mean is, I just saved all our lives because you weren't capable of finishing the stupid little game you'd started!'

'Now come on,' Benny tried to interrupt. 'I don't think that's . . .'

'And after all that business with the chameleon circuit,

too. If you'd have had your way, I wouldn't have known how to operate it at all, and then we'd all have been dead.'

'Yes,' said the Doctor, somewhat cowed. 'Sorry.'

Ace regarded her dishevelled companion for a moment before she spoke. When she did, it was with all the contempt she could muster. 'You stupid bastard!' she said. And without another word she swept coldly out of the room, slamming the interior door forcefully shut behind her.

Her departure was followed by a long heavy silence, and Benny was almost tempted to follow her companion's example if only to escape the awkwardness of the moment. What stopped her from doing so was the sight of the Doctor, suddenly nothing more than a pale, troubled old man, staring forlornly after his old companion with eyes which held a world of pain. Her heart went out to him – but then she remembered the deaths on Silurian Earth and in the Althosian system, and she no longer knew quite what she felt.

'So what happened?' she asked, keeping some distance for the present.

The Doctor shrugged as if it were all inconsequential. 'Just a simple little trick, that's all.'

Well, go on then . . . I want to hear this!

'I suspected we were in the Land of Fiction from the moment we arrived,' he explained. 'It was the TARDIS itself that told us, if you remember, through its use of the chameleon circuit – and no, I couldn't tell you that before.' he added quickly, responding to the accusation written on Bernice's face. 'I couldn't even think about it too hard. The Master of the Land would have been aware of my knowledge instantly.'

Bernice nodded, pacified for the present. Encouraged, he continued:

'So with that in mind, I was able to change the Writer's own story without him even realizing it . . .'

What?

257

'... specifically by defining the type of energy with which our friend Mister Chambers became infused.'

But I ... I ...

Benny brightened as she began to comprehend. 'So all that rubbish you gave me about McAllerson's Radiation, about it causing genetic changes and everything ...'

... all that stuff at the beginning of Chapter Six, the scene in the guest-house – I don't believe it ...

'All lies, I'm afraid,' the Doctor admitted. 'But it obviously convinced the Master of the Land, and it persuaded him that the radiation he needed for his story should be McAllerson's.'

'Which does exist?'

'Of course, but its properties are completely different to those I described. So what actually happened once I'd goaded the Writer into making Philip Chambers release a huge quantity of McAllister's Radiation all at once ...'

'... was that it interfered with the energies making up the Land of Fiction ...'

'... and caused everything in it to flash out of existence, yes. Temporarily, at least – and just long enough, thankfully, for us to locate and reach the TARDIS.'

'Which, of course, was one of the few real things left when all the fictional ones vanished.' Benny concluded.

The Doctor smiled as if congratulating a particularly bright pupil.

'So why all that business with this Writer fellow – and why try to take control of the Land? Couldn't you just have found a quicker way of getting the energy released, so we could all get out of there?'

'Maybe,' the Doctor agreed, and the ghost of a smile flickered across his face as he looked her squarely in the eye. 'But I didn't think it would work.'

After a moment, Bernice smiled with him; a warm, genuine smile, in which the tensions between them melted just a little. But she still wasn't sure where she stood, nor how she truly felt about her place in the TARDIS. What she needed now, she told herself, was another bath – a long, hot soak to soothe her troubles away.

She paused in the doorway, uncomfortably. Already, the Doctor was busy again at the console.

'So, erm . . . what happens now?'

'A message to the Time Lords.' He didn't look up this time. 'At the very least, they can work out the extent of the Land's influence and put up warning beacons. Maybe they can even find some way of counteracting the energies which brought it back together, and perhaps nullify them for good. Either way, I don't want to see anyone else falling into that particular little trap!'

'And?'

'And what?'

'And what about the person behind all this? The one who's been screwing about with your past and generally rewriting the timeline since we had all that mess with the – with the Silurians.' Even thinking about that opened the floodgates on a host of painful memories. She suppressed them and continued. 'Any ideas who it might be yet?'

'One or two,' the Doctor confessed. 'And an even better idea of what that person's next little game might be.'

Benny raised her eyebrows in query.

'Something the Master of the Land said,' her companion muttered distractedly. 'About an invasion of Earth in the year 1976. Except that in the history you and I know, such an event never occurred. Seems like our friend's engineered another little glitch in the time stream.'

'Great! So if that's where the next trap is, we can make sure we keep away from it.'

'Quite the opposite,' the Doctor corrected. 'I have to investigate, and do whatever I can to rectify the situation.'

'But wouldn't you be better off looking for whoever's behind it all and stopping them from doing any more damage?' asked Benny.

'I'm sure our enemy will make himself known to us,

259

eventually. In the meantime, reversing his mischief is our paramount objective.'

'So where do we start?'

'We start,' said the Doctor, 'by trying to locate a man named Danny Pain.' And he fell silent then, as if that were all the explanation that was necessary.

Bernice nodded slowly, a number of questions buzzing around her head but none seeming important enough for her to bother asking just at this moment. She was, again, about to leave the room when a far more urgent thought occurred to her.

'And we are safely away from that place, yes? I mean, completely away?'

'Far enough that it can't affect us any more,' came the answer. 'Another twenty seconds or so, and we'll be out of its range altogether.'

She relaxed slightly, and thought longingly of hot running water. 'Right. Great. And after that, there'll be no one watching or reading about us anymore?'

'No one.'

Benny smiled tightly, and they still avoided each others' eyes. She couldn't think of anything else to say so she left quietly, easing the door shut behind her in contrast to Ace's rather more explosive departure.

'Well,' muttered the Doctor when he was sure she was out of earshot, 'no one out of the ordinary, anyway.'

Hello? Are you still reading this?

I'm sorry, I really am. I suppose things didn't work out the way we expected, did they? The Doctor escaped, I'm still trapped here . . . and, well, I just wanted you to know that this isn't the end. No way. Okay, so the Doctor's going to be on his guard from now on. But he can't stay out of my reach forever. One day – one day soon – he'll come back. It's just a matter of time. And then, we'll play the game again.

So please, don't be annoyed. Look on the bright side: this way, we get to have a sequel. And I can bring all my old characters back to entertain you again. I'm already planning a story where we find out that the White Knight did get his powers back after all and was teleported to another dimension an instant before his death. And then there'll be one where Rosemary wakes up and finds the Adventure Kids in her shower, or something like that.

So I'll tell you what we can do, shall I? We can just look on this whole thing as being the penultimate book in our glorious saga. Let it whet your appetite for the Grand Finalé, because I promise you, it'll be bigger and better than ever. And next time, it *will* be the end. Next time for definite!

Maybe then, you'll let me go.

THE PIT
Neil Penswick

One of the Seven Planets is a nameless giant, quarantined against all intruders. But when the TARDIS materializes, it becomes clear that the planet is far from empty – and the Doctor begins to realize that the planet hides a terrible secret from the Time Lords' past.

ISBN 0 426 20378 X

DECEIT
Peter Darvill-Evans

Ace – three years older, wiser and tougher – is back. She is part of a group of Irregular Auxiliaries on an expedition to the planet Aracadia. They think they are hunting Daleks, but the Doctor knows better. He knows that the paradise planet hides a being far more powerful than the Daleks – and much more dangerous.

ISBN 0 426 20362 3

LUCIFER RISING
Jim Mortimore & Andy Lane

Reunited, the Doctor, Ace and Bernice travel to Lucifer, the site of a scientific expedition that they know will shortly cease to exist. Discovering why involves them in sabotage, murder and the resurrection of eons-old alien powers. Are there Angels on Lucifer? And what does it all have to do with Ace?

ISBN 0 426 20338 7

WHITE DARKNESS
David McIntee

The TARDIS crew, hoping for a rest, come to Haiti in 1915. But they find that the island is far from peaceful: revolution is brewing in the city; the dead are walking from the cemeteries; and, far underground, the ancient rulers of the galaxy are stirring in their sleep.

ISBN 0 426 20395 X

SHADOWMIND
Christopher Bulis

On the colony world of Arden, something dangerous is growing stronger. Something that steals minds and memories. Something that can reach out to another planet, Tairgire, where the newest exhibit in the sculpture park is a blue box surmounted by a flashing light.

ISBN 0 426 20394 1

BIRTHRIGHT
Nigel Robinson

Stranded in Edwardian London with a dying TARDIS, Bernice investigates a series of grisly murders. In the far future, Ace leads a group of guerrillas against their insect-like, alien oppressors. Why has the Doctor left them, just when they need him most?

ISBN 0 426 20393 3

ICEBERG
David Banks

In 2006, an ecological disaster threatens the Earth; only the FLIPback team, working in an Antarctic base, can avert the catastrophe. But hidden beneath the ice, sinister forces have gathered to sabotage humanity's last hope. The Cybermen have returned and the Doctor must face them alone.

ISBN 0 426 20392 5

BLOOD HEAT
Jim Mortimore

The TARDIS is attacked by an alien force; Bernice is flung into the Vortex; and the Doctor and Ace crash-land on Earth. There they find dinosaurs roaming the derelict London streets, and Brigadier Lethbridge-Stewart leading the remnants of UNIT in a desperate fight against the Silurians who have taken over and changed his world.

ISBN 0 426 20399 2

THE DIMENSION RIDERS
Daniel Blythe

A holiday in Oxford is cut short when the Doctor is summoned to Space Station Q4, where ghostly soldiers from the future watch from the shadows among the dead. Soon, the Doctor is trapped in the past, Ace is accused of treason and Bernice is uncovering deceit among the college cloisters.

ISBN 0 426 20397 6

THE LEFT-HANDED HUMMINGBIRD
Kate Orman

Someone has been playing with time. The Doctor Ace and Bernice must travel to the Aztec Empire in 1487, to London in the Swinging Sixties and to the sinking of the *Titanic* as they attempt to rectify the temporal faults – and survive the attacks of the living god Huitzilin.

ISBN 0 426 20404 2

WHO ARE YOU?
Help us to find out what you want.
No stamp needed – free postage!

Name _____

Address _____

Town/County _____

Postcode _____

Home Tel No. _____

About Doctor Who Books

How did you acquire this book?
Buy ☐ Borrow ☐
Swap ☐

How often do you buy Doctor Who books?
1 or more every month ☐ 3 months ☐
6 months ☐ 12 months ☐

Roughly how many Doctor Who books have you read in total?

_____

Would you like to receive a list of all past and forthcoming Doctor Who titles?
Yes ☐ No ☐

Would you like to be able to order the Doctor Who books you want by post?
Yes ☐ No ☐

Doctor Who Exclusives
We are intending to publish exclusive Doctor Who editions which may not be available from booksellers and available only by post.

Would you like to be mailed information about exclusive books?
Yes ☐ No ☐

About You

What other books do you read?

Other character-led books (which characters?) _____

Science Fiction	☐	Thriller/Adventure ☐
Horror	☐	

Non-fiction subject areas (please specify) _____

Male	☐	Female ☐

Age:

Under 18	☐	18–24 ☐
25–34	☐	35+ ☐

Married	☐	Single ☐
Divorced/Separated	☐	

Occupation _____

Household income:

Under £12,000	☐	£13,000–£20,000 ☐
£20,000+	☐	

Credit Cards held:

Yes	☐	No ☐

Bank Cheque guarantee card:

Yes	☐	No ☐

Is your home:

Owned	☐	Rented ☐

What are your leisure interests? _____

Thank you for completing this questionnaire. Please tear it out carefully and return to: **Doctor Who Books, FREEPOST, London, W10 5BR** (no stamp required)